Siren of the Waters

Siren of the Waters

Michael Genelin

Published by
Soho Press, Inc.
853 Broadway
New York, NY 10003

Library of Congress Cataloging-in-Publication Data

Genelin, Michael.
Siren of the waters / by Michael Genelin.
p.cm.
ISBN 978-1-56947-484-6
1. Women police chiefs—Fiction. 2. Police—
Slovakia—Fiction. 3. Slovakia—Fiction.
4. Prostitution—Fiction. I. Title.

PS3607.E53S57 2008
813'.6—dc22

2007043004

10 9 8 7 6 5 4 3 2 1

For the two ladies in my life,

SUSY AND NORA,

who manage to keep me together,

and to

NOAH,

who always makes me laugh.

Acknowledgments

My special thanks for their friendship, help, and inspiration go to Miro, Adriana, Dano, Jana, Emilia, Mirjana, and Professor Mathern, to all the judges, procurators, and legislators I worked with in Slovakia; and to those very committed Slovaks involved in building a wonderful country. And a very special acknowledgment to my editor, Laura Hruska. Blame me for the bad parts, thank her for the good ones.

Chapter 1

The cold wind surging down the black ice-covered highway was like a blast from some frozen hell. All Jana could do was plunge her hands deeper into her state-issue winter coat and talk loudly enough through the muffler she had wrapped around her face so that the other bundled officers clustered at the accident scene could hear her. The Traffic Police generally don't call on the Criminal Police for anything, particularly in Slovakia with its communist-based tradition of compartmentalizing everything; but the number of bodies frightened some Traffic Police supervisor enough for him to make the call to her. Jana cursed him in the same breath that she cursed the sub-zero cold, wishing the request had come on some balmy evening instead of an icy night.

She looked at the Mercedes van that had hydroplaned off the two-lane highway, through snow drifts, smashing into the small cluster of trees. There was no immediate way to check how fast the van had been going: no skid marks on the ice, so there were no telling physical references except the smashed condition of the vehicle, a large van that had nothing left to identify its make except the logo of the circle with the Y on it that protruded above what was left of the hood.

The blaze that the vehicle had become was, surprisingly, still going strong, and the bodies that had been thrown from it were scattered in such disparate locations that they looked like indicators of the time on some fiery sun-dial clock.

A flash went off; one of the police photographers taking pictures of the scene that was dimmed by the falling snow. Even with the flash and high-speed film, there would be a certain amount of blur from the hard-blowing white sleet that stung the uncovered portions of her face. Where the hell had Seges, her new warrant officer, got to? A bad time to bring a novice in on a death investigation, particularly a police officer who had the work habits of a Seges. The man had transferred in from working pickpockets and thought all he ever had to do was to stand around in crowds looking inconspicuous, and the criminals would invariably reveal themselves by sticking their hands in his pockets.

Jana trudged through the snow, circling the wrecked chassis, trying to spot Seges. She went over what she knew of him: He had come with a mixed bag of personnel reports from his past postings, all of his writeups couched in the vague jargon of bureaucratic supervisors who wanted to push the man on to his next assignment and were afraid that bad writeups would saddle them forever with his presence. So they propped the man up and shoved him out, his promotions coming with time. And now, courtesy of departmental rotations, he was here to make Commander Jana Matinova's life harder.

The anger Jana felt in the pit of her stomach was the only warm spot on her body. She scanned the scene. Still no Seges. The man made mistakes that even newly transferred officers should not make. Securing the scene, for one. Jana had been unsatisfied with the way the danger flares had been set out on the highway so she had told Seges to have the traffic cops reconfigure them. Reluctantly, he'd gone off to comply with the order. That had been twenty-five minutes ago, long enough for the man to take several pees in the snow if he had to. She rather hoped his cock had frozen when he took it out of his pants, then had broken off like an icicle.

She smiled at the thought, than shook herself back to reality. She was his designated training officer. New transfers were supposed to report back to their commander after their assignments were completed. She let herself get slightly annoyed at his failure to follow protocol. Not the thing to do, Jana ruefully reminded herself. She didn't believe much in rigid rules. They were just another way for authority to limit a police officer's originality or inventiveness. Rules over results.

Nonetheless, procedure had to be followed now. Time to finish this phase of the investigation. Seven people dead. There would be lots of questions she would have to answer later.

She moved around the bulk of the fire, finally noticing Seges's pinched shoulders crouching over one of the bodies. Lo and behold, Seges was apparently making notes. Maybe there was some hope for the man. She crossed over to Seges, pulling her six-cell flashlight out, shining it over the body before she knelt next to him. Not good. She knew the face of the dead woman.

"I recognize her." Jana pulled her scarf down from her face so she wouldn't have to yell over the wind. Seges did the same. "It's the Jedlik girl, Marjana. Last I heard, she'd become a prostitute, working one of the houses outside of Bratislava." No surprise she knew the girl. Everyone knew everyone else or was someone else's cousin in Slovakia. That's what you got in a country of less than five and a half million: too much familiarity.

She ran her flashlight over the body again, then back to the face. Everything was at odd angles, broken bones from toe to neck, except the head which did not have a hair out of place. Absurd things happened in auto accidents. She'd once found a man's head inside the headlight of a truck that had smashed into him. The head was face out, a bizarre commentary on his failure to see the huge vehicle before he'd run out in front of it.

Seges went back to taking notes, his writing hand bare so that he had to blow on his fingers every few seconds in a futile effort to keep them warm. "Seven bodies: six women, one man. My guess, he was the driver. All thrown from the car, so obviously no one was wearing seat belts."

She stopped him. His failure to use his eyes combined with his lack of experience was irritating. No, he would not learn easily. She'd probably have to rewrite all the investigation reports herself just to be sure he didn't screw them up. "Seatbelts wouldn't have mattered in this wreck. And a woman was the probable driver. One of her high-heeled boots was pinned under the driver's door when it was torn off. Part of her foot went with it."

Seges's face took on the supercilious look of a teacher who was a pedant, irritating Jana even before he spoke: "She could have been anywhere in the jumble of people that was in the car when the vehicle went off-road. The shoe could have flown off on impact and become lodged under the door."

Jana listened quietly, promising herself she would not get angry, which was not an easy promise to keep with this man. "If you are insistent on our reaching conclusions this early in the process, at least have something, anything, to base your conclusion on. If the powers-that-be question you about it, you will look like you were born a poor Gypsy. Change it!"

She watched as Seges reluctantly crossed out what he had written. With a certain amount of misgiving, she plunged on. "Did the man have a driver's license among his papers?"

"I haven't looked, Commander Matinova."

"Look, Seges!"

Seges finally managed to pull a sheaf of papers from his

pocket, the bits and pieces already double rubber-banded so they would not scatter with the wind. Cold fingers are awkward, and his attempt to shift the rubber bands in order to unwrap the papers was fumblingly slow. To fill the waiting time, he began to recite what else he had learned.

"Several half-empty bottles of alcohol were found in the area around the car."

"What kind of liquor? What proof were they?"

"Slivovitz. 110 proof. What's the difference?"

She fell into her instructor mode. "Alcohol absorption rates of the bodies. Maybe we will be able to tell when they began drinking? Maybe they weren't really drinking at all? Maybe they were drinking something else, somewhere else?" Seges was new, but he should have known this. Jana tried not to show her impatience, wondering what other important items he might ignore or misinterpret.

"Always assume you, and anyone else who reads your reports, doesn't know anything. If you are unsure, write that down. Don't, and you mislead any officer who reads your report."

"I will be more careful in the future, Commander Matinova." He finished thumbing through the papers. "No driver's license. But the man had two passports." He passed them over to her. "I don't like people who carry two passports. They don't owe allegiance to anyone. You can't trust them."

"How many people have you have met, in the course of your duty as a police officer, who you can trust with just one passport?" Jana thumbed through one document, then the other, holding them both side by side open to the primary personal information pages. "These days, it's not unusual to claim two nationalities. But two different *names* means he's a crook."

In his hurry to keep his fingers out of the cold, Seges had

seen that both passport photographs were the same, but had neglected the simple task of comparing the names of the individuals who had been issued the passports. She riffled through both documents again, put one of them in her pocket, and then tossed the other back to Seges, who scrambled to look at the name on the document as if to prove she'd made a mistake. Inside herself, Jana felt anger rising. Incompetence. Too many botched cases because of too many sloppy or lazy officers.

"The dates of birth are the same; same physical description. One gives his place of birth as Kremenchuk, Ukraine, the other as Tirana, Albania. One has a Ukrainian name, the other Albanian. Both passports have tons of visa stamps. He liked to visit lots of countries."

Jana stood, her muscles anesthetized by the cold, her knees stiff. She began to beat her body with her clenched fists, trying to force the return of circulation. She had given up stamping her feet; they were numb to the bone.

She felt the cold more these days than when she was younger. "Put all the papers together, then leave them on my desk."

"We have to give them to the coroner."

"He can wait. I can't."

"It's a simple case, with just a body or two more than usual. Seven people. Drunk. Driving too fast. Ice. Blam!! They are all dead."

"There is too much 'blam!' here."

He stood. "We've both seen it before."

Jana noticed he had risen without much effort, which made her more irritated. The energy and recovery power of youth is indeed wasted on the young, but particularly on the young and stupid. "Tell me, why the fire?"

"Cars catch fire."

"Why such a long-lasting blaze?" She pointed at the still-burning car. One of the traffic police was unsuccessfully trying to douse the flames with a hand-held extinguisher. The flames would not die. The cop finally threw the empty extinguisher into the dark.

"Make a note," Jana murmured, with a half smile at the cop's frustration. "The officer will have to pay for the extinguisher." She hadn't really meant it, but Seges scribbled furiously in his notebook.

Jana looked in the direction of the mountains. "I think it will be light soon. Hopefully it will warm this goddamned place up a little." She started toward her car, then stopped, sniffing the air. "Smell," she commanded Seges. "Eyes, ears, nose, the senses. That's your main toolkit. Learn to use them." She inhaled in an exaggerated manner. "You can smell it. Gasoline from the car but also *not* gasoline. Something else. Get one of the arson people on it."

A fire truck finally arrived. Everything is late in Slovakia; even the men climbing off the truck to douse the blazing vehicle seemed to realize it. They were backseat spectators in this drama. No need for haste, their movements through the snow took on an exaggerated slowness. It was like an odd, primitive dance to the elements, the fire personnel ringing the blazing pieces of the vehicle with their equipment, priapic hoses slowly coming erect, finally spraying their juices over the remnants of a death sacrifice.

Jana watched, noting a salient fact: Even when they finally started to spray the vehicle with a chemical retardant, the flames seemed to resist, insisting on their angry prerogative of burning whatever substance was fueling them. Someone had wanted to make sure this car burned.

When the flames finally died, she walked to her car.

Seges eyed her as she left, nesting his hands under his

armpits, trying to warm them back to life. She was like all the rest of his supervisors had been: Short on trust, she ignored his good qualities. Matinova was going to be looking over his shoulder. All she would do with his life as an officer would be to make more work for him.

Chapter 2

The man in whiteface, wearing an imitation Austrian army uniform circa 1800, stood on a small wooden box in the middle of the main square of Old Town, Bratislava. Except for the few passersby, the empty space, with its wind-driven, drifting veils of snow, looked gloomier than it generally did, even in winter. The statue of the armed knight looming over the fountain had been taken down and stored for the winter; the fountain itself had been covered over to prevent ice from forming inside, expanding and then splitting the stone.

The corpse-like leafless trees dotted through the square gave it an air of deep melancholy which even afflicted the clown figure performing on the box. Well, clowns had never made Jana laugh. Too sad or too scary. They had made her dislike going to the circus when she was a child.

Off to the side, Jana had been watching the man for some time, marveling that he was continuing his act even in this miserably cold weather, his only reward the rare coin that a pedestrian threw into his alms box out of pity.

The man was working with two cats, and he had them doing remarkable things, tricks that any household cat lover would tell you were impossible to teach.

He would stand the cats straight up, and they would remain immobile. He'd drape them around his neck, first one and then both of them, like a feather boa. Or he would sit them erect, face to face, and they would hug each other. He would extend his arms out from his body with a cat lying along each arm, and the felines remained absolutely immobile, neither giving any sign of discomfort or fear, each looking like a frozen piece of statuary shaped like a cat.

Jana finally stepped out of the doorway and walked over to the man, stopping in front of him. She looked up at him for a few seconds. The street busker gave her only the slightest indication that he'd seen her, continuing on with his act.

"Come off the box, Jurai," she finally ordered. "You need to be told something."

"I'm working," he hissed at her. "This is what keeps me in bread. *I* don't get paid by the state." He draped the cats like bracelets around both wrists, then transferred both to a single wrist as a double bracelet of cats, then again as a double necklace around his neck.

"Very good, Jurai. Now come down or I will have to kick the box out from under you and bring you down."

Reluctantly, this time mumbling to his cats, the man climbed off his makeshift stage. "All police are the bearers of bad news. It's a disease they have." He sat the cats where he had stood; neither moved from where it was placed. "Patience. I will be back in a moment." He turned to Jana again. "What is it now?"

Jana stared at his face. Up close, even through the white makeup, she could see the three-inch scar on his forehead. She knew where to look. She had put it there.

The clown watched her eyes, knew she was studying it, and involuntarily touched it with his fingertips. "You marked me for life."

"Blame it on the communists."

"You were the one who hit me."

"You were stealing from the mail. The communists would

have charged you with an act against the state if I had arrested you. You would have gone to prison and they would have thrown away the key. Prison for a man with a young family to support was the greater of two evils, so I hit you."

"You should have let me go."

"Then they would have punished me."

"They would never have found out."

"You would have been caught eventually by another police officer, you would have sought a favor, a lesser sentence to save yourself, and you would have told them about my letting you go. Not something the communists would have liked. So the deeds, present and future, required punishment. Your wife thanked me."

"She was stupid."

"You were the stupid one. She doesn't have a scar on her forehead."

"She's dead."

"I heard. Last year. You were not at the funeral."

"We were separated."

"Now your daughter is dead."

The clown swayed just a little as if the wind had picked up and changed direction.

"You saw her dead?" He had to make sure. "No question it was her?

"No question."

"How?"

"A car wreck."

He stared at her as if waiting for the next blow. "You keep giving me scars." He thought for a minute. "You have more?"

"She was working as a prostitute. Who was her pimp?"

He shook his head, then shrugged his shoulders to indicate he did not know. "I haven't seen her in a year. She would not work. She would not go to school. She left."

"You threw her out."

"Maybe."

Jana held up the passport she had taken from Seges, opening it to the photograph of the dead man, holding it up in front of the clown's face.

"Who is this man?"

He looked at the photograph, trying to decide what to disclose. "Are you putting me in danger if I tell you?"

"Clown, your daughter is dead. Who is the man?"

He considered his options, finally deciding that the present danger of not giving her the information outweighed any future threat.

"I think he owned the wine bar across from the English pub."

"You saw him with your daughter?"

"Never. He asked me to do my cat act for him at his bar one evening."

"Who was there?"

"No one I'd seen before or since."

"Slovaks?"

"All foreigners."

"I am sorry about your daughter." She put the passport in her pocket. "I remember her when she was little."

"She had become a whore."

"And you were a thief."

He shook his head stubbornly. "She slept with anyone who paid her. A whore."

"At least she gave something in return for what she got." Jana looked down at the cats. "Show me one of them." The clown hesitated. "I will leave you with another scar if you don't show me the cat."

Reluctantly he bent down and picked up one of the cats,

handing it to her. The cat did not move. Jana examined its face, petting the red and brown patchwork head.

"Poor thing. Poor little thing." She stepped closer to the clown, almost nose to nose. "It's blind. They're both blind, aren't they?"

"So they're blind. As long as the spectators are blind as well, who cares? They're just cats."

"They can't see, so they must stay where they are, clinging to you, to each other, hoping you won't drop them."

"I feed them. They would be dead otherwise."

"How did you blind them? A pin in each eye when they were kittens? Just half a centimeter into each pupil, right? Blinded as children so they would not know any better." She paused. "They are your children so you can do what you want with them, right? Did you sell your daughter to the Albanian?

"I am an honest man."

"Never."

Jana reached over to the platform and scooped up the other cat, then walked away carrying them both.

"Where are you taking my cats? They belong to me. I own them."

Jana kept on walking.

"You are taking my livelihood away."

"Maybe you don't deserve to live."

She continued out of the square. The passersby wondered why a police officer was carrying a pair of cats.

Chapter 3

Back when the communists were in charge, there was no Easter. No Christmas. Religious holidays ceased to exist; people could not celebrate. The communists delighted in denying reality, substituting mirages, false celebrations created specifically for what they perceived was the state's benefit. All false; everything distorted. Bureaucrats ruled the world. And, for the common man who had to eat, he who did not steal from the state stole bread from his family. That was the only rule the people could follow to fight back.

Communist Slovakia. A strange time and place for her to decide to become a police officer. Then again, maybe not. In a land of distorted values, it at least offered some certainty as long as you stayed away from the political side. She had tried, and look where it had gotten her, even under the new rule of winner-take-all capitalism: She was just another gray bureaucrat in a cubbyhole.

Jana looked around her office: dull, drab, paint peeling, an old cabinet for police procedural publications, a few never-framed dusty pictures on the walls depicting bucolic scenes. She had hoped they would add freshness and light. But as soon as she put them up, they had taken on the characteristics of the room, becoming overcast themselves.

The two blind cats she had rescued from Jurai were curled up in a corner on two-week-old newspapers she had culled from the visitor's room. Jana had found a small bowl for water and shredded some lunch meat, laying it out on a cracked saucer from the coffee room. The cats had sniffed at the meat, one of them taking a small bite; then both of them had gone to sleep. They had not made a sound during the whole time she had them. When cats are blind, she asked herself, are they also deprived of the ability to make sounds?

No. Blindness has nothing to do with speech. To be blind was to simply not see. Unseeing and unseen. You looked in a mirror and still saw nothing of yourself, of your future. When she had first met Daniel, she had been blind.

Daniel had also been sightless. But his lack of sight had been assumed as part of a role he was playing at the National Theatre. He was performing Hamlet, the youngest Hamlet in the history of that theater, and in his interpretation of the tragic prince he was playing the role as if the young Dane were blind, a boy turning into a man who makes his life mistakes not only because of his own emotional incapacities but due to the actual failure of his sight. And it had worked. Oh, how it had worked.

That night, everyone in the theater felt for that slender, dark-haired man on the stage. His limpid brown eyes showed such pain and anguish, even though the eyes were unseeing.

How incredible he was when he moved; how sensual he was when he touched things; how he walked from object to object on the stage supposedly not knowing they were there, yet reaching every destination using an actor's artifice that was completely accepted by the audience. Dano, as she later called him, was even believable in the play's denouement, the dueling scene, somehow conveying that he could hear the blade coming at him, parry, than slash back at his unseen opponent. And, finally, when he was about to succumb to the poison administered by the scratch of his opponent's blade, every man in the audience believed they had seen the ultimate ennobled prince, and every woman was dismayed that she was about to lose her heroic lover before their romance had reached its fulfillment.

In his penultimate dying speech, to the last person in the last row, everyone in that audience died a little.

If thou didst ever hold me in thy heart,
Absent thee from felicity awhile,
And in this harsh world draw thy breath in pain
To tell my story.

With the play's final sigh, the audience sighed with him, No. It can't be over. Let us have more. We love you! The applause that greeted the final curtain, and the appearance of Dano, was a huge wave that resounded through the aisles. The subsequent rhythmic, synchronized clapping that is so characteristic of Eastern Europe continued for a good ten minutes. They were all Horatios and Ophelias, promising not to forget him.

Jana had come to the theater with Monika, a friend who was, even before this performance, in love with Daniel. And, as usual with Dano and women, he had already moved on to his next conquest. There was never any animosity on the women's side when these brief romantic dalliances ended. The women he blew a farewell kiss to were always convinced they were parting because of an uncontrollable set of circumstances, their love now to become a deep friendship which, in actuality, soon faded away.

Monika, who led Jana backstage to meet the blind hero, was now going through the end of the deep-friendship phase with Dano, still wanting to maintain a modicum of closeness by showing up after the play to at least kiss the man of her past dreams on the cheek.

Dano was surrounded by well-wishers. Monika ran over to embrace him and congratulate him on his wonderfully felt and interpreted performance. After a moment, ever so gracefully, she was gently ushered aside to allow the next courtier to greet the prince.

Jana had lagged behind, not wanting to mix with the royal heir's entourage. She was interested in what Daniel was really like, but this was not the place where anyone could find that out. So she focused on the surroundings that had created the illusions of the play: the false walls that conveyed the strength of Elsinore Castle, the flats, the throne itself. She even picked up one of the rapiers the prop master had not yet collected and, for a moment, engaged in an imaginary duel, thrusting and parrying with her unseen enemy, stopping only because she realized that the stage had become silent.

Jana turned, and there was Dano staring at her, his league of admirers behind him, all of them waiting to see what their hero would do.

He continued to look at her, not eyeing her up and down, simply watching her face. In turn, she stared at him: tall, face even more expressive up close, his hair darker, his eyes deeper. He finally gave her a slow smile; she smiled back.

"I think I like you," he said softly.

"Impossible." She shook her head, smiling anyway. "Too early."

"I wish we had met sooner." He said it as if he truly meant it. "We will be friends."

Jana felt her smile getting even wider, happy with his attention, but unsure how to respond. She knew she was pretty, with an athlete's trim figure, but women police officers, even in civilian clothes, have a look and a posture that tends to drive suitors away. So she was not quite prepared for a Dano in her life.

Their next meeting was at police headquarters. Jana had just finished working up a background on one of her defendants,

a farmer who had killed his son because the boy had disre-
spected him. The mother, in hysterics, had related how her
husband had hit her, then hit her again. Their son, a fourteen-
year-old, had stepped between the two to stop any further
injury to his mother. The father wasted no words. He went
to his bedroom, came out with his shotgun, and killed the
boy. The mother still had blood spattered on her clothes and
kept patting the spots, gently rubbing them, as if her son
could feel her touch and be comforted by it.

So Jana was not in a great mood when she saw Dano standing outside the doors to the building. Her bad mood gave way
to surprise, then surprise turned to pleasure at seeing him.

Dano was too busy acting out a part for the police officers
stationed at the front door to notice her at first. She watched
him continually changing characters, first by pretending to
be a Golem, his next role; then transforming himself into
seventy-year-old King Lear; then into the gangster Mack the
Knife in Brecht's *Threepenny Opera*. He was in the middle of
singing the opera's signature theme song when he saw Jana.

Dano danced over and finished his performance of the
song for her. When she told him she was too busy to see him
that evening, he pretended to cry, then wandered around the
lobby acting the part of a distraught country swain begging
for the support of the other police officers in the lobby, all of
them eventually urging her to give in.

The chorus of support was so loud that Jana finally agreed
to go for coffee. Dano held out his arm to her, the rest of the
cops applauding and shouting approval as the two walked
down the steps together. Dano charmed her into pushing the
farmer's wife and her son's tragedy into the back of her mind.
And, despite his reputation, Dano kept his distance during
the evening they spent together. Jana drove him home and
he only kissed her on the cheek.

Their next date was at least planned. The two of them went rollerskating along the Danube, both laughing and giggling at their awkwardness on skates, finally stopping several kilometers upriver to sit on a cold bench that required them to bundle together for warmth.

And always they talked, nonstop. Dano was filled with the idea of leaving the National Theatre and starting his own company; Jana spoke about her cases, Dano taking an intense interest in them. The two worlds mixed and matched, very different but both intense with action, with pathos, with sudden passions of love lost and regained, with tragedy lurking at every intersection of people's lives. And with joy. How wonderfully surprising it was to them both that their worlds, so different, could be so alike.

Jana brought Dano home to meet her mother, who had seen Dano onstage and was already talking to her friends and neighbors about the growing liaison between Jana and the most promising actor in Bratislava. The older woman went out of her way to cook halushka and to bake up a storm so that Dano would see the kind of hospitality he could expect as a son-in-law.

The courtship lasted one month. They were married without fanfare in a civil ceremony. Jana was rapturously happy, married to the handsomest man in Slovakia. She knew about his past reputation, his romantic grand passions. He swore they were over. And she believed him. She did not care about the government, the world, politics, and certainly could not predict what would happen to them.

Chapter 4

The phone rang. Jana quickly picked it up, afraid its insistent clamor would wake the cats. "Yes, right away, Colonel Trokan." She hung up and reached into the top drawer of her desk to pick up the decedent's papers that Seges had left for her. She walked to the door just as Seges came in without knocking. He was still doing things the wrong way.

"You didn't knock."

"Sorry."

"I'm going to see Colonel Trokan." She went past Seges. "Whatever it is, I'm sure it can wait."

Seges followed her into the hall. "All the men are talking about the blind cats. They think they should be put to sleep."

"I'll decide that." She began walking toward Trokan's office. "No one lays a hand on them except me."

"Naturally, Commander Matinova." He followed her for a few steps. "The coroner wants the papers of the decedent. He keeps phoning me, citing office regulations."

"Tell him to call me. I've dealt with him before. Not a problem."

"He says that's why he called me. I think he's afraid of you." He waited until she was almost at Trokan's door. "I found out where the Albanian lived. I am going there."

Jana stopped at the colonel's door, raising her voice just enough so that Seges would hear the no-nonsense quality of the command. "You will wait until I finish with the colonel! Understood?"

"I can toss the place myself, you know."

"You are to wait." Everything with Seges had to be repeated twice. "Or I will feed you to the department dogs."

She knocked on the door, waited a full five seconds, than went into the colonel's office.

Stephan Trokan had been a colonel of police for ten years now. Three months ago, he had been put up for promotion to general by the minister of the interior. Unfortunately, the president, who approved all promotions at that level, disliked the minister of the interior because of an imagined slur he was thought to have uttered about the president's party in Slovakia's coalition government. So he refused to sign the promotion, sealing Trokan in his colonel's rank until this government fell or the president died. Since the president was a born survivor and the next government might be even worse for Trokan, he had decided to stop being ambitious, at least for the moment.

Not that Trokan, a robust man despite his bureaucratic responsibilities, was disheartened enough to become angry or frustrated, or ready merely to let the years go by until he retired. He shrugged it off as a part of life and decided to enjoy the job he had. Which was good for everyone he supervised: No anger was directed their way. Although a fearsome reputation as a martinet continued to follow him, his subordinates were now surprised to discover that he had a sense of humor. Jana walked into an example of it when she entered his office: He had a London bobby's cap perched on his head.

She took a seat, ignoring the cap, as Trokan pretended to finish something he was writing until she noticed. Finally, to break the stalemate, Jana reached over and took the cap, putting it on her own head.

"It's mine," Trokan mumbled, pushing the papers away. He looked up to take in her appearance wearing the cap, then gave her a fleeting smile. "It came from a British cop who is over here with the EU to tell us how bad our police practices are and how we have to become more like the English, or the Italians or the Germans, in order to catch more criminals."

Trokan leaned back in his chair, ogling her. "Women do look better in hats than men. However, if one of our officers should walk through the door, they would begin inventing stories about us to explain why you look a little strange."

She took the hat off, carefully laying it on the desk. Trokan immediately put it back on his head.

"Police colonels are allowed to be a little strange."

"The face below the hat is too Slavic. You would never pass as British."

"Nothing wrong with looking Slavic."

He placed the cap on a shelf behind him, in line with a number of police caps he had collected from other countries. "The English always look too prissy." He swung back to face her. "They know they can't bribe me with money, so they try to get me to change by offering these little gifts I have to take."

She eyed the shelf of caps. "Dust catchers."

"Spoken like a housewife, not a police officer."

"I've not been a housewife for a long time," she reminded him.

"I know." He cleared his throat. "How is our daughter Katka?"

"My daughter is still *my* daughter." Trokan was not her daughter's father, but he had seen so much of her when she was in her pre-teens that he liked to pretend she was his.

"You haven't heard from her in a while?"

"A year."

"No cards, letters, phone calls?"

"One, from her husband, when she had the baby. I sent presents. I called. She wrote back once, a standard store-bought thing with her name written under the printed 'Thank You.' I think her husband forged her signature. Americans are very polite. The family is in France. He's the American consul in Nice."

"Very warm in Nice; sunny most of the time. Good sea air."

"They eat lots of fish." Jana hesitated, then asked, "How is your wife?" It was no secret that his wife and Trokan did not get along.

"Always a madwoman."

"Too bad." She laid the papers, collected from the bodies that had been in the burning van, on his desk. "I thought Seges would have filled you in on the details of the case by now. And informed you, because of all his brilliance, how he was close to clearing it." They both knew that Seges had come to her with a reputation for going behind his supervisor's back and claiming credit for other people's successes. "I suppose a medal would be in order for him, from his perspective, of course."

"He told me everything from his perspective," Trokan amiably agreed. He looked a bit uneasy. "We both know he is a sneak. Since I don't trust his perspective, I thought I might ask you."

"Why do you have to assign all the problem people to me?"

"I gave a problem child to a problem child. That way, I only have to focus on one place to determine where grief is coming from."

"When was the last time I gave you trouble? Are you complaining about the way I do things?"

"Of course. Everything is a major event with you. At least

that's what Seges implied." His belly jiggled as he chuckled gleefully. "I think he said you were making mountains out of molehills."

"You want to give the case to someone else?"

"No."

They always had this argument at the beginning of a case. Trokan took pleasure in needling her. He would have come up with a reason to do so even if Seges had not complained. She took it in good humor, because it always ended up with Trokan letting her have her way.

"You can't complain about the results," she reminded him.

"It's my job to complain."

"As long as it's only a little bit." She eyed him, knowing he had something more to tell her. "What else?"

"One *working* girl dead, no problem. Two dead, a sigh but good riddance. Three dead, a little uncomfortable. Four, and we are sweating. Five, and the building is falling down. Here there are six of them. Time for the government people, the newspapers, everyone, to run to an insane asylum and take lessons from the inmates. Throw in the man and there are major earthquakes, particularly with the Western community. The EU is already asking questions."

"All the women were probably prostitutes."

"That is your call."

"Not for sure yet. Seges was supposed to run the records. He told you; he didn't tell me."

"He's busy scoring points. He knows the Interpol man in Lyon. They did a hurry-up job for him. All the women were prostitutes. Most from other countries." Trokan paused, then smiled very broadly. "That Seges does like to suck up to me. In a way, it is very comforting. He makes me feel like I am important. You should try it once in a while."

"Too late for me."

"It never hurts."

"If they were all prostitutes, it means it might be a trafficking case as well. Perhaps part of a motive for the killings?"

"All murdered?"

"I have begun to think so."

She went to the door.

"And get rid of the blind cats," he threw after her.

"Is that an official order?"

"I just make suggestions."

As soon as she walked out, Trokan got on the phone to the minister. "I spoke to her, Minister." He listened. "I know. Pressure from the UN; pressure from the EU; pressure from the Americans. We did sign the Rome Treaty on Human Trafficking." He swiveled in his chair, absently taking the bobby's cap from the shelf and slipping it on again. "I think she will have to be the person we send."

He pulled a small mirror from a desk drawer and peered at his reflection wearing the hat. "No. Those are not the types of waves she would make." He put the mirror down, than slipped the hat back onto the shelf. "Who cares what the French say? Less? Even less, who cares what the British say? They are not Slavs." He settled back in his chair. "I know, the EU is important. Yes, the treaty. Yes, the UN." He took a deep breath waiting for the minister to finish, smoothing the hairs back that had been dragged out of place by the cap. "Yes, Minister, I will push this. Thank you, Minister."

Trokan dumped the phone back onto its cradle, then picked up the mirror, studying his face, this time without the cap. "English is okay; Slavic is better." Satisfied, he put the mirror back in the drawer.

Chapter 5

Jana and Seges were unable to locate the landlord of the "pimp's" third-floor apartment on Strakova. They assumed that was what he was, as he had been in the car with six probable prostitutes. Unfortunately, there were no keys to the apartment among the dead man's possessions. And no landlord meant no passkey, and that meant they had to use a crowbar to snap the double lock combination on the heavy door. Not a problem by itself, but the neighbors had to be assured that they were police officers on official business.

As usual in Slovak culture, no one ever gives information to the police unless their lives absolutely depend upon it. Once the obligatory identifications were made, immediately after their denials of ever seeing anyone living in the pimp's flat, the tenants' doors shut. As far as the neighbors were concerned, the apartment had never been rented.

Inside, the place was filled with the cheap modern furniture sold by places like IKEA to furnish the expensive rentals in Slovakia. In the cheaper rentals all you got were heavy furnishings, dark remnants of the prior Eastern bloc status, which hulked about in a grim way to remind the user that any place else would be more cheerful.

"Expensive." Seges nodded his approval at the look of the apartment. "Must be a thousand dollars, maybe twelve hundred dollars a month." The landlords all took their tenants' money in dollars or Euros, cash only, so they wouldn't have to declare it on their income tax. Ownership was an attractive investment for those who could afford the initial cost. "I'd like to have a few rentals like this. Give up police work and live the easy life."

"You would be an instant target for the Tax Police. Ex-police officer, no other source of income. And then they'd ask where you got the money to buy the properties in the first place. Good-bye apartments, hello prison."

"Hell," Seges complained. "Half the force is taking graft."

"Consider it carefully. They get away with it; you wouldn't." She finished her first look around, then took a quick tour through the apartment: living room, kitchen. Seges followed her, oohing and ahhing at the conveniences.

Everyone hides things in the bedroom or the kitchen. This time the bedroom was their first choice. Seges searched the clothes in a freestanding armoire; Jana took the dresser.

Neat and tidy. So neat and tidy, it bothered her. There was nothing out of place, socks were paired neatly, shirts arranged by color; every piece of underwear bore the same label. All the brand names were foreign. She smelled the drawers' contents. No cologne scent, no aftershave. She checked the collars on the shirts. No abrading or discoloration. Everything was new or nearly new. She walked over to the armoire as Seges finished.

"Anything?"

"Good-quality clothes. Italian suits. They cost money." He shrugged. "My dream life isn't this good. Tonight I'm going to shake things up, make my fantasies richer."

"Richer doesn't mean better."

"You could fool me."

"His expensive suits didn't keep him alive." She reconsidered her conclusion. "If they were indeed the dead man's clothes." She checked the cuffs on the trousers of the suits.

"No wear. Again, new or nearly new." She inhaled. Unlike the drawers, there was a faint bouquet of cologne in the closet. She checked each of the jackets until she identified the one giving off the aroma. She pulled the jacket and matching pants off the hanger, laying them on the bed. From inside the breast pocket she took a single coin, from Croatia. All she knew about that country came from a Dubrovnik woman who bragged about how nobody in the world could cook fish like the Croats and told elaborate stories about the beautiful Dalmatian coast and its islands.

Seges began stripping the bed as Jana walked through the living room into the kitchen. She began searching through the drawers and cabinets. Again, everything was neat. Nothing in the sink, not even a glass left out to dry. Detergent under the sink, never opened. Full bottles of this and that, still sealed. This was a person who ate out all the time. Her last stop was the refrigerator.

She could hear Seges begin to toss the living room as she opened the freezer compartment. Frozen food was piled up in a haphazard way. Not like the contents of the rest of the apartment. Jana began pulling out the boxes of frozen food, dumping them in the sink, finally emptying the freezer. Nothing.

She stood back and eyed the refrigerator, both of its doors open, wondering what she had missed. The only item stored on the shelves of the refrigerator door was a small kielbasa in clear plastic wrap.

Jana pulled a knife from one of the drawers and cut herself a small piece of the sausage, chewing it as she walked back into the living room. She had a sudden pang of memory: her daughter, Katka. Always snacking on little pieces of sausage in the kitchen. Now she was grown and gone. Jana pushed the memory away.

Seges was on the floor in the living room, the couch upside down. He was pulling at a small notebook that was taped to the underside of the sofa, finally tugging it loose from the fabric.

He grinned, satisfied with himself. "How about a piece of sausage for this book?"

Jana cut Seges a piece, passing it to him in exchange for the notebook. Then she sat at the dining table and carefully opened the cover. Seges leaned over her shoulder, chewing loudly on the sausage as she slowly leafed through the pages.

"You like the sausage?" she asked offhandedly.

"Very good."

"He's not Albanian."

"The sausage maker?"

"The dead man or whoever put the sausage in the refrigerator."

"You can tell from the notebook? The clothes? The apartment?"

"The sausage. It's pork. Albanians are mostly Moslem. Pork is forbidden."

"He could be part of the Christian minority."

"Perhaps. Except Christians from there don't eat it much because it offends their neighbors. So, when they leave Albania, they haven't acquired a taste for it. They continue not to eat it. Habit."

She went back to her focus on the book: columns of numbers, names, sums. But nothing that had a point of reference to allow her to give it meaning. Seges pointed to one page's entries.

"Truck, table, table, vegetables, stone. A shopping list? No," he answered himself, his speech a little slurred from the kielbasa he was chewing.

"Nobody tapes a shopping list to the underside of a couch."

Jana opened the book's rear cover, touching the inside, holding it up to the light. "It's water-stained. Still damp. It was taped to the couch recently. Not long ago enough for it to dry out. Our man in the car died a few days ago. Unless he was resurrected in the morgue, he could not have taped it there."

"So?"

"Maybe it was the man who had the jacket with the coin in it? I think the book was originally in the freezer. Frost got on the cover, then melted when it was removed from the refrigerator."

"Why would the man put it in the freezer in the first place, then take it out and hide it under the couch?" He thought about it. "Maybe the fellow was afraid we wouldn't find it in the freezer," he joked, "so he taped it under the couch knowing we would look there." Seges laughed at his own silliness.

Jana silently noted Seges's response. He was too easily convinced he was wrong, even when he was right. She decided to give him a pat on the back. "Good for you, Seges. Maybe he *was* afraid we wouldn't find it in the freezer."

"I'm right?" Seges tried to conceal his surprise with false jocularity. "You see, you will have to listen to me from now on. I'm a certified genius."

"Absolute genius. The Einstein of the Slovak police." She continued to study the contents of the book. "Can you decipher the writing?"

"It's in code."

"Brilliant, Seges. I will have to rely on you more and more." She got up, handing the book to him. "We must find someone who can decode the thing. Maybe the Americans in Austria? The FBI in Prague?" She tossed the sausage to him. "Rewrap the kielbasa and put it in evidence."

"It will smell up the file."

"They have a small refrigerator in the evidence room." She tried to keep a straight face. "Tell the custodians that it's poisoned so they won't eat it."

Jana took a last look around. No ashtrays. Not an ashtray in the entire apartment. No smoking inside. Unusual for a Slovak household. She walked over to the French doors leading to a balcony, stepping outside.

Seges was right about one thing, at least. The apartment, by Slovak standards, was a jewel. The wind had died down and there was a clear panoramic view of Bratislava: Maria-Theresa's castle on the hill to her left; the tall Soviet war memorial on the hills across the valley celebrating the Russians driving the Nazis out of the city in the Second World War; Michalska Gate, the last gate standing of the old city's defensive wall, directly in front of her. And below, the winding streets with their air of decay almost hidden by coats of snow. And the occasional new building, with the hope it represented, stretching up out of the soiled snow.

Jana looked down. There was a man at the corner gazing up at the building. From the angle of his head, Jana could swear he was focused on this apartment, on her. The man turned, then went around the corner and out of sight. For some reason, Jana visualized the man wearing the jacket with the cologne smell and the coin from Croatia. No proof, but for some reason she thought it was his. She shrugged it off. Just a feeling; nothing to act on.

Seges stuck his head outside. "You ready to go?"

There was a large planter on the balcony, the ice-covered vegetation it contained long dead. Jana checked the dirt. No cigarette butts. People sometimes came outside to smoke, then put their cigarette butts in a planter. Here, nothing. Again, lack of real habitation, the apartment almost like a stageset built to fool the audience. Jana was ready to believe there was a stage manager orchestrating events. Except, the dead bodies were real, Jana reminded herself.

"Too many people to track, too many dead bodies, too much of nothing," Seges grumbled. "Where's the writing on the wall?"

"The writing is there."

"Invisible ink, then?"

"We find out how to make it visible."

They left, Seges still grumbling. More problems, he thought. This case was going to wind on and on and on. Working the pickpocket patrol was better. Even if they did try to put their hands in your pockets, with them things came to a quick conclusion.

Chapter 6

The call rang on Jana's mobile when she was eating a late lunch at Hrubulas, the small soup and sandwich place she frequented. The proprietor shrugged at her in sympathy. She was always being interrupted. His shrug was even broader, accompanied by a roll of the eyes, when the minister's black BMW sedan, one of the ubiquitous BMWs that ministers in Slovakia have a penchant for, picked her up.

As she left, the owner added a nod of approval to his shrug. Jana was moving up in the world. "Next, a helicopter," he yelled after her, as the sedan roared off.

Government cars get to places very quickly in Slovakia. They simply dare pedestrians to get in their way. When it is a minister's car, the chauffeur's hubris is intensified, the driver appearing to aim at pedestrians who even look like they are going to cross in front of "his" limousine.

The interrupted lunch and the near-suicidal jumping of the traffic lights by the chauffeur did nothing for Jana's spirits. So, arriving at the Ministry, she was already irritable when she was directed to a conference room, and became just a touch angry at not being told about a scheduled meeting which she had had no time to prepare for.

Jana entered the room to find the chairs at the conference table filled, forcing her to edge around several cameramen, taping the proceedings for public consumption on some dull news day, to find a seat along the wall. She felt superfluous, an afterthought on the agenda of a session that had evidently been going on for a good portion of the day before they even thought of summoning her.

Jana tuned into what was happening. Nothing vital. Some bureaucrat from an isolated department was doing what so many of the Eastern European government cadres did when they had to give a talk: reading in a monotone from a paper that he had spent a week writing and which had then been cleared by all his supervisors. The man was afraid to leave out a word of the approved script. Democracy had not changed the embedded legacy of mediocrity in which the communists had buried the nation.

"We are determined that the principles will prevail. Transactions in human beings are remnants of feudalism that we, as individual states, cannot condone. We must work together on this issue." Even though the speaker's last words were supposed to be a thrilling call to arms, they simply trailed off, everybody in the room heaving an ill-concealed sigh of relief.

Jana took time to scan the room and then checked the participant biography handout that had been laid on her chair. Virtually all of the attendees except the media occupied government positions. All of them looking gray or brown, even their skins picking up that dusty, muted appearance so many civil servants have. Trokan was there, sitting on the other side of the room. He was one of the few who still had a vivid life force that made him appear animate rather than a mere robot.

The person who interested Jana the most was the only other woman in the room. She sat behind a small table-flag indicating that she was from the EU. Jana checked the paragraph about the woman in the biographies. She had no academic degrees, but had put together a network of groups in the EU countries that were interested in fighting trafficking of woman and children. Because of her activities and expertise, the president of the EU had personally taken a hand in appointing her to her current position.

While Jana was checking the woman out, Trokan nudged her, indicating Jana with his head.

The EU woman stared at Jana, each of them looking directly at the other. The woman smiled. Jana nodded at her, she nodded back, polite but contained. Jana found herself assessing her: a formidable person, a woman who was self-assured, even in this group of powerful people, but also a pleasant person not afraid to smile at someone she did not know.

Jana checked out the woman's clothes: neat but fashionable. No wedding band, but a ring on her right hand, an oval of diamonds surrounding a large center stone. Tasteful but expensive. The wearer knew that people respected wealth but that they did not like being slapped in the face with it.

The woman had taste, determination, and competency, or she would not be in the room as a representative of the EU. As well, she had the drive needed to get to this level of power, a formidable person who had to be taken seriously by the minister sitting at the head of the table. And Trokan's pointing Jana out to the woman meant that she was interested in Jana. Jana sensed that the woman was the reason the minister had summoned her this late in the session.

The people at the table, out of politeness, asked the speaker a few questions, and his answers were now droning to a close, a smattering of applause following him from the rostrum. As if afraid someone would raise another issue or generate an unwanted discussion, the minister quickly closed the meeting. People broke into small groups and began to filter out of the room. The EU woman approached the minister, the two of them joined by a man who, Jana remembered, was a UN representative from Vienna. The three talked amicably as they left. Jana remained seated. She would find out soon enough why she had been summoned.

Trokan made his way around the table, dropping a word here and there to other participants, finally sitting on a chair next to Jana. "There is some coffee still left in the pots." He indicated the coffee setup in a corner of the room. "Cookies if you like."

"The coffee will taste burned by now, the cookies stale."

"They tasted that way from the beginning of the meeting. You saw the woman?"

"Yes."

"Her name is Moira Simmons, an official with the EU. From Strasbourg."

"She expects to meet me? The minister's doing?"

"Yes."

Trokan got up, Jana following his lead, the two of them edging toward the door, Trokan pausing every few steps to say a word or two to the other people who were also moving out.

A colonel from Customs she hadn't seen in some time mouthed a "hello" at her. "You will love Strasbourg." He patted her on the shoulder as she passed. "But you will have to dress less like a police officer there," he warned.

Jana nodded and smiled. Then, to Trokan, "I didn't ask for any assignment to Strasbourg. Why?"

"It's always a 'why' with you. Things happen. The minister will tell you."

"Does everyone here know about it but me?"

"Most of them."

"A miserable way to run a police department."

"We specialize in being miserable to everyone, including each other."

Jana thought of Jurai, the man she had taken the blind cats from. He had said something similar. Maybe it was true. She hoped the cats felt better being with her rather than with the street busker. Then again, maybe blind cats can't tell they are miserable.

Trokan and Jana finally made their way into the hall, picking up their pace as they walked toward the minister's office.

"Why am I going to France?"

"You speak English; you speak French."

"I took French twenty years ago at the university."

"I told them you spoke it fluently."

"Why?"

"We decided you were the only one to go. Everyone else would fake interest in the topic just to get to France, even if it is Strasbourg and not Paris."

"I have no reason to go to Strasbourg."

"You don't even know what the topic is, so you can't say you have no interest. And the more you try to turn it down, the more they will want you. It's human nature."

They walked into the minister's suite, his secretary opening the office door after a brief knock, then ushering them into the inner office. The minister was seated across from the woman from the EU. The man from the UN sat next to her, waving his arms, puffing out his cheeks, obviously telling an amusing story from the half-smiles on everyone's face. Jana suddenly remembered his name: Foch. He was a man who giggled all the time and had once told her he was related, in some distant way, to Marshal Foch, the commander of the French Army in World War I. Nobody believed him.

The minister stood up, looking at Jana. "Good morning, Commander." Foch stood, a polite Frenchman, listening to the minister's introductions as if he hadn't met Jana before.

Moira Simmons, the EU representative, nodded at Jana again, studying her intently. Motioning Trokan to close the door, the minister wasted no time with small talk.

"You are going to speak at a conference in Strasbourg."

Jana decided to protest the minister's decision. "The methods used by the Slovak police are not of interest to Strasbourg, unless we are talking about dialogue for a musical comedy. And I am not an entertainer."

Moira Simmons finally spoke. "Unless I am mistaken, you have been assigned to the case of the prostitutes killed in the car accident?"

"Car crash," amended Jana. "We still have to determine it was an accident."

Simmons inclined her head to allow for the correction and continued speaking. Her English had a lilt that only the Irish have.

"Slovakia has become a country of transit in human trafficking from the East. Most of them are refugees from poverty, from war, from famine, people trying to make a new start for their families. We find them when they have suffocated in the backs of trucks, in the holds of ships, in containers made to be used for machinery, not people." The woman's voice became more impassioned with every word. She conveyed a strong belief in what she said, and what she was trying to do.

"Women, children, men looking to send money back to save their families. Prostitutes being traded on the open market. All so many items; numbers, not people. Millions of dollars made from people being treated like something much less than human. And they are now beginning to come through the chute that Slovakia provides to the West. It must be stopped."

"Look at a map. This country is bordered by the Czech Republic, Hungary, Poland, Ukraine, and Austria. It is a pivotal state, particularly with flesh peddlers, for dispatching their *goods*."

Moira Simmons continued, a true believer addressing the heathens, trying to convert them. "The numbers are increasing, a sea of people, all of them being abused, all of them just raw product on the market. And the flesh peddlers earn millions of pieces of silver from their misery."

Simmons took a breath. Jana used the opportunity to raise a small objection. "I understand. They are being criminally exploited. But you must understand that I have had no experience with human trafficking. It's a textbook subject to me."

Simmons brushed her remark aside, intent on her own agenda. "People from all over Europe are coming to testify before our committee on human trafficking. Slovakia has been notably absent from our common approach to this problem, and it is time for a country that is new to EU membership to become involved in it, particularly since it is a country being used by the traffickers."

Foch put his two cents in. "A bad record in this area will certainly affect Slovakia in a negative way as Slovakia tries to take its equal place among the other member nations." The smirk left over from the joke he'd told had not left his face. "The UN is also gravely concerned about this issue." He did not look gravely concerned. "Everyone wants to hear more from this country." He leaned back in his chair.

Trokan's eyes seemed to have fastened on a spot on the wall, his fascination as intense as if he were studying a Rembrandt. The minister shifted on his seat, eyeing the cell phone in his hand, wondering when he could finally get on with the rest of the day's business. Moira Simmons could read his body language. Time to sum up. She had made her points, gotten her commitments even before she had met Jana. If nothing else, Jana would follow orders.

"We need a field person, not a diplomat, to discuss the problems. Nitty-gritty stuff. The case you are investigating is perfect. We would like you to report your progress to us, describe the police procedures you are using in your investigation. Periodic reports would also help. You can explain how you locate where the prostitutes were shipped from, how they came into the net of traffickers, where they were going, and why they died."

The minister looked over to Jana. "You heard?"

"I heard, Minister."

"Then it is done." His waved at Trokan. "Give Matinova the resources she needs. Keep the lines of communication open."

Jana and Trokan nodded at the people in the room, walking out past the smiling secretary who had somehow known when to open the door for them to leave.

Chapter 7

One door closes; another door opens. The past ends; the future begins. The first months of marriage to Dano had been even better than Jana could have hoped. Her mother moved into a room on the second story, selling the family house to them for a mere promise from Jana and Dano to pay over the coming years. Miracle of miracles, unlike most newlyweds in Slovakia, they had their own place. Every night, when Jana got off duty, she and Dano would rush into each other's arms, make love like it was the first time, then spend the rest of the evening gabbling nonsense at each other until it was time to make love again. And she was rapidly advancing in her career in the police.

She was promoted to second warrant officer, and her new supervisor was Lieutenant Commander Trokan, a man she immediately liked for his quick mind and an air of seriousness which never descended into pomposity. Unlike most of the communist cadre in the police force, he was even able occasionally to demonstrate a dry wit, often at the state's expense. It was good to have a supervisor look after your back, becoming a mentor, particularly when that man was a newly-wed himself. Trokan also understood the need sometimes to get off a little early to enjoy life, even though there were already rumors that Trokan's new wife was a bit of a harridan.

It was the end of the year. The New Year's celebrations were about to begin. A number of parties were being given by police officers, but Dano grumbled that they saw enough of police officers during the year. They decided to see a play. Tickets were free to Dano, and Jana loved the theater, and what better way for an actor and his wife to begin the new year than to enjoy an evening at the National.

One of Dano's own mentors, Vaclav Saitz, an older actor, had the leading role, and the two lovers met Saitz backstage. The three of them then rushed off to join a group of other actors, musicians, directors, and a room full of other theater folk in a small cellar theater that had been borrowed from the resident theater company for the party.

Saitz immediately began chasing an actress who was young enough to be his daughter's daughter, leaving the two of them with a group of others in the screened-off lobby. That was when Jana felt her first real pang of anxiety about mixing with theater people. Jana recognized a woman at the table. She knew her only slightly. Her name was Zibinova. She worked for the Secret Police. Zibinova recognized her as well, turning to her companion, a short, heavy-set man who purported to be a director, whispering in his ear.

All the party noise, the clamor of the celebrants, the too-loud music, became nothing but background static, Jana's thoughts muting everything except her own fear. Zibinova and the man were there to investigate, and the only thing they would be interested in was possible anti-state activity. With the Secret Police, the possible nearly always turned into the probable, the probable into arrests and charges. Guilt would be found by them. It was the nature of that beast.

Jana had to get Dano out of there. He would make a comment or a joke, or smile at someone else's comment or joke relating to some political issue, however remote, and that was all their kind of police needed. They might involve everyone at the table. Even if you didn't speak or make any type of supportive gesture, you were subject to sanctions for your failure to object to a perceived anti-state remark or activity. Jana could not tell Dano about Zibinova. He would tell his friends, they would tell theirs, and it would all come back to this night, and to Jana.

The only course of action Jana could think to take was immediate and drastic. No one was looking at her, so she put her finger down her throat to provoke a gag reflex. The bad wine she had been drinking helped, and Jana threw up on the table, everyone scattering to get out of the way. Dano, standing, looked down at her, shocked at the sudden-ness of the event.

He took her home, disappointed at not having his evening of fun. Still the newlywed, solicitous about her health, he helped her get her clothes off and put her to bed. She lay there, unable to sleep, reviewing events over and over again, obsessing over every conversation at the table, trying to determine if one of them had said or done anything which could be construed by the Secret Police as a cause for action.

Two days later, she was called to Trokan's office. He was polite, referring to a folder on his desk from time to time. "I understand you went to a party and got sick."

"I appreciate my commander's expressing sympathy for my being sick."

He looked up at her, a sly smile on his face. "You recog-nized her?"

"Who, Commander?"

"The lady at the table, Zibinova. Just before you got sick."

Jana paused, as if to reflect. "Ah, that's who she was. I thought I knew her, but I wasn't sure." Jana adopted a rueful expression. "She must think I can't hold my wine. Not good for a police officer to have that kind of reputation."

He looked down at the notes in the folder, trying to hide

his broadening smile. "The fact that she is a comrade in the Secret Police had nothing to do with your becoming sick, did it?"

"Nothing whatsoever, Commander."

He was now trying to suppress laughter. "She wrote in her report that she believed you might have problems being an alcoholic and that we should monitor you for possible excess drinking, particularly on the job." He finally got control of his laughter, managing to wipe the smile off his face. "It's not good to get on the bad side of these people."

"I agree completely, Commander."

"Rest easy. There is nothing in the report that implicates you or your husband in any form of illicit or anti-government activity."

"I didn't think there would be, Commander. Thank you for telling me anyway. If I had recognized who she was, I would have been very worried."

He nodded thoughtfully. "So would I, in your shoes. It's not good for a police officer to be involved in a hotbed of the disaffected."

"Is it a hotbed, Commander?"

"It always is, with theater people. They are all malcontents, otherwise they wouldn't be actors. At least that's what the Secret Police think." He snapped his fingers, as if remembering something. "Ah, your husband, he's an actor. Yes, a good one, too." Trokan's voice hardened. "Keep him out of trouble, if you can."

"I will, Commander."

"As to Zibinova, and this conversation, it never took place. Understood?"

"Absolutely."

He waved her out of the office. Jana managed to get back to her desk, pulse rate elevated, sweat staining her blouse, and, unlike the night at the party, truly feeling sick to her stomach. She was grateful to Trokan for giving her the information in the report, and for the warning. She had been cautioned: Stay away from theater people. Except that her husband was a theater person. And his friends were theater people. How could she keep him away from them? How could she keep herself away from them? She could not see any clear path; she had no answers.

Chapter 8

The body was found wedged against a Novy Most bridge pylon on the Petrzalka side of the Danube. The woman still wore a flowered dress. The dyes in the flowers had run together, creating a dark, impressionist tent shape over the obese mountain of flesh it still attempted to shelter. The woman had one hand missing, severed at the wrist. The other wrist still had a weight attached to it, although it had also been partially severed by the thin wire connecting it to the weight.

Stomach gas, perhaps more than usual because of her bulk, had bloated the corpse until she became so buoyant that she carried the weight with her when she popped up to the surface to lodge against the foundation of the bridge, the last bridge to be built in Slovakia by the communists before they finally floated into history.

When the body was turned over to the coroner, the patrol officer, who knew her son, had already put a tentative identification tag on her which included the son's telephone number. The coroner called the son. Jana and Seges were waiting for him when he entered the coroner's waiting room.

After briefly introducing everyone, the coroner led them all to the autopsy area. Apologetically, he explained that they would ordinarily have put her into one of the body storage drawers, but she was so bloated that she might jam the drawer's mechanism. Instead, his assistants had merely laid her out on a table, after stripping away her clothes and covering her with a rubberized sheet.

The coroner asked the son if he was ready. The son, a maintenance man who worked for the city government, finally understood what the coroner was asking and nodded. When the sheet was removed from her face, the man merely nodded again without changing expression. After the rubberized sheet was replaced over the face of the woman, the son gave the coroner the needed preliminary information: full name, address, Ukrainian nationality. She had married his father in Bratislava a year after he was born.

The man shifted from one foot to the other, momentarily stumped about his mother's age, finally figuring out that she would have been 63 next month. He supplied the coroner with his mother's maiden name. As Jana and Seges walked the man back into the hall, the coroner called after them, telling the son when the remains of his mother would be available for any funeral services that might be planned.

The man continued to talk in a monotone to the two police officers. "Yes, she traveled to Ukraine, to Kiev, several times a year." There was no emotion in his voice, no sorrow, no love for the woman in the morgue. He was already beaten by life to the degree that nothing really mattered except survival. "No, I don't know the friends she visited there. My mother and I did not talk much any more. She owned an apartment that she rented out and lived on the proceeds."

He looked back at the door of the room where his mother's body was lying, a sudden look of comprehension, then release, upon his face. She was dead. He was free; a burden had been lifted from him. "She had a terrible temper. Always hitting, screaming. I tried to stay away." And, no, he had no idea who the tenants were who were renting his mother's apartment.

They let him go, promising to get in touch with him if they heard anything about who had killed her. Just before he walked out, he asked them when he could claim his mother's apartment. His face changed with the pleasant light of aware-ness, the promise of deliverance, of compensation for his years of tolerating the woman on the slab. "It's mine now. The fur-niture, her bank account, everything. Right?" They told him to get a lawyer and walked back into the examining room.

The coroner had removed the sheet from the body, quickly going over the salient points. "One hand gone. Torn off. She was weighted at the wrists, the body's bloating created a strong pull, the wire cut into her wrist, chemicals in the river didn't help, and the hand was severed from the wrist."

"The wrist was not cut off?" Seges wanted to be sure.

"It was torn off. Jagged. No knife, no saw, no question." He turned the head to one side, pointing to a hole behind the ear. "A small bullet in the back of the head. She was almost certainly dead before she was tossed into the Danube. I will know absolutely when I examine the lungs, but it's a reasonable assumption, I think." He pulled the sheet back over the head.

"The man who was brought in from the car wreck. Have you finished that autopsy?" The doctor walked to a body drawer, Jana following him, Seges a step behind her. "I want fingerprints."

"No fingerprints. Burned off in the car fire."

"In the car fire, or before?"

"Can't tell. Many broken bones, chest caved in. His face went through the window. Also fire-damaged."

He pulled the sheet away where the man's face would have been. There was not much left. "The women are in a little better shape." He scratched at his bald head. "What's to know about the bodies? Nothing that couldn't be caused by the accident. I will send you fingerprints of the females after the technician takes them. Also a complete set of photos of the bodies."

"Thank you, Doctor," Jana nodded. "Very professional."

"We are all professionals here. Even the dead are professionals at being dead." He chuckled at his little joke. Jana wondered how often he told it. "None of them have ever tried to pretend to be anything other than what they are: carcasses."

Chapter 9

Trokan didn't like it. And after he told the minister what the investigation seemed to be suggesting, the minister liked it even less. They now had one definite murder of the woman pulled from the Danube, and seven possible murders from the car holocaust, all requiring investigation, and all on their plates. Knowing the Slovak penchant for blaming everything on corrupt officials bribed to cover things up, and with the EU and the UN looking over their shoulders, they had no alternative but to listen with open minds to Jana's request.

Identification had been made of the remaining dead prostitutes. Aside from the Slovak, there were four from Ukraine, and one from Moldova with a last known address in Ukraine. From what they knew of the driver, he was either from Ukraine or Albania; the woman who had been shot behind the ear and tossed into the Danube was originally from Ukraine. Too many coincidences, Jana argued with the minister and Trokan. She had to go to Ukraine.

The minister was very definite in his response. "Too expensive. We have mutual legal assistance treaties with them. Use the telephone. Use the fax. Use e-mail. Have *their* officers investigate." Jana sat without moving, looking at him. "So?" he finally asked.

"The militia in Ukraine is up to their balls in criminality themselves. The ones who are not corrupt are notoriously slow in doing anything about their own cases, much less another country's." Unblinking, she continued to stare at the minister. "Only through personal, face-to-face contacts, which I have established over the years—"

"Nonsense!" the minister got out.

"—which I have established over the years, will we get quick, relevant information." She not so subtly added, "Strasbourg is going to want to know a little more than that we have positively identified six dead bodies. One of their secretaries could have done that with a few well-placed phone calls."

The minister slumped in his seat, caving in. He couldn't afford to take another beating in the press, considering the current shaky state of the coalition government.

The minister authorized the expenditures, and blamed Trokan, in front of Jana, for not being able to control his subordinates. When they finally left the office, Trokan was so angry with the minister that he was grinding his teeth. Trokan's mood became even worse when Jana indicated that she had brought her bag to the office in anticipation of being given permission to go to Ukraine. She was leaving at once to catch her plane.

"Leave! Leave!" he growled at her. "But you better come back with something." He thought about it. "Anything!"

The building had a rotating elevator with open cubicle platforms that never stopped descending, one cubicle quickly dropping after the other. Trokan jumped on one of the moving platforms, yelling that he was going to have to leap from the top of Michalska Tower if she returned from Ukraine without something solid. He then kicked at one of the walls. Her last sight of him was his descending head mouthing something that could only be a promise of more violence, this time directed at her.

She was not troubled. Trokan recognized the necessity for

her to go to Ukraine. He would eventually forgive her for the minister's behavior.

To get to Kiev, the capital of Ukraine, you must fly either Aeroflot or one of its affiliated airlines. Singly or combined, they have one of the worst safety records of any airline, and they appear not to encourage their passengers to think that they are trying to improve that record.

Jana tried to take her mind off the flight by going over the facts of the case. Unfortunately, she was constantly distracted by a low level of panic generated by the rough air pockets the plane went through, and by the way the flight attendants constantly took smoking breaks with the passengers on a non-smoking flight. Someone had a cat, which kept yowling from fright in its carrying case. As well, Jana's seat belt was missing, the windows were scratched to opaqueness, the upholstery was torn, and, finally, there was the dive-bomber approach by the pilots to the Kiev airport as the striking climax to a very interesting flight. The only thing she had to be happy about was that Mikhail Gruschov met her when she walked down the steps to the concrete passenger disembarkation area.

"Janka," he thundered from his 190-centimeter height, his militia uniform adding to his authority and bulk. Everyone exiting the plane gave him a wide berth. Mikhail's generally grim police face was for once modified by a huge grin. "I love you, Janka."

Mikhail was the only person she knew who still used her nickname. He grabbed her in a bear hug, almost smothering her against his chest. "Janka, I am so glad we could see each other again."

Jana took a deep breath when he finally let her come up for air. "Me too, Mikhail." He looked like he was going to hug her again, so she thrust the box of candy she had brought from Bratislava into his hands. "For Adriana. Milk chocolate with nuts."

"She will love them," he bellowed. It was the one characteristic of Mikhail that Jana always had problems with: He refused to speak below a roar.

Mikhail swept Jana through customs ahead of everyone else and without an examination, then to a car waiting for them at the front entrance to the terminal. "We rented the apartment downstairs for your stay. The woman, reliable, I've known her for years, has a nice place. Clean. A big bed. Better to sleep there than on our couch."

"A hotel room would have done."

"Not in Kiev!" His roar was only slightly muted in the car. "Better to rent an apartment than fight the bedbugs, thieves, and smell of alcohol and disinfectant in those places. You would need a gas mask to survive."

"I am a born survivor," she advised him.

"So am I," he allowed. "Except it is always better to survive in the most pleasant circumstances one can obtain." He switched gears, becoming more professional. "You know, the stuff you are asking for is not going to be easy to come by. It's not my department. I supervise traffic cops. Everybody here guards their own farm. If you control information, you control your job. So they hold it close to their chests. However, there is a guy I know who owes me small favors. His wife got drunk and drove her car into a storefront. I helped him quash any problems."

"You are becoming corrupt, Mikhail."

"A little corruption in the right places never hurts. It allows me to do my job. I help him; he helps me. One hand washes the other. How does it hurt to aid a comrade's wife? Besides, he divorced her."

"For a younger woman?"

"Young but ugly. She's already drinking." His laughter was an even louder roar, the sound's impact causing the driver of the car to swerve. "Watch your driving!" he yelled at his chauffeur. "You could get us all killed."

Jana looked at Mikhail with disapproval. Mikhail's face adopted a faked, comically sheepish look. "The driver, he needs to keep his eyes on the road. What if someone threw a bomb at the car? Would he flinch from the noise?"

"Not after having to listen to you, Mikhail."

"That's good to hear. Now we can continue on with confidence." He took her hand in his huge paw, the two of them old pals, sitting in comfortable silence the rest of the way to police headquarters.

Chapter 10

The nightclub was drab, to say the least. Grimy was probably a better description. Nothing indicated that it was a place where a fun time was going to be enjoyed by all. The putative decorators had hung multicolored streamers from the ceiling in a feeble attempt to disguise reality. Unfortunately, the ambient light made the streamers look like a demented spider's web, with a huge tarantula waiting in a corner to scuttle across the strands and drop on an unsuspecting customer to devour him.

There were the usual complement of B-girls sitting at a small bar, half asleep because there were no available single men for them to fasten onto. The few customers in the place appeared bored, dressed in clothes that looked like they were from a vintage thrift shop that sold third-hand apparel. None of the customers were listening to the performers, too busy with each other or with drinking to care.

Jana watched the performers pretending to be the life of a party that only existed in their own minds. A man who was too old for the job sang a duet with a young blonde who had her eyes lined with kohl and her lips darkly painted to make them look ripe and sexy. The four-piece group backing the duet wore huge T-Shirts on which "Vadym's Place" was painted in fluorescent Cyrillic.

It was Vadym they were waiting for.

"He is a clod," Mikhail's wife hissed. "An hour eating this

terrible food, drinking this awful wine." Adriana, normally very cheerful, had been happy when Mikhail suggested she accompany them to the club, but the place had an aura that made her uneasy and anxious. Vadym's lateness was not helping. So she complained. "If he does not come in the next ten minutes, I want to go home."

Mikhail rolled his eyes, shifting his bulk, trying to get comfortable in the cramped booth. "He will be here. He's always late. He's that kind of person."

"Late!" She spit it out. "That means he's a bad police officer."

"My sweet, there are good police officers who are always late." The look on her face indicated that Mikhail's attempt to appease her had failed. He kept trying. "He is very proud of this place."

"What kind of police officer owns a nightclub? There are whores at the bar. They must work for him."

"Prostitution is not illegal in this wonderful country of ours. They are independent. They pay a small rental fee for the chairs. It's good for business."

Adriana took out her compact and began to fix her makeup, turning to Jana. "Do you remember when you two met in that school in Budapest? How we all had fun at night? Those places we went to, they were cheerful. Not like this filthy cave." She turned back to Mikhail. "I promise you, Mikhail, I will leave here if he does not come in five minutes."

"Vadym will come."

"The International Law Enforcement Academy in Budapest. Good people; a good learning experience." Jana smiled at Adriana. "And, yes, good fun. Young police officers can still have fun."

"Budapest was a wonderful city." Mikhail smiled, remembering. "A good place for a friendship to start."

"I was jealous," Adriana sniffed. Her eyes roved over to Mikhail, who looked embarrassed.

Jana shrugged. "We have always just been friends, Adriana."

"Just friends," echoed Mikhail.

"Good." Adriana, satisfied, slipped her hand into one of Mikhail's big paws. "I knew it. I just wanted to hear it." She went back to her least favorite person of the moment. "You were in the police academy in Kiev with Vadym. You told me the instructors did not like him, Mikhail."

"What do instructors know about who will really make a good police officer? They guess."

"They liked you."

Mikhail looked embarrassed again. "Vadym was always a little pompous. He would try to correct the instructors to show them how much he knew. They didn't care for that."

"And they didn't like his showing up late," Adriana added.

"That too," Mikhail agreed.

The orchestra took its break. "Thanks to God, they are finally stopping," Adriana muttered under her breath so she would not wound any of the performers by her criticism. Then she turned back to Mikhail, pointedly giving him his etiquette lesson for the evening. "When he arrives, if he comes at all, you will have to tell Vadym the performers were wonderful. We are not hypocrites, it's a lie in a good cause. I don't want any of them to lose their job because of an irritated woman's complaint."

"Of course, sweetheart," Mikhail agreed.

A small man, erect, looking a little like a pouter pigeon, came through the double set of winter drapes at the door, looking the place over as if he were the emperor of all he surveyed. A waiter rushed over to him, grabbing the man's briefcase when it was tossed to him, barely managing, as the pouter pigeon shrugged off his coat, to snatch the heavy leather garment before it hit the floor.

The man walked straight to their table.

Vadym looked even more overstuffed up close. In love with himself, yes. Pompous, filled with self-importance, a preposterous little porker, yes. But, aside from the vanity he projected, his eyes showed a sly intelligence as well as impatience to get to the point. Odd, thought Jana, for a man who was perpetually late.

"I am Vadym," he announced, then nodded at Adriana, as if regretting the energy spent on having to acknowledge her, then, with more cordiality, at Mikhail, managing to get Mikhail's name out in greeting. He stared at Jana, patronizing and attentive at the same time. "You are the police officer from Slovakia? I am Vadym Grisko. You may call me Vadym."

Jana stared back at him for a moment. Italian tie, expensive shoes. Too costly for a police officer who did not have an outside income. Probably graft. This nightclub itself, a part of it. She hoped he had not sold out their case already. "You may call me Jana, or Matinova, or Commander. Whatever you feel comfortable with."

Grisko caught the irony in her voice. He stared for a second too long, wondering whether to take offense. Finally he sat, laying his briefcase on the table. Without preamble, he pulled out a number of photographs and a stack of reports that had been stapled together under a cardboard cover that bore the name "Makine, Ivan." In capital letters, at the center of the page, was the name "KOBA."

Grisko looked over at Mikhail while Jana examined the photographs. "You will remember what I have done for you?" Vadym was making sure that Mikhail acknowledged that he owed him now. A favor would require a favor in return.

Mikhail sighed. "I find myself always in your debt, Vadym."

"I am a generous man." Grisko maintained his grip on the reports, his fingertips impatiently running back and forth across their cardboard cover. "Good to see you with your wife." He did not bother to glance at Adriana. "Have you danced together this evening?" He looked pointedly at the dance floor.

Mikhail nodded. Grisko wanted to talk to Jana without another set of ears around. Mikhail was being asked to leave. "I think that is a wonderful idea." He turned to Adriana. "We must take advantage of the opportunity a club like this gives us, sweetheart."

"The band is not back yet, Mikhail."

"We have music in our hearts, my love. Who needs a band?"

Adriana, suddenly comprehending, walked stiffly with Mikhail to the center of the dance floor. The two of them came together and began swaying to unheard music.

"A nice couple, don't you think?" Grisko declared.

"Lovely." She decided she liked the man even less. "They are good for each other." She spread the photos in front of her on the table, then nodded at the reports Grisko was fingering. "Photographs are good, but they are much better if you have text with them."

"I have had difficulty in obtaining these documents. Everything is in disorder. A hard place to do business, Ukraine."

"Slovakia appreciates the effort. What is the old saying? 'To give is to receive.'"

"I like that philosophy. Have you noticed that people, no matter how different, think the same?" He went on without waiting for her to answer. "I have a cousin." He stared at her. "A stupid man."

"Cousins get into trouble," she suggested.

"Always. But one must help family."

"True."

"An altercation. He hit a man."

"Cousins do that."

"As I said, not a very bright individual. He was sentenced to three years of prison in Slovakia."

Jana considered it thoughtfully. "A terrible place to be, prison." If Grisko's "cousin" had been sentenced to three years, he either had a long record, was a gangster involved in organized crime, or had injured his victim seriously. If Grisko was interested, it was probably all three. She didn't want to put that kind of man back on the streets. "Once a man is sentenced, it is hard to bring him back. The courts generally will not allow us to do it."

"His family is mourning their loss." Grisko brought his hands to his eyes, bowing his head in mock grief. When he brought his head back up, he winked at her. "So we must help the whole family over this bad period. Just a small favor, not a big one."

"Small mercies are all anyone can hope for."

"One can only hope." Grisko pointed at photographs, his manner becoming direct. "Interesting photos, these, particularly of the fat woman." He slapped his hand lightly on the table for emphasis. "My cousin. He needs a change of prisons. The one he is being kept in, there are people who are also being kept there who are trying to do him injury."

"His bad temper, again."

"Naturally. He can be somewhat aggressive."

"Under the circumstances, a small favor, even for an aggressive man like your cousin, is not out of order. I think this one can be arranged."

"Wonderful. To the Czech Republic?"

The Czech Republic. The prisoner had very dangerous enemies if Grisko wanted him shipped that far. Yes, Jana thought, organized crime. Perhaps a war between factions. No other reason for a Ukrainian officer to make such a request outside of official channels. She decided to put more cards on the table. "If a man gives information to the authorities, we can possibly help in this way. I only say 'possibly' because you are asking us to send him to another country."

"'Possibly' is not good enough."

"It would depend on the information your cousin had."

"Narcotics. My cousin hates narcotics and would like to put an end to the dealing in drugs."

"Slovak authorities would welcome that."

Grisko pulled a small envelope from his jacket pocket. "His name, prison number, and so forth. I assume you will act on it quickly?"

"No later than tomorrow." The prison authorities would get the information from the prisoner. Grisko knew it had to be good, so there was very little doubt in Jana's mind that the prisoner's transfer would be worth the cost.

Grisko slid the reports over to her, confident that they had finalized their arrangement. "I like dealing with fellow police officers. We understand each other." He pointed at the photos again. "The women we identified, all have minor criminal records. One for petty theft, another for working with a group of pickpockets. And so on and so on. They worked the tourists that came into Kiev. My guess is that all of them, including the one from Moldova, had gone into prostitution. A natural progression for ambitious young ladies looking for a profession." He laughed at his joke. "The old fat one you showed me, the one dumped in the Danube, we know her as well."

"She was also Ukrainian?"

"Born in Kremenchuk. But most of her activities were also here in Kiev."

"One of our man's passports said he was from Kremenchuk."

"I will get to him in a minute." Grisko was saving the best for last. "First we finish with the old woman. Also a prostitute when she was younger. She then graduated into all types of petty criminal acts. We have a lot of paper on her. The last time she was here, she was questioned about stolen vehicle sales.

"The group she was involved in was, and is, reported to be stealing cars to order, like an agency. They steal them in Western Europe: Mercedes, Peugeots, BMWs, top of the line. They then slip them over the border from the EU or Prague or Sweden or wherever, into an Eastern bloc country, go through a fraudulent sale, and, in a flash, you have legitimized ownership of the vehicle which can now be brought back to the West.

"Amazing what you can purchase a new Mercedes or BMW for in Ukraine. The last entry on her sheet was two years ago."

"According to her son, she would return to Ukraine maybe twice a year," Jana said.

"Probably. We just didn't pick her up."

"Did the man killed in the auto burning have anything to do with her or the dead prostitutes?"

"Ah, the man, Ivan Makine. Better known as Koba. Koba! An ugly name. Fitting. He picked it up from God knows where. You win the lottery with him. And with me.

"I met him once." Grisko paused to savor the moment, enjoying the surprise on Jana's face. "The most dangerous man I have ever encountered. Absolutely evil. A killer. He left bodies in his wake wherever he went. And we knew he traveled, so he left many bodies, whether he did the killings himself or had another person do it for him. The street knew he was responsible, and they would tell us."

Jana felt excited. Finally, positive information on the man in the car. "You recognized him from the passport photos?"

"Who can tell from a shit passport photo? And it has been a long time since I saw him. But it looks a lot like him." He laughed at himself. "Now you know why all police officers hate I.D. testimony from witnesses. Like me, they are never quite sure."

"Tell me the circumstances of your meeting with Koba."

"Patience, dear fellow officer." He was enjoying his story, prolonging it. "He wanted people to talk about him. Fear! Fear was a tool for him. The crowds in the streets parted for him wherever he walked." Grisko half closed his eyes, reliving the event.

"It was not your normal type of meeting. I was in a restaurant. The owner had not paid his protection money, and he was just brave enough and just frightened enough to talk to us. That's why I was there. Koba walked up to the owner, while I was standing there, and drove an ice pick into the man's eye. No talking; no bargaining. He simply killed the man in the cruelest, most public way where everyone could see, and so everyone would forever after be afraid of him."

"You arrested him?"

"A very difficult thing to do. A young woman had a gun to my head. A pretty woman. The women loved Koba, or Makine if you prefer. I very quietly watched them leave."

"Your police looked for them?"

"For both of them. I never saw either of them alive again. If any of my associates saw him, or her, they never reported it. Koba—poof—was gone."

"Even the police were frightened?"

"Anyone would be. His reputation was so ferocious, he was

reported to be impervious to bullets and knives. A fiction. He was very, very bright; he was at the center of the criminal world, involved in every type of depravity. He played with the police in Hungary, Romania, Russia, the Baltic states, for years."

"How do you know, if no one ever saw him again?"

"Always the rumors."

"I am interested in the woman who held a gun to your head."

Grisko stared at the ceiling, going off on a tangent. "Maybe I should add a water motif to this place. All blue, with the moonlight gliding over the ripples. It would be pretty." He looked back over to Jana. "What do you think?" He didn't wait for a reply. "I like rivers. Lakes also. It's the soothing nature of water. Of course, I only like them in the summer. Too cold in the winter."

He finally returned to the woman who had held a gun to his head. "We know nothing about her. Believe me, we turned the country upside-down. Nothing."

"So you stopped looking."

"When he died, there was no reason to look any further." Grisko laughed. He watched the expression on Jana's face, enjoying the fact that she didn't quite comprehend what he was saying.

"You thought you had the first case in which he died. No. I did." He continued watching her face as she tried to piece what he was saying together with the facts she had.

"Died? You mean in Slovakia?"

"Here. In Kiev. Seven years after the ice-pick murder. Near the monastery; everybody knows the place. All the tourists go to see those dead monks in the catacombs. You should go there. Quite a sight. I went there as a boy. Frightened me when I realized even holy men die." He ran his fingers through his hair, patting a few strands down, then wiped the hair oil off his fingers onto the tablecloth. "He was killed in a collision with a fuel truck. The driver was killed as well. Bad fire. Identification by documents."

"Just like the Slovak burning."

"Maybe he was killed here? Maybe in Slovakia? I'll tell you what: I'll let your country have the credit."

"Maybe he was not killed anywhere." Jana thought about the crash in Slovakia, then came back to Ukraine. "Witnesses?"

"One, a monk from the monastery. Out on some errand for his patriarch. The monk saw the crash. The car came down the street, slid on the ice, and boom! Accident. The monk's name is in the reports. He would seem to have been a reputable witness."

"I can find him at the monastery?"

"He drank himself to death a short time after the crash. By mistake: He drank cleaning fluid."

"A bad way to die."

"All ways to die are bad."

"You are sure he drank the cleaning fluid without being coaxed into it?"

"You know better than to ask that. There are no crystal balls in our pockets. I practice police work, not astrology. In this business, there is nothing sure."

"Did you believe Koba was dead?"

"At first, I thought, possibly. I wanted him to be dead. After the monk died, not so much possible. Now, maybe no."

Her business with Grisko was over. Not very satisfactory, but a piece of information or two. Koba was taking shape. Jana looked at the dance floor to invite Mikhail and Adriana back to the table. They were not there.

She quickly checked the rest of the club. The B-girls were no longer sitting at the bar; the waiters were gone. There were no other customers. The room was empty except for her and Grisko. A flicker of fear went through her.

"Grisko, get up!!" She stood. Grisko, a little bewildered, stayed seated.

Jana reached over and pulled him to his feet. "Everyone is gone, Grisko. No one is here but you and me." She let him go, yelling for Mikhail and Adriana.

Grisko looked around, comprehension suddenly dawning. Frightened and wide-eyed, he came out of his seat as if he had been ejected. "Bad!! We have to get out."

He started to go for the front door. Jana grabbed him. "Through the kitchen, not the front." Grisko responded by bolting toward the kitchen, with Jana following him.

The pouter pigeon ran surprisingly fast as they scrambled through the kitchen area. Food was still steaming in the pots. There were no cooks. "Everybody is gone." Grisko ran even faster, scuttling through the rear door.

The two of them skidded into a dark alley, Grisko caroming off a garbage can, sliding to his knees, scrabbling to his feet again as they ran toward the light in the nearest side street. As soon as they reached it Jana saw Mikhail and Adriana leaning against a car across the road. Jana ran toward them; Grisko followed.

"Up the street!! We need to go further up."

Mikhail immediately reacted to Jana's sense of urgency. He didn't wait for Adriana to respond. The huge man picked up his wife and carried her an additional fifty meters, running. Finally, they all stopped, panting. Jana and Grisko looked up and down the street, then back to the club. They saw no one.

"Nothing," Grisko said between gasps.

Jana stepped into the middle of the street, trying to find an angle that would allow her to observe a larger arc of space.

"Where did the people go? Your waiters, cooks?" She turned back to Mikhail. "Why did you go outside?"

Adriana responded for him. "There was no music. Why stay there?"

"Adriana wanted to leave, so we left. She didn't like it there."

The fear had begun to ebb from Grisko. He looked at Jana accusingly. "You spooked me! I should not have left my own club like that. Undignified. There was nothing wrong."

"There is still something wrong. I know it; you know it."

"I don't know any such thing." Grisko's ego started to reassert itself, puffing him up into his pouter pigeon stance. He started back toward the club.

"Grisko, where did everyone go? *Why* did they go?" She took a step after him. "Wait a little longer. Let's make sure."

"It's my club. I am going back!" he called over his shoulder. He began to walk faster, swinging his arms, more and more the little Napoleon.

He had gotten half the distance back to the club when the place erupted in a huge ball of fire that curved up and around the whole structure which, for a moment, seemed to continue to exist, stable on its frame, until it erupted, in an eyeblink, into a shredding of plaster, brick, wood, tile, becoming part of a huge, shattering, burning tornado, the blast tossing cars parked by the club onto their sides, debris raining down like hot pieces of magma rejected by Hades, too hot even for Hell.

Mikhail covered Adriana with his body, fiery pieces bounding off him. Jana was thrown to the ground, the heap that was Mikhail and Adriana between her and the fiery debris of the explosion, saving her from its direct assault. She waited until the primary momentum of the blast was past, then picked herself up to stagger through the still-falling shards of wreckage toward Grisko.

The Ukrainian was sitting up, alive, soot-covered, his face

blackened, clothes torn. He was no longer a pouter pigeon. His chest appeared to have sunk. Through the grime on his face, his skin had gone pale and a small trickle of blood descended from a bloody eyebrow. Grisko finally focused on Jana. "My club," he got out, teeth chattering from fear. "Gone."

"Gone," she agreed.

Grisko wiped his eyes, thinking. Finally he said, "They were right. He is indestructible." It took him a while to get his lips and tongue wet enough to spit his conclusion into the inhospitable air. "Koba is alive."

They continued to crouch, watching the fire, as people began emerging from the surrounding buildings, awed by the blaze, coming closer and closer to the magnetic pull of the flames, staring wide-eyed at the conflagration.

Grisko eyed the bystanders, trying to satisfy himself that the bomber was not one of them, all the while checking his arms, his face, his legs, surprised that he was still a living creature, still whole. He muttered, repeating to himself: "They were right. The man is indestructible. Koba lives."

Chapter 11

The fear that comes from being watched is contagious. It spreads like a virus whose symptoms are paranoia and anger, eventually becoming an epidemic that kills the spirit of everyone it contacts. Relationships disintegrate, nations break up, civilizations shake, all because of this contagion of human emotion. With Jana and Dano it was no different. They were not superhuman.

It began and ended with their friends.

Dano would come to her, smiling, saying he had met so-and-so, a budding playwright, a dramaturge who had a wonderful concept for a Schnitzler play. Or he had met an actress who was a leading lady in a film being produced in Prague, and she wanted them to meet the director. Or they were invited to a cast party for the close of a show, or a celebration in SNP Square, or a jazz concert where he knew several of the musicians. Maybe it was an old friend from school days who needed help, or his mother's cousin, a Slovak who had produced a play in Moscow. All of them suddenly represented a possible danger.

Trokan had given her fair warning. And now, if they had reports on her, they had reports on Dano. The entries in the secret dossiers had to be stopped. The more paper, the more serious the charges would be. And that meant calling no further dangerous attention to themselves, an impossible task to demand of an actor.

The budding playwright was the one who first increased the pressure on them. Dano came home elated. One of the new writers—a friend of Vaclav Havel, the world-famous Czech author—had seen Dano as Hamlet, and the man wanted to write the lead character in his next play with Dano in mind. They would stage the play in Bratislava with a mixed company of Czechs and Slovaks. Czechs and Slovaks understood each other's languages, so each would speak in his native tongue.

The play would be about unity: unity in the family leading to unity in the country and the world. It would fit in with the current SSR concept of a unified republic, and when the writing and staging problems had been worked out in Bratislava they would take the play on the road to Prague. It was the next step for his acting career, said Dano breathlessly, and he had invited the playwright to their apartment. Jana and her mother were to provide the meal.

It was a wife's duty to help her husband, so Jana, despite the increasing caseload and responsibilities she was taking on in her own job, accepted the task. When the day came, Jana bought the wine and, with the rare good fortune that crime had taken a day off, she managed to get home early, in time to aid her mother. Together, they made a number of Slovak and Czech dishes to carry out the theme of the play.

Except that, when the playwright arrived, he came without Dano, but with an entourage of eight people whom Dano had neglected to tell Jana about. Adjustment time. She and her mother made do, her mother scrambling to the neighbors to borrow this and that, additional silverware and crockery to supplement their meager supply. All the while, their guests smoked up a visible, acrid haze which invaded every corner of the apartment. Every thirty seconds, Jana would run to the phone, trying to find out why Dano was not there.

He arrived an hour late, with two other actor friends in tow, as well as a man who claimed to be a director, and who was, in fact, Zibinova's informant, the secret police officer from the cast party. Jana was angry with Dano for being late; she was more afraid than angry when she saw the director. Everything that was said or done that evening would appear in a report and become part of their dossier.

Dano, making up for being late, was even more charming than usual. He apologized to everyone individually, claiming that the artistic director of the National Theatre had insisted on talking to him about their new season, indicating the roles he thought Dano was suitable for. Dano said he had laughed at the man. Time for me to think of Prague, he had informed the artistic director; time for me to develop my own vehicles. He left the man, Dano said, with his own vision, the one that Dano held of his personal future. He was now no longer sure that he would take any of the roles the National Theatre had just offered since, as Dano put it, he was the "premier young actor in Slovakia."

His apartment audience, particularly the Czech playwright, cheered Dano on, all of them gabbling about the need for change in the system, a change that would give the actors more choice of the roles they were asked to play and of the plays themselves.

While Dano and the others talked, Jana watched the agent provocateur, knowing he was taking mental notes of who was saying what and who was agreeing. The fat weasel would nod, and smile, stimulating more and more extravagant statements.

Jana could no longer tolerate her anticipation of the terrible mischief that might be generated by the viper they had taken into their apartment. She pulled Dano from his audience, not an easy task with an actor who has had too much to drink.

She half-dragged her husband into the bathroom, locking the door. Dano misunderstood her actions. "If you are still angry with me for being late, I apologize again, my sweet, sweet wife." He began giving Jana little kisses on the forehead, mouth, ears, eyelids, neck, shoulders, and hands, only stopping when she pushed him away. "Look at us," he joked. "All alone in the bathroom. A wonderful opportunity for us both, and my wife pushes me away."

"You know I love you?" Jana said. Dano started to come closer. She held him off with a straightarm. "Listen to me, Dano. I need a promise from you."

"I promise never to be late again." He tried edging around her arm, then used her arm to pull her closer. "I'm trying to make up."

"What I tell you now, you have to promise to tell no one else at this party, or afterward."

Dano only half-listened to her, preoccupied with his friends in the other room. "I have to get back to the party. They will be asking for the host." He tried to unlock the door. Jana held it shut.

"I need that promise, Dano."

"Promises, promises, always promises." He touched his forefinger to his lips, then the same finger to her lips. "For you, I promise."

Jana relaxed slightly at his seeming willingness to keep his word. "You will say nothing?"

Dano was now impatient. "I promised. When have I ever broken a promise to you?" He tried to push past her and out of the bathroom. Jana held up her hands, palms out.

"All right, Dano." At that moment she wished she had never become a police officer. "There is an informant here." Dano looked at her not quite comprehending. "There is a Secret Police informant here among our guests."

Comprehension set in. Dano pulled away from her, his face registering both anger and fear. "Why here?"

"Why not here? They are everywhere." She again tried to impress on him the necessity of keeping the informant's presence a secret. "The Secret Police are aware that I know him. If you do anything to let on that you know, or tell anyone else, or try to do anything to him, they will take measures against you, and me. And my mother. You understand?" Dano's eyes had lost their focus. Jana shook him to emphasize the seriousness of his promise. "You know nothing!"

When they returned to their guests, things seemed to go well at first. The playwright was holding forth on the concept of his play; Dano let the man hold center stage. But Dano's silence and his heavy, continuous drinking were not like him. She could see the tension building. Only when Dano left the room could she relax, even if for a few minutes. Good, she told herself; they would get through the evening without more damage. The tension would ease overnight, and she and Dano could discuss their circumstances and how to deal with them in the morning after they'd had their night's sleep and were fresh and open. But when Dano walked back into the room, he held Jana's service automatic in his hand.

Before Jana could do anything, Dano had walked over to the agent provocateur and put the gun to his head. There was a silence, then nervous giggles, a few of the guests thinking this was a part of a performance. The little man with the gun to his head was initially a statue, afraid to move, afraid not to move. Then a tremor began building from his legs, his feet jiggled, then tremors went through his stomach, chest, shoulders, and up to his eyes, which began to tear. The longer Dano remained silent and the longer the gun was held to the man's head, the more pronounced the fat man's trembling was and the more his tears flowed.

Jana slowly rose, preparing to walk over to Dano and take the automatic from his hand, when he cocked the gun. She froze, as did everyone else, all of them becoming aware that this was a real-life event and not a piece of theater. Their focus was now on the pistol, eyes fixed on Dano's hand, waiting for his finger to pull the trigger.

Dano placed his face close to the informant's. "Get up." The man struggled to his feet, wobbling and weaving, his body shaking more than ever. "You are to walk to the door. When you get to the door, you are to leave this house, this city, and the theater. There is no place for you." Dano waited a moment, to let the words sink in. "You understand?"

The agent provocateur nodded, managing to take a few little steps in a jerky start, than began a staggering run to the door, and out.

Jana slowly walked over to Dano, who had not bothered to look up when the little man had left, took the gun from Dano's hand, and uncocked it.

Eventually, he looked at her. "I broke my promise, didn't I?"

Chapter 12

The plane was late arriving in Bratislava. Nothing new. However, this one was long past its estimated arrival time. They had bumped through the air pockets, the pilot trying to make up time. As usual, the late arrival was due to a delayed departure from Kiev. The passengers had been forced to sit in the plane on the runway at the Kiev airport while additional defrosting of the plane's wings and engines was completed. The wait had given Jana time to think.

Mikail had told Jana that Grisko had gone into a meltdown worse than the one at Chernobyl. His club being destroyed was secondary to the belief that he had now been targeted by Koba. All the man could think of, as he raged through police headquarters, was that he could no longer walk down the street for fear he would get an ice pick in his eye or a bullet in the back of his head.

Grisko had remembered other stories about Makine, the man who had become the legend called Koba, some of them so vividly related by Grisko to Mikhail and passed on to Jana that they now came up again and again in her own memory: Koba had dismembered one of his rivals, cutting off an arm, a leg, his nose, all while the man was still alive; another, about cutting off one his prostitutes' breasts when she tried to hold money back from him; the third, about Koba walking into a rival's apartment, and when he came out the man's infant son and two-year-old daughter had both been raped while his rival was forced to watch.

What kind of a man had Koba been? No, what kind of a man was he still? A man? No, a creature bred from the netherworld whose sole task was to make people regret that they were alive. Was this creature still living? Still robbing the world of its security, its sanity? And where was he now, this minute? On the plane with her? Even though the seat next to her held an old woman in a babushka, Koba's spoor contaminated that seat, and the one in front and in back. And why had Koba chosen to reappear and follow her to Ukraine? How had he known she was going there?

The day after the attack, Grisko slept in his office in police headquarters with the door locked. Even after Grisko's subordinates informed their chief about their boss's crazed behavior, Grisko refused to open his door to his supervisor. It took an hour-long plea by the man to convince Grisko that he was not an agent of Koba.

The hysteria did aid the investigation in one way: The other officers were moved sufficiently to give a semblance of help. They brought in those who were believed to be former associates of Koba, all of whom were shown the photograph of the man and asked to identify him. Each one reacted with fear. They yelled, cried, growled, and squealed that they had never seen the man before, never heard his name before, and had no information they could give to the police.

No additional leads were developed, and no further evidence resulted from the inquiries, with the exception of the belief that Koba had been some kind of dread presence in their lives and still existed inside them in a twisted, monstrous way.

Some cities are just dirty. Others are more than dirty, they are unclean in a spiritual way. Jana was convinced Kiev was now one of the latter, the cracked, grimy buildings sinking deeper into a dreadful swamp that was rising up to engulf every part of it. And its inhabitants were warped people, shuffling through the grubby streets, becoming more and more like the ruins they trudged through.

Jana was glad to be out of there, glad to be returning to Bratislava and the fresh, clean snow on the airport tarmac. Trokan was waiting for her in the terminal. He immediately caught her mood, and they sat in silence for most of the drive to the city. About halfway there, she realized that he was taking her home instead of to police headquarters.

"I thought you wanted me to write up my report."

"Sleep, then the report." They continued to sit in silence until they glided to a stop in front of her house. "I am now taking care of your blind cats."

"My brilliant aide was supposed to feed them."

"He is sightless himself. Besides, he knows nothing about cats, much less blind ones," Trokan allowed. "Animals need nurturing."

She smiled. "What do you know about cats?"

"Nothing." He thought about it for a moment longer. "They remind me of you, so better in my hands than his."

They reminded him of her? A new Trokan riddle. Always surprising her; always surprising his other troops. He liked to keep them slightly off-balance before making his point. "I may not be blind," she pointed out. "However, I may be obtuse. Please explain the comparison."

Trokan waited until they were fully parked, then he emphatically hit the automatic trunk release preparatory to retrieving her luggage. "The cats, they never saw my office before I took them there. But they are beginning to find their way around using smell, hearing, touch, memory."

"So, on this case I am feeling my way around? Bumping

into the furniture? The bombing of the club is like the cats crashing into your desk chair? If so, just a little bump."

"A large bump."

"Okay, a large bump."

"Did it frighten you?"

"Bombs scare everyone, me included."

"Good. You are still in touch with yourself. So are the cats when they go bump in their perpetual night. Despite the bumps, the cats keep trying, and so do you. I am amazed at them; I am amazed at you."

"Bumps are a part of being a police officer. A part of life. We both know this."

"I can take you off this case. Do you want that?"

She shrugged. "Like the blind cats, I want to continue."

In Trokan's mind, victims deserved at least a small reason, an explication given for their murders. Some deaths required more of an explanation, required a more complete investigation and a more competent, caring investigator. The bombing had not destroyed Jana's desire to get to the bottom of all these deaths. Jana was still whole. She was still the investigator for this case.

Trokan relaxed. "Maybe you are not a blind cat after all; then again, maybe it is not so hard, being blind." He exited the car, pulling her bags from the trunk, placing them at the beginning of her walk. Jana continued to sit in the car, staring down the block. Trokan checked to see what she was looking at. There was nothing unusual to see, so he walked over to her door and opened it.

"Time to stop thinking and go to bed. Sleep is good for the soul, and your soul has been up for a few days too many."

Jana finally focused on Trokan. "We questioned the employees, the bar girls, the musicians. The manager said he had received a phone call from Grisko before he came to the club that night. Grisko was suffering from a cold, so his voice was hoarse. Grisko, or the man pretending he was Grisko, told the manager to have all the employees, everyone, leave the club when he came to my table to talk with me.

"The manager said he knew enough not to question Grisko, so that was exactly what he had everyone do. Grisko swore he'd said no such thing. I believe him. He was too frightened to be lying; I also believed the manager."

Jana slid out of the car, again looking down the block, checking the street, looking for anyone performing surveillance on her house. Trokan, trying to reassure her, joked, "I don't think the mad bomber is spying on this street right now. Too many nosy neighbors. The broom brigade would be after him in minutes."

"I want to try an experiment with you."

"It depends on the nature of the experiment. I am getting too old to try certain things."

"I would like you to run to the middle of the next block as fast as you can."

He eyed her, skeptical about her motives. "I am a police colonel. Have you noticed the fat around my middle? It comes with my desk. People expect me to live at my desk. If I do what you ask, they will think I have gone crazy and will report me to the minister."

"Okay, then. I want you to time me. Start when I say 'Go.' After that, wait until I raise my hand and yell. I want you to note the time from beginning to end."

"I hereby declare you officially crazy. However, I will humor you, Matinova." He focused on his watch. "Any time."

Jana took a breath. "Now!" she yelled, and started running, reached the corner, crossed the street without looking, and ran another ten meters. Then she turned around, crouching, her eyes shut.

Trokan began silently counting the minutes off. At two and a half minutes Jana was erect again, taking a few steps, slowly at first, then striding, before she suddenly stopped. Her arm went up and she shouted "Time" to him. Trokan checked his watch as Jana jogged back to him.

"How long?"

"Three and a half minutes. So, the reason?"

"Grisko and I ran out of the club to where we stopped, then waited. Then Grisko began to walk back to his club. Then came the explosion."

"And the reason for timing the actions?"

She picked up her bag. "Why did the blast come *after* we left the club?"

"Bad timing when they set the bomb."

"I disagree. Grisko is notoriously late. So, there could be no way to predict when he would come. There could be no accurate timer on the bomb. Therefore, the bomber had to set the bomb off in person. Whoever it was, was there, watching.

"There is more. Whoever set off the bomb had to have the time to plant it. Which means the bomber knew well in advance that Grisko was going to meet me, and where. Probably it is someone Grisko works with."

"A police officer?"

"I think so, yes."

"Any idea who?"

"Grisko told everyone at the station he was going to meet the Slovak officer. Theoretically, it could be anyone."

Trokan eyed her. He thought about the events. "Why set the bomb off after you ran out?" He answered himself. "The bomber wanted you out of there when it exploded."

"They wanted to make sure everyone got out, including Grisko and me. Then, when Grisko started back, the bomber triggered the explosion. Not to kill him; to frighten him. He didn't want to kill; otherwise, why get rid of the employees?"

"To frighten you as well; maybe to warn *you* off."

Jana walked to her front step, carrying her bags. "There is an inconsistency here. Was it to stop my looking into the death of Ivan Makine, our Koba, if in fact he did die? Or to make sure we started looking for him if he is still alive? I do know one thing: Whoever set the explosives and blew up the building is involved with the man or his legend, one way or the other."

"And the man is?"

"Still too early. Not enough proof yet."

Jana opened her front door, sliding her bag inside. She looked back at him, smiling, deliberately keeping Trokan on tenterhooks.

Trokan scratched his head in an exaggerated gesture of puzzlement. "Okay. Don't tell me today. But remember, if you don't, I still have your blind cats. No answers, and I will feed them rusty nails and shoelaces."

Jana looked up at the sky, dragging out the moment. There was going to be more snow coming from the west, but it would be a lot better here than in Ukraine. She looked over at Trokan. "Koba is a man who kills without hesitation. He would not care about the cook and bottle washers. Or me or Grisko. The bomber was not Koba. Whoever it was warned us, warned us that he could also stretch out his hand and kill if we did not heed the warning."

Jana stepped into the house, only to pop her head out again. "So there are at least two antagonists here, not just one. Maybe a whole separate set." She waved good-bye at Trokan. "And make sure you feed my cats well while I'm asleep."

She shut the door behind her.

Chapter 13

The aftermath of Dano's broken promise was as Jana expected. When the informer fled, he told Zibinova what had occurred. Rather than arrest Dano and try him for assault, the government opted for another solution. After all, bureaucracy never wants to embarrass itself. Dano was a national figure on the stage: the young Romeo, a figure their own critics had labeled the "Savior of Slovak Drama." So their way was a simple but vicious one: They simply forced the National Theatre to give him only minor roles, and even those were offered more and more infrequently.

Dano refused to take his cue and leave voluntarily. With the word out that he was becoming a non-person, the critics began to berate him, even in the small parts that he was now playing. They went out of their way to be spiteful. After a year and a half, the National shipped him to a regional theater in the north of the country. Six months later, they dropped him completely.

Jana's punishment was lighter. As soon as Trokan was made aware that Dano had threatened the informant with her gun, he had Jana transferred to Preshov, a small city in the East, and dropped one grade for storing her service weapon in an unsafe way, allowing it to be used in a criminal act.

Being apart is difficult for all married couples. However, in a small country, it is easier to get together, even if it is for just one day a week. And because of that day, and the sexual heat that absence increases, Jana became pregnant with Katerina. The pregnancy revitalized her relationship with Dano, strengthening their bonds. For Dano, it was as if he had been cast as the leading man in a major production. He told anyone and everyone about his newest creation, almost as if Jana had nothing to do with it. Jana did not mind. It gave Dano renewed hope, and he traveled all over Bratislava again, trying to revive his career.

On those days when they could be together in Bratislava, they would try to meet with all the people who might take a chance on Dano, despite his being in disfavor with the state.

Their first effort was the producer who had a new concept for a Schnitzler play. It would be based on the play *La Ronde*. Except it would take place in a war-torn setting, and the actors would play couples accidentally thrown together, their frantic sexual needs generated by war and devastation. It would be a comedy, like the original, but with such a dramatic background that the comedy inherent in the play would be intensified and the audience would accept a more explicit sexual content.

Dano tried to sell the concept to an actress who was the leading lady of a comic film that had just been made in Prague. She grasped the idea and went to her lover who had made the film, to convince him that this would first make a wonderful play, and then a film. Unfortunately, based on the success of his film, her lover decided to defect to the West where his opportunities would be greater, taking the very willing actress along with him.

Then there was his mother's cousin, a sometime producer of plays in Moscow, who wanted to go on the road to bring her productions to the rest of Eastern Europe. She had access to all the scenery and costumes at a ridiculously cheap rate, so that mounting a production in Slovakia would be inexpensive. But the authorities in Moscow confiscated the warehoused material, saying that, to their amazement, they had discovered that the producer had filched them from a Moscow theater. Dano's mother's cousin had to flee.

Then there was Dano's old friend from their school days. He had fled from Poprad to Bratislava to hide because he had embezzled money from the band he worked with. He swore to Dano he had not stolen the money, but the manager of the band had tricked him into signing incriminating documents, and now it looked like all the evidence pointed to Dano's friend as the thief. Except, his Poprad friend winked, he still had access to some of the stolen funds and maybe Dano could use them to finance a stage or movie production.

As soon as Jana found out about the friend running from the Criminal Police, she told Dano that he had to either turn in his Poprad friend or never see the man again.

Jana's pregnancy convinced Dano. She warned him that if he continued flirting with the thief, he would be endangering the future of their child. As desperate as he was for a project, for once Dano listened to her.

Then there was the rock concert, all proceeds to go to the building fund for an alternative theater to the National. Dano and his friends obtained a commitment from an American celebrity touring Europe to bring her show to Bratislava on an open date. They spent an entire night putting up posters advertising her appearance. When the posters, and the concert, came to the attention of the government, the performance permits were immediately canceled. The government wasn't about to allow the decadent West to invade Slovakia, especially to benefit a project the state had not sanctioned.

Possibilities began to peter out, and Dano became bored

and depressed, looking for any way to get himself out of his personal morass. Grasping for straws, they decided to get out of the house, agreeing to attend the traditional SSR May Day celebration in SNP Square.

Normally, on their one day together, Jana did not want to waste their time on an event like this, an event neither she nor Dano really cared about. However, Dano, who was dragging himself around the house, was clearly unhappy, and he insisted on going.

There was to be added interest to this event: Dano had heard that there might be a counter-demonstration, and he wanted to see how loud it got and whether the people were going to support it. A location where a counterrevolutionary demonstration might be held was not the place for an off-duty police officer, a woman seven and a half months pregnant. But when Dano told her he was going, with or without her, she went along. She saw little enough of him, and Jana told herself that at the first sign of trouble, she would leave.

The square was filled, the band playing martial music and the first speaker standing on the dais, when a commotion started in the rear of the crowd. First fruit, then bottles, were thrown; a group of young people began chanting slogans. Then the special riot police moved in, clubs flailing. People scattered, screaming; there were several shots, and the dispersion of the people in the square became a panic.

Jana tried to escape, her advanced pregnancy and its unwieldy bulk impeding her. Dano led her, straightarming panicked men and women out of the way, protecting her as best he could. But there was no way to get her to safety. The fleeing people barged into her as she fled. The two were suddenly parted, the crowd intervening between them. Jana was knocked down. It got even worse. People fell on her, kicking her, trying to get up and save themselves from being trampled. Jana finally lost consciousness after being kicked in the head.

An hour later, she was in the hospital, along with dozens of other injured people who had been hurt in the riot. But, unlike the others, she was in the maternity ward. Fifteen minutes after being taken by ambulance to the hospital, Jana gave birth to Katka. And despite all that Jana had gone through, Katka was a healthy baby.

Jana and Dano were ecstatic. The baby was even more beautiful than they had thought she would be. Even Trokan, who Jana had not seen since she was sent to Preshov, came to visit, a happy smile on his face.

Chapter 14

L ate-night calls are part of police work. You accept that,
but you don't have to like it. Jana had gone through her
notes and begun writing the rough draft of her report. It was
1:00 A.M. before she went to bed, so when the phone rang at
3:00 A.M. she was in the middle of a deep sleep. It took her a
while to realize where she was and what had awakened her.
Finally, she scrabbled to pick up the receiver, the remnants
of sleep making her voice hoarse as she grumped out
"Matinova."

The caller first spoke in French, then switched to English.
After a few seconds, she could understand it despite his
accent. His name was Jacques, and Jana was now authorized
by her department to go to Strasbourg, France, at 1600
hours today. The tickets were prepaid and waiting at the
Vienna airport, the Strasbourg hotel room reserved.

Jana scrambled for a pen, eventually getting most of the
travel particulars down before the man hung up. Then she
proceeded to get angry at herself, realizing that she hadn't
been given enough information about the subject of the
meeting, other than that it was about the human slave trade.

She lay back in bed, looking at the darkened ceiling. An
authorized trip meant the minister must have briefed
Trokan; so she called Trokan, and got his wife, Paula.

Jana winced as soon as the woman's voice came on the
line. Trokan's marriage was not a happy one, and his wife was

notorious for resenting the hours that he put in at work. Since Jana was often involved in the time her husband spent away, Paula had fixed on Jana as one of the major causes of her marital unhappiness. In the background, she could hear Trokan trying to persuade his wife to hand the phone over and Paula adamantly refusing. She cursed Jana for daring to call at that hour and awakening her husband, who had just gone to sleep, and then hung up in the middle of Jana's attempt to explain how important it was for her to talk to the colonel.

This had happened before to other officers, and there was an established protocol for dealing with "Trokan's Domestic War," as it was called. Jana waited a full five minutes, anticipating what was happening at the other end of the line, before redialing, confident that by now the colonel had rescued the phone. Trokan answered. In the background, Trokan's wife was still screaming.

This morning, Paula did not give up easily. She hurled gutter abuse at Trokan, scuffled with him for the phone, and yelled obscenities into the receiver when she got close enough. Trokan finally fended his wife off sufficiently to be able to talk.

"Commander Matinova, is that you?" Trokan was very formal with his staff, particularly the women, when his wife was around. It didn't help. The background ranting became even louder. "We only have a short time," Trokan got out. "My wife is a little annoyed."

Jana tried to hurry, abbreviating her sentences. "Interpol called. A meeting tomorrow. You know about it?"

"The minister signed off on the expenditure." There was a sudden grunt; Trokan's wife had apparently hit him. He covered the receiver with his hand, but not soon enough to prevent Jana from hearing him swear at his wife to get away from him. When he came back on the phone, there was a mixture of irony and resignation in his voice. "I'm being assaulted. If I kill her, remember that I acted in self-defense."

Jana choked back a giggle. Through it all, Trokan was maintaining his sense of humor. He muffled the phone again, then came back on. "She is promising to leave me forever, and is now packing her clothes. God grant that she keeps her word." There was a long sigh. "I have about a minute before she goes to the kitchen and gets cups to throw at me. So, quickly. As discussed, they want to share their information with yours from Ukraine."

"I can send them the report I've written."

"Not good enough, nor complete enough. They also want you to meet someone who may have seen Koba. He may be able to provide other information as well. You are to stay in Strasbourg as long as they need you."

"I have other cases."

"Seges will continue with them."

"I cannot agree to that, Colonel."

"I didn't ask for agreement." There was the sound of crockery breaking in the background. "She is now throwing cups at me."

"I am sorry."

"I didn't ask for that either. Just follow your orders. The command comes from the minister as well." There was another crash; this time, the phone was dropped. Trokan yelled at his wife, then came back on. "It's a command, Inspector. Do it!" He hung up.

Jana slept fitfully the rest of the night, then rose early to call Seges and tell him to pick her up. She took a cold bath to fully wake up, re-packed, and moved her suitcase to the front door. Seges was five minutes early and in good spirits. He cheerfully picked up her bag and stowed it in the car. Jana decided Seges was too happy to see her leave and wondered what he was up to at the office, before deciding he was just glad to see her depart.

Before they drove into Austria and to the Vienna Flughafen, where her flight was scheduled, she directed Seges to take her to the wine store that Makine, or Koba, as she now thought of him most of the time, had operated in Bratislava's Old Town.

"I am supposed to see a witness this morning. It would be better for me if I drop you at the airport so I can get back on time to interview the witness."

"On which case?"

"The shotgun murder of the son."

"The pretty niece? You're planning to see her? A good-looking girl, the niece."

"The niece is good-looking; yes."

Seges's cheerfulness was now explained.

"She can wait. The wine shop!"

Seges lost much of his happy expression but drove to the wine shop through the winding streets of Old Town. The place had just opened for the day. A hostess was setting a large sandwich board in front of the shop to advertise the wine tastings of the day and promote the Italian imports they were trying to fob off on the public as premium wines.

Jana and Seges walked inside. There were two employees in the shop: a hostess still bustling around with her opening chores, and a chunky man with a shaved skull and features that looked like they had been pressed flat with an iron. The man stood behind the counter drinking a beer. Not much of an advertisement for his wines. Jana walked to the counter and sat opposite the man on one of the tall wooden stools at the service bar area for customers.

Jana stared at the flat-faced man, whose small, almost

colorless, eyes stared back. She recognized him for what he was: an enforcer type, a bouncer and general all-around thug who would beat you to a pulp if his employer wanted it done. Killing would not be beyond the man if he was paid enough. The hostess came over to Jana, her best smile on her face.

"We have a tasting of a dessert wine today. Hungarian. Their best," she bragged. "Only 10 crowns for a glass and if you buy, we deduct it from the price of the bottle."

The flat-faced man growled at her, "They're police. They don't want wine."

The hostess's eyes widened and she backed away, holding the bottle she had proffered as if it might contain mouthwash. "Sorry," she mumbled.

Jana continued to stare at the thug. The man looked down, pretending to be busy, pushing glasses around, moving bottles, only looking up after he realized that the police officer sitting in front of him was not going to go away.

"How did you know I was a police officer?"

"I'm good at that."

"Lots of dealings with police?"

"Some."

"Your name?"

Seges whipped out his pad and ballpoint. The thug's bald head swiveled between the two cops, coming back to Jana as the one who presented a threat.

Yes, a thug, Jana confirmed to herself. The man was waiting for a blow; he had received blows in the past, and he had picked her as the one who would signal when the beating was to begin. She had his attention.

"I asked for your name. You are too slow. Now I want your identity card."

The thug reached into his pocket and held it out to Jana. Jana deliberately waited, increasing the man's tension, before indicating that the card was to be given to Seges. Seges jotted down the information from the card.

"The owner of this place, he died in a car crash."

"I know."

"When did you find out?"

"Two days ago."

"Who told you?"

"The new owner."

The hostess decided she would give Jana a drink after all, sliding a small glass of Tokay onto the bar in front of her. "No charge for you. House compliments." She skittered away.

Jana continued to look at the thug as she picked up the glass, inhaled the bouquet, viewed the light amber color, and finally took a sip. She made a face, setting the glass back on the counter, glad to be rid of it.

"Despite what the bottle says, it is not Hungarian. Probably Slovak. From the border area. Maybe they slip it over to Hungary so it can be 'bottled in Hungary' to add to its price." Jana let her irritation show. "Who is the new owner?" she continued.

"I don't know."

"Then how did you know there was a new owner?"

The thug blinked as he considered the question. "He telephoned. He told me he was now the owner; he knew the old one had died."

"That's all? No name?"

"Nothing. No name."

Jana held out her hand to Seges for the thug's identity card, scanning it, then looked back at the thug. "Is this your real name?"

"Of course."

"How do you know it is your real name?"

"It's on the card."

Jana laid the card on the countertop, face down. "Not because of the card. You know your name because your mother told you so."

The thug thought about Jana's statement as if it were a new concept. "She told the government, and they gave me the card?"

"Good. Now, who told you the man who called up was the new owner, besides the voice on the phone?"

"The old owner. He said he might sell the business to a Ukrainian."

"And the man who called you was Ukrainian?"

"He could be. Well, he had some kind of accent."

Jana looked over at Seges. "Give him your card." Seges pulled one of his cards out of his breast pocket, slapping it down on the bar in front of the man. Jana slid off her stool. "Have the new owner call Warrant Officer Seges when he finally arrives at 'his' new business."

The man's head bobbed slightly on his thick neck to indicate that he understood.

Jana walked out of the shop, Seges behind her. "This man, the 'owner,' will not call."

Seges jerked his thumb back in the direction of the bar. "I don't think that clod in the bar knows how to dial a phone, or read, or anything that was taught in primary school. That's the reason we win, you know. It is not that we are so smart, but they are so dumb."

"Perhaps." Jana agreed, but didn't like Seges's patronizing tone.

They got in the car, Seges put it in gear, and they headed down the street toward the highway that would take them into Austria and to the airport.

Jana settled in for the ride, mulling over the new information, trying to fit it in with everything else. "The owner knew, before he died, if he truly was the one who died in the crash, that he was leaving and that someone else would become the 'owner.' Again, an organization is at work. Someone was prepared to take over. They didn't want to give up that miserable little wine shop with the doctored bottles of wine. Why? Because it makes too much money for them."

"Not from that wine."

"They use the store's account books to launder money, criminal proceeds from other activities. It costs them nothing for a crap inventory. They declare nonexistent, very large sales to their imaginary high-volume customers, and then bank sums of gray money, funds acquired from criminal enterprises."

"What do you want me to do?"

"Call the Financial Police, then the Tax Police. Tell them about the place and what we suspect. They need to do a workup on the records, registered ownership, licenses, books, past tax reports. Everything."

"They will take months to act on my request, if they act at all."

"Maybe there will be a miracle." She looked back at the town as they swung onto the highway, still feeling fatigued from the last few days of nonstop turmoil. "A nice place, Bratislava." She closed her eyes and sank back into her seat. "But, I think after all, I will be glad to get to Strasbourg."

Chapter 15

It is not an error that has simply "occurred," he thought, when the information came to him. Everything is deliberate, purposeful, as it always was at times like this.

He looked out the large French doors of the red-roof-tiled, white adobe-like building toward the Adriatic and the Dalmatian coast of the mainland hidden in the distance. Small whitecaps were starting to appear, pushed by an East–West wind, but it was still calm enough, he decided, for a swim.

The man opened the doors and walked down the steps carved into the island's black lava base leading to the edge of the small inlet. There he shed his white pants and light blue sweater, laying them neatly at the base of a scrub bush. He paused for a moment—slim, streaks of gray in his hair, very tanned—to look back at the house once more, remembering when he had acquired it. Nothing had needed to be done to the structure, and the furniture had come with the house, enabling him to step through the front door and be comfortable.

It was good that way: no chores, no need for workmen to disturb him, nothing to be shipped in except the necessities of life. And, except for additional communication equipment he had acquired over the years, and the piece or two of furniture that use and age forced him to replace, or a tile on the roof that needed to be repaired, the place was unchanged.

He had appreciated it when he obtained it, so why change? In many respects, he was like an animal that maintained a consistent lifestyle. His usual routines had worked to keep him alive, and he would continue to follow them.

He slipped into the water, walking until it was up to his waist, then smoothly, silently, dove into the sea, effortlessly breast-stroking to the outer limit of the inlet. As anticipated, the water, cold by other people's standards, was perfect for him. His metabolism had the uncanny ability to adjust rapidly to extremes of hot and cold.

When he got past the last protection of the inlet, the water began to exert a more insistent push. No matter, the exercise was good, toning up his already supple body; he merely lengthened his steady stroke to accommodate the swell. After stroking a kilometer beyond the inlet's breakwater, he dove, swimming along the seabed to visit his Venus.

He had found the marble statue of a half-nude woman, a Venus, standing upright on the seabed a year after moving to the island. Of course, he had never mentioned her presence to anyone. That would have meant visitors and the disturbance of his interludes with her. Once in a while, he conjectured about her origin: She might have been part of some ancient shrine, but he thought not. She was probably cargo on a ship that had foundered eons ago, depositing her in the sea, the wreck and its other contents long since dispersed.

As he always did, he swam up to his marble "Siren of the Waters," as he thought of her, kissing her on her water-warmed lips, then gradually left her below as he rose to the surface. When he broke the surface, he faced his island and immediately saw the two men darting from one part of the outside of the house to the other, depositing packages that somehow adhered to the walls.

It was clear to him what the men were doing; it was equally

clear that he neither could nor would try to do anything about their actions. Finished on the side of the house within his vision, the two disappeared around the corner, and he heard the faint sound of a small boat engine starting, quickly passing out of his hearing. From the direction of the sound, he assumed that the men had been put ashore from a larger boat on the windward side of the island.

No matter for the moment. He turned his back to the island and, angling to his left, began swimming toward a very small islet barely visible, about two kilometers from where he was. Not a big swim for him, and he could rest on his back from time to time if he needed. Abruptly the sky lit up with a series of flashes, muted rumbles following the light. He paid no great attention. The house was over with; the island the house had stood on did not exist for him any more. The smaller dot on the sea he was swimming to was all that mattered—and, of course, the materials which he had providentially stored there. From that island, he would go to Dubrovnik, walk down its marble-paved center street, find a restaurant he knew where he would enjoy a fish dinner, then rest and do what he always did: Like Jesus Christ, he would resurrect himself.

Chapter 16

Strasbourg is a French town still leaning to Germany. It is an old town trying to pretend it is a new one, all the while trumpeting its ancient traditions. It is a small provincial town wearing the clothing of a large cosmopolitan one. And even though it is located on France's border with Germany, and so is a backwater for much of France to its west, it is now the home of the European Parliament and the European Court of Human Rights. No fools when it comes to money, the French had the EU foot the bill for the modern edifices that house the bureaucracy and its showpiece necessities of fountains and statues and flags dotting the area to make it impressive to tourists.

Once again, France could legitimately claim to be the center of the world, albeit the EU structures of this capital had been built through the good offices of other nations. The French had done one thing for themselves: They had slightly modernized the airport to take care of the increased traffic into the area, intending to make it easier for the traveler to find his way into the city proper. The innkeepers who were ever ready to sell travelers Strasbourg's accommodations, particularly its well-regarded cuisine, appreciated their government's efforts.

Jana arrived at the Strasbourg airport slightly over an hour after leaving Vienna, then wandered around trying to find out how to get to her hotel. She was finally pointed toward a minivan that took her to the small hotel that had been booked for the conference delegates near the central train station.

At the hotel, there was barely time for a brief bath. She had to quickly change into a simple suit and matching shoes she saved for events like these, then use a large over-the-bureau mirror to apply her makeup. She sighed, realizing once more that she had now crossed into that region that people called middle age. Nothing she could do about it, she sighed again; then she caught a taxi near the hotel. She showed the taxi driver her card, on the back of which she had written down the meeting's location.

As the taxi pulled up to the Palais de l'Europe, Jana dashed out and into the building. The lobby guard checked her credentials, then called up to the contact person whose name Jana had been given. After a brief conversation, the guard looked up from her phone, smiling at Jana in a sympathetic way. She first informed Jana in French, then in English, to make sure that Jana understood, that she was very sorry but the meeting had been postponed until the next day at nine hundred hours.

Worse than the bureaucracy in Slovakia, Jana thought. She remembered the brief relaxation of the hot bath she had had to rush through. A simple call, a note left at the desk of her hotel to tell her not to come today, would have been nice. She looked around the lobby, trying to decide what to do with herself for the rest of the day. She had reread her reports on the plane, reviewed facts, and generally prepared for questions that might be asked in the meeting. She would not have to go over them again. That put her in the lazy category of tourist.

Jana's eye caught that of a younger man. Decent-looking, but, she thought ruefully, out of her age bracket. Yet he kept on staring. Her recent inspection of her features in the hotel-room mirror had again disabused her of any notion that she was still beautiful, so why was he looking at her with so much interest? She stared back at him, and he quickly turned away, piqueing her interest. Bashful? Maybe. The man turned to look at her again. This time, he did not back off when he realized she was studying him.

He reminded her very strongly of someone she knew, but she could not yet quite place him. When the answer came, it jolted her. He looked like Dano, a little taller, his hair a little lighter, but his nose, eyes, the set of his chin, even the way he held himself reminded her of Dano. She started toward the man, than realized she was being crazy.

Jana willed herself to change direction, rushing through the doors and into the street. Off to one side was the Parc de l'Orangerie. She headed for the grass and trees, too many memories crowding her head, the need for open space and a brisk walk her immediate remedy for the momentary confusion she had just gone through.

She walked for a few minutes, not really seeing anything, finally angling through the park to the quay along the river, maintaining a steady pace for a good ten minutes, the water on one side, the trees on the other muting the traffic noises and the rest of the cacophony of the city. Then she slowed down, realizing that she had worked up a fine sweat, and was just about to change direction and head back toward the Centre Ville when she heard footsteps behind her. Once consciously heard, Jana realized that she had been aware of them keeping pace with her for some time. Now they were closing in on her.

Police officers naturally develop and refine a sense of caution over the years: Defense must be automatic, without thought, or the policeman loses the fight. Jana's first impulse was to swing around and confront the pursuer head-on, to ward off any imminent attack. But she had passed through the park and was in the open, it was daylight, and there were other people passing by, so this was not the time or place an attacker would choose for an assault. She was not likely to be in danger.

However, a small amount of caution is a good thing. She was passing a bench. Jana walked behind it, turning to face her pursuer, keeping the bench between them. It would give her an extra moment to prepare a defense in case she was wrong.

Again, Jana was jolted. Her pursuer was Dano's look-alike, the man from the lobby. He hesitated a moment, then came toward the bench.

Closer, he looked even more like Dano, down to dark shadows under his eyes which created a soulful look, that appearance of sensitivity that made women want to embrace him.

"I've been following you," the man got out, seeming to be embarrassed. "I think I know who you are."

"Who am I?

"Jana Matinova." He watched her reaction, her response confirming that he was right. He finally smiled, a shy smile, which softened his face even more. "You don't know who I am."

Jana shook her head.

"I'm Jeremy Conrad. Your daughter's husband."

Chapter 17

It had been a different time; things seemed to be getting better for Jana. She was back in Bratislava. She had a charged-up ten-year-old who insisted on being called Katka, not Katerina. And she and Dano were trying to reestablish their relationship, which still suffered from Jana's long exile in the hinterlands of Slovakia.

Katka had grown to be "Daddy's Girl." She had a sixth sense about when Dano was about to come home, running around the apartment to get everyone ready, making sure the house was neat, giving orders to her mother and her grandmother about items which, in her mind, needed to be prepared, from how to set the table to having a flower cut so she could give it to Papa, all the while running over to the window to see if Dano was walking up to the front door.

The years had not been good to Dano. He had been unable to get a job in state-sponsored theater since he had put Jana's gun to the agent provocateur's head. He had continued to act, but only in the nonfunded, unsponsored theater. These small, storefront troupes were always in trouble with the state authorities, and Dano's participation in them, in turn, ensured his place on the state's enemies list. There *had* been a minor benefit to all this: Dano had built a small following of people who would come to his plays and, at least for his ego's sake, he had kept his name out there in the Slovak theater world.

There was one additional misfortune for Dano. Because his theater appearances earned no money, except for meager voluntary contributions from the audience, Dano had to go onto the "will-work list."

To help all those made "nonpersons" by the state, the "will-work list" had come into existence. It was informal, passed on by word of mouth through people who needed workers and wanted to pay them less than scale, or needed people to work in unsafe conditions, or simply wanted a worker who could never complain, could never talk back, and could be terminated on a whim. The "will work" laborers were available for any job for a pittance and would never go to the authorities. Working on the "list" had left its scars on Dano. He'd had to clean out too many septic tanks without the proper tools, put up with too much abuse. It was not a good role for one of the premier actors in the country.

Yet Dano could not get or keep any legitimate job, no matter how menial, because the authorities checked on new hires and when his name came up, word was immediately communicated that he presented a potential problem for his employer. No employer could take the risk of irritating the state. Dano would be unceremoniously fired, sometimes with a surreptitious small payout to him from the more decent employers, who also didn't want any fuss. Most of the time, when Dano was fired, he forfeited his wages. It was used as an opportunity to cheat him.

It was easier for Jana. She had been allowed to come back to Bratislava as a police officer two years earlier. Trokan had tried to help her when she was in "exile," throwing special assignments her way.

The Criminal Police had become notorious for their use of criminal charges filed for political reasons. Combining that with their corruption and their ineptitude, there was a need for an honest detective, even one who was in disfavor. So Trokan had first pulled Jana out of Preshov and sent her to Poprad, from Poprad to Zilina, then to Banská Bystrica, from there to Nitra, then to Trnova. And now she was finally back in Bratislava. The journey had been one of forgiveness and repatriation.

It had not been easy for her, but better than what Dano was going through. At least she was working in her chosen field. And she was climbing the ladder once more. Jana had worked case after case, establishing her credentials as a police officer who knew how to successfully investigate the most complex cases. Her nominal superiors thought she was hard to control, unconventional, perhaps better to stay away from because of her "contacts" in Bratislava. But they did have to respect her. The water poison cases, the Mafya killings in the Hungary and Ukraine border areas, the political killing of a mayor, they all fell to her and were solved. Promotions eventually began to come to her again, and she was now a sublieutenant.

Back in Bratislava she had to confront conflicting emotions. Her relationship with Dano had deteriorated. Perhaps too much time had passed, too many non-shared experiences; perhaps it had to do with the youth that they had left behind and the turns each had taken in different directions.

When Jana returned, Dano had begun to drink heavily. She had seen it on occasion, been warned about it by her mother and others. But the presence of Katka and Jana seemed to make a difference. Miracle of miracles, he stopped. Unfortunately, they were still not yet out of the woods. One trouble with incipient alcoholics is that they all too often use heavy drinking as a drug to shelter them from the perception of an unhappy reality. And when they stop drinking, that perception returns with a vengeance.

Suppressed anxiety, hidden anger, and the pain of depression strike; without the escape of the bottle, formidable emotional changes take place. For Dano, sourness set in. A sarcastic, angry cast colored his attitude. He would lash out, then regret his actions, then, a moment later, lash out again. He did this with everyone except Katka.

That evening, Dano came up the walk carrying a package. And even before she wrestled the door open, Katka knew that it had to be a present for her. She jumped on her father at the door. Dano swept her up with his free arm, the two of them dancing a quick jig around the room. Katka hugged her father around the neck as hard as she could squeeze, kissing him on the cheek, and finally, when he was out of breath, let go to slide down to the floor. Of course, the first questions she asked were: "What's in the package, Papa?" and "Is it for me?"

"For you?" Dano pretended to be surprised by the question. "I'm not sure. I guess I've forgotten."

Of course it was for her, and Katka pulled it out of the loosely tied paper wrapping. A dramatic purple skirt, long and flowing when it was unfurled, more an adult's skirt than a ten-year-old's, but Katka loved it anyway, squealing with joy, running to kiss Dano again, running to show it to Jana and her grandmother, finally slipping it over her head, holding up the hem so she wouldn't trip over it, parading around the room as if she were a royal princess.

And Jana loved him again, because she could see the sparkle in his eyes, reveling in the fact that he had made their daughter happy. This was the Dano she had known before, the Dano who was Hamlet and all the other great stage heroes that he had portrayed, standing there in their living room that evening. She went to him, as her daughter had done, and gave him a long kiss.

Dinner that night, even though not graced by any particular holiday dish, was as festive as any they'd had recently. There were lots of giggles from Katka, jokes from Dano about his latest rehearsals, and local gossip from her mother about who was having an affair with what married man in the neighborhood. Jana generally had nothing to offer at the dinner table because the nature of her work was not conducive to the appetite, but tonight Dano insisted that she tell them what was going on in the "dreaded halls" of the local police.

Jana finally gave in, laughing while she told them a story about Trokan and his wife. His wife had come to his office, and everyone could hear an argument building up between them, with Trokan's wife getting louder and louder. Finally, Trokan had broken away, steaming out of his office, telling his secretary he was not going to return that day, leaving his wife behind. Thirty minutes went by, with the wife still inside, everyone starting to make bets on how long she would remain. When she emerged from the office, she turned back as if Trokan was still inside behind his desk, yelling at the phantom Trokan, "And if you come home late this evening, don't count on spending the night in your bed." With that, she'd stormed out, a self-satisfied look on her face as if she had gotten the last word in the argument.

Katka wanted to know if the woman could have been speaking to a ghost, like Hamlet had talked to the specter of his father in the play. Dano, who had gone over his favorite role many times with Katka, indicated it was possible, but more likely the woman was a little crazy. Jana's mother chimed in with "more than a little," cackling about poor Trokan coming in the next day not knowing the embarrassment he was facing. And Jana suddenly felt depressed.

Husbands and wives often share terrible events, events they can never get out of their minds as much as they try.

Dano's cheerful mood dissipated, as if sensing what she was thinking, the almost perpetual gloom returning to his face. And Katka, seeming to sense that she shouldn't be around the adults for the rest of the evening, announced that she was going to bed and would be sleeping in her new purple dress. Princess-like, she imperiously demanded not to be disturbed for the rest of the night, and went off to her bedroom.

Jana's mother began clearing the dishes from the table, both Jana and Dano stopping and starting to speak, stuttering sentences trailing off. They no longer had the confidence, or the ability, to maintain a pleasant, comfortable conversation.

"Would you like to know where I got the dress for Katka?" Dano finally ventured.

"It's very pretty," Jana quickly got out, realizing she hadn't said anything about the dress before.

"The National Theatre's wardrobe warehouse. They shouldn't have let me come back." He laughed, awkward in confessing to an act he should not have committed. "I stole it for Katka. You see what I've become because they won't let me work: a thief." He thought about his confession. "Are you going to arrest me, Jana?"

"No. I think, perhaps, they owe you more than what the dress is worth."

"I agree," Jana's mother chimed in. "They owe you."

"Thank you," Dano nodded. He turned his seat around, still facing Jana, his arms now folded over the back of the chair, his enthusiasm starting to return. "I have decided to do more than steal a dress. I am going to fight back."

Jana's mother was the first to react to his statement. Suspiciously, a little afraid of what he meant, she approached the table to face him. "What do you mean you're going to fight back? Who are you fighting? How are you going to fight?"

"I'm joining a political group that is going to form a new party."

"And what will its political platform be?" Jana's mother demanded in a pugnacious tone.

"To bring down this government. It will be called the Revolutionary Democratic Party. There are already fifteen of us who have subscribed to its platform. As time goes on, we will attract others. And then we will pull this government down."

Jana's mother turned white, her voice taking on a frantic edge. "Are you a madman? Have you forgotten Dubcek? Have you lost your memory of the Soviet tanks rolling into Prague? Has it slipped your mind what they did in Hungary? They don't tolerate *other* revolutionaries."

Dano ignored his mother-in-law, addressing Jana. "Do you understand why I have to do this? If you have gone through what I have gone through, what I am going through, you must act against them. I am not a contented lapdog any more, nibbling at a bowl of chopped meat before napping in a corner."

Jana's mother's voice rose even higher. "You are doing it again, aren't you? You have not learned the cost? Lunatic! Lunatic! Lunatic!"

"Stop. Stop now!" Jana found herself yelling. "Katka will hear." Jana could feel what remained of her relationship with Dano slipping away. "He has a right to act as he feels, Mother. He should not be talked to this way. Dano is a man of respect."

"To hell with this 'man of respect' nonsense! Look what he did to us the last time! He nearly buried us with his actions. They sent him away from the theater, but they exiled you from your home, your friends, your job. And you have been fighting your way back ever since. Listen to this man: He is proposing that he do it to us all over again!"

"That remains to be seen, Mother."

"Are you also a lunatic? You cannot hope to survive again!"

Dano hung his head for a moment, his shoulders slumped. Then he looked back up at them both. He held out his hands, palms up, as if to say "What else can I do?" "That's why I have to leave," he said. He looked directly at Jana. "You see that. I must go. Otherwise you will be tainted by what I do."

"No."

"Yes."

"I agree, yes," said her mother. "Emphatically, yes!"

Dano packed his clothes and left that night. He wrote a note for Katka, explaining that he had work that required him to be away for a while, kissed Jana on the cheek, and walked out of the door. For some reason, Jana found that she could not cry. Ever afterward, Jana felt she had not done enough to stop Dano, to keep him home, safe.

Jana's mother told all the neighbors that they had finally thrown that no-good actor out of the house, that Jana and she were tired of supporting him. Then she went to the local police station and informed the registry people that Dano no longer resided with them, making sure that all the police officers knew that they had rid themselves of the nuisance of his presence. For Katka's sake, her mother demanded that Jana tell her supervisor and everyone else she knew at the police department that her husband had been thrown out. They needed to make a public break from him and whatever his activities were going to be.

The next day, Jana told Trokan that she and Dano had parted, and took his picture off her desk. When she put it in a drawer, she felt like she had gone into mourning.

Chapter 18

They had lunch in an old Alsatian restaurant in that corner of the Grande Ile called Petite France. Her son-in-law drove like a madman through the streets, never worrying about traffic, the diplomatic plates on his small car giving him immunity from French prosecution. He came close to colliding with other cars at least twice. Jana wondered if all Americans were suicidal when they drove. She finally decided that it was the Dano in him that was so reckless.

The restaurant had a folksy interior, combining old French and German décor. Jana didn't really listen to the waiter's suggestions, absently nodding her head so that when he filled the table with food, she was surprised at all the dishes. All Jana could really concentrate on, most of the time, was Jeremy. His resemblance to Dano, even up close, was remarkable.

Jeremy spoke almost nonstop about the Gods of Serendipity, who must have been working overtime for him to have recognized her in the lobby, since he had only seen a few old photos that Katka still had. Of course, he would have met Jana tomorrow anyway. Yes, more serendipity, she agreed, when she realized what the word meant. They would both be attending the same meeting. Jeremy surmised that he would probably have recognized Jana at the meeting tomorrow because Katka looked so much like a younger version of her.

Jana managed to fully focus when Jeremy stopped talking and began eating.

"A few simple questions. First, how is she?"

"For the third time, Katka is marvelous."

"This time I'm asking about the baby."

"Daniela is super. Healthy, advanced for her age, etcetera. You can add all the rest of the things to describe her that any doting father would use to describe his child."

Named after Dano, Jana reflected. No need to ask who had suggested the name. "And you; why did the Americans select you to come up from Nice to Strasbourg?"

"We're stationed in Paris now. With the embassy, naturally. One of my responsibilities is civil rights and law-enforcement problems in France, which meant it was my turn to come up here. Political officers do all kinds of things. We stay current on smuggling dope, trafficking, stolen cars, and lots of other criminal stuff. We've got the FBI over here, but the meeting tomorrow is at the diplomatic level." He smiled one of his Dano smiles. "And I've heard from other sources that I'm now sitting with one of the premier detectives in Slovakia."

Jana ignored the compliment. "Does Katka talk at all about me?" she asked.

He paused, considering the question. "Some of the bitterness has faded." He tried to use diplomatic language and found himself unable to. "You come up rarely. She has mentioned telling Daniela about her grandmother, but the baby is too young, so the time hasn't come yet."

"I would like to see them both. There won't be an opportunity like this again for a long time, if ever. I am in France, here, now. My granddaughter is close by. Perhaps I can come to Paris?"

"Katka is in Nice right now, with the baby. It's warmer than in Paris. And we have another month left on our lease for the Nice place, so while I'm in Strasbourg, she went south. I'm returning to Nice tomorrow, after our meeting."

Jana located Nice on her mental map, a dot on the French Riviera. She pictured palm trees and sunshine, with Katka walking Daniela in a stroller by the blue Mediterranean waters of the Côte d'Azur. Odd to think of her daughter in that storybook setting.

"Will she see me if I go to Nice with you?"

Jeremy winced. "I don't think that's a good move."

"You said the bitterness was fading."

"But not gone."

Jana nibbled at a piece of chicken with some sort of cream sauce, not out of hunger, but to play for time. Surely she could figure out a way to get to see her daughter, and her daughter's daughter, after all these years. The chicken was still tasteless. She drank a sip of Alsatian white wine. Tasteless as well, to her. She surveyed the almost-untouched dishes on the table in front of her, thinking: What a waste.

Jeremy tried to resolve the family impasse. "Let me talk to her. Katka does not take well to surprises. You probably know that she likes everything to go according to a plan."

Jana ran through all the possible scenarios, regretfully concluding that Jeremy had to know Katka better than she did now.

"I have to go back to Slovakia soon. You will talk to her quickly? About my seeing her?"

"I promise."

"Time heals."

"And sometimes it doesn't."

"Yes," she had to agree.

They sat in silence until Jeremy finished eating and the waiter arrived with the bill. She reached for it, but Jeremy got to it first.

"How often do I get to treat my mother-in-law, courtesy of the U.S. government?" He slapped a credit card on the waiter's plate, which was immediately picked up and run through a portable machine, Jeremy punching in the bank numbers. "I can justify paying the bill with taxpayer money if you and I can talk about Koba's organization for a minute."

"I don't know much to talk about." Jana tried to switch the focus of her thoughts from Katka and her grandchild to the investigation. "Koba is dead, or he isn't dead. Nobody is quite sure. Yes, I believe there is an international crime ring. But I am not positive. How many people are in it? Who are they? We don't know, but it seems to exist in at least four countries, and, if I am right, in many more. Whoever these criminals are, they know how to plan, and are quite ruthless in carrying out that plan. In fact, there may be two groups, perhaps at war with each other. That is about all I know."

"What we want. . . ." He smiled ruefully at his use of the royal "we," beginning again. "Well, what the U.S. wants, is to track this group, to find out if they're already functioning in America, or if they are about to move into our country. Who the hell are they? Koba and Company have to be identified so we can track them."

"I thought the U.S. could track anybody, intercept all communications, color the world red, white, and blue, if it wanted to."

"My favorite colors," admitted Jeremy. "Except in the nursery. But, no. The red, white, and blue is not all-powerful. We have no magic wand. We can't even come close." They both rose at the same time. Jeremy helped her on with her coat. "How about us touring the old cathedral together while we're here? That's a nice touristy thing to do."

"Only if you agree to come to Slovakia where things are even more antique." They both headed toward the door. "Maybe I could arrange for you to visit one of our castles for the day? We have a castle that Dracula was supposed to have inhabited."

"I thought Dracula was from Transylvania."

"They stole the idea from us." She laughed. "Everybody stole from us. It's why we are so poor. Maybe that's good. There is nothing left to steal, so now we don't have to worry."

They walked over the canal bridge to the main island, turned toward Place Gutenberg, and from there toward the Cathedral de Notre Dame.

"I think I know one of them; one of the group involved," Jana acknowledged after they had been strolling for a while.

"A name, any name, would look good in my report. Who's the man?"

"It's early. I need to make sure."

"We can help."

"I hope so. I will be sure to ask for help, if I need it later."

"Maybe other things will happen to help us."

Jana nodded. "The cracks will widen. If there is a war between criminal factions, it will go on. More casualties. Hopefully, we will pick up the remaining pieces."

They stood in front of the cathedral, looking up at the sculptures and stone scrollwork enhancing the high walls. The main panels above the door depicted the final judgment of saints and sinners, with the sinners falling down to Hell.

"You see," Jana continued, "all the evil people are punished in the end."

"Not everyone," murmured Jeremy. "Just the ones who get themselves carved in marble."

"No." She thought of herself and Dano. "I think everyone is caught in the end, one way or the other."

They went into the cathedral.

Chapter 19

Of course, the meeting began late. Those who knew each other exchanged greetings, others drank the coffee or tea provided, people searched for their namecards indicating where they were to be seated. Finally everything coalesced and the group was called to order. Jana was not surprised to see Moira Simmons as the Chair.

Moira's name plate stated that she was the head of the "Human Rights Anti-Trafficking Committee" of the EU. There were about twenty people at the table, mostly from Western Europe, along with representatives from a number of the former Eastern bloc countries, including Dmitri Levitin, a large-headed, lanky young man from Russia. He nodded at Jana as if he knew her. Politely, Jana nodded back. Jeremy had still not arrived, although his name was placed in front of the seat next to Moira. One other chair remained vacant: that of Foch, the representative of the UN from Vienna.

The seat that interested Jana most was occupied by a man whose nameplate read Aram Tutungian. The man was olive-skinned, with coal black hair and eyes. The eyes were oddly set, off center, looking at you, but not looking at you directly. Tutungian and Jana exchanged glances. The impression that she received was one of lack of feeling. No emotion came from him, there was nothing to connect with. Jana was glad to look away.

Moira Simmons began, going through the usual litany of

why they were here and who the speakers were on the day's agenda. Jana was scheduled for later in the day, her subject listed as "The Problems with Investigating Violence in Human Trafficking." Inwardly, Jana groaned. She was not yet even sure she could establish that the killings in her case were motivated by anything to do with human trafficking. All she had were unverified suspicions. She decided that her speech would be as short as possible.

Tutungian was announced by Moira as a surprise witness, on the agenda for the next day. He was, Moira Simmons said, going to reveal the secrets of his brethren in the nether world of trafficking. Tutungian sat without acknowledging the introduction, his eyes drifting around the room without focusing on any one person. He was doing his best not to appear interested.

The first speaker of the day was a Dutchman who began relating methods the smugglers were using to transport people across borders. He went into the statistics of people coming from Moldova, from Russia, Belarus, Georgia, Lithuania, Macedonia, Albania, and on and on. At first, the sheer numbers and the amount of profit, in the tens of millions, surprised her, and then it numbed her. Women, men, children, for one purpose or another. As for Slovakia, surprisingly, just a few reported cases, mostly Gypsy women. In the charts he displayed, the Dutchman listed Slovakia as primarily a conduit. Unfortunately, along with the human beings, these same routes were also used for narcotics, stolen goods, and every other criminal venture known to man.

The Dutchman had shifted to problems in the Asian sphere when Jeremy arrived. He glanced at Jana, then walked quietly over to Moira Simmons, and whispered in her ear. Moira's body straightened as if she was experiencing a massive muscle spasm, her face registering shock to the degree that everyone stopped listening to the Dutchman, wondering what it was that Jeremy had said.

Moira sat for a moment, gathering herself; then she beckoned to Jana, signaling her to come outside. Moira and Jeremy walked out, Jana following. Surprisingly, Levitin rose from his seat and left close behind Jana. Outside the room, Moira registered no concern at Levitin's presence, ignoring the Russian as they walked to the end of the hall. There Jeremy dropped his bombshell.

"Foch is dead. He was killed. They found his body a few minutes ago downstairs in the main-floor stairwell."

Death, violent death, is always a shock to everyone. It is a particular shock, even to a policeman, when you know the victim. Jana tried to visualize Foch as a murder victim. She couldn't quite manage it. Who would kill the inoffensive-appearing Foch? She pictured him telling his jokes. Vapid, a typical "don't make problems for me" bureaucrat. Not the type of person who would get himself murdered, especially not in the setting of this building.

"How was he killed?" asked Levitin in perfect American-accented English.

"Stabbed, I think. I saw people running to the stairwell and pushed my way through. He was just sitting there, on the bottom step, as if he were dozing, his head down, but there was something sticking out of his eye."

Levitin addressed Jana: "Perhaps you and I could go downstairs and have a peek. Maybe it will tell us something."

The way Jeremy looked at Jana, he wanted her to go. Moira nodded in agreement. "A good idea. We need to know what happened, and why." Her voice was strained, scratchy, as if she had a cold. At the news, her calm control had been lost; her face was slack. "Poor Foch. He was a weak man, but nice." Then she managed to pull herself together. "We can't let this affect the conference. It's too important. Foch would have wanted us to continue." She hurried back to the conference room, gathering momentum as she went.

Jana pictured Foch worrying about the conference continuing. When he was alive, he would not have cared one way or the other if the conference was a success. Dead, he would care even less, if possible.

"Are you coming?" asked Dmitri Levitin, as he headed for the elevator. Jeremy wore a rueful expression as he looked at Jana, already regretting what he was getting her into. Jana patted him on the shoulder, assuring him that it would be all right, then hurried after Levitin, who was holding the door of the elevator open for her.

Levitin took several keys from his pocket and began trying them in the floor-designation panel, finally finding one that fit.

"They will have the main-floor entrance to the stairs blocked off. And they won't want us to interfere."

Jana nodded. "So we take the elevator to the basement, than walk up. Yes, better not to have to depend on second-hand information."

Levitin turned the key, than punched the basement button on the panel. With the key inserted, the elevator descended without stopping.

"Where did you get the key?"

"I bribed a maintenance man when I arrived." His Adam's apple bobbed in his throat as he swallowed. "I don't like riding up and down with crowds. I get claustrophobic and scream very loudly. This always creates a panic in the elevator, so it's much better if I ride with as few people as possible." He smiled slightly at his joke.

"You are a police officer," Jana stated. "From Moscow?"

"St. Petersburg."

"Not good for a police officer to bribe people, even if they are French. You will bring bad habits from us to them."

"Too late. They already have the habits."

"How do you know me?"

"My supervisor received a call from Colonel Trokan. Trokan obtained an attendance sheet, saw I was coming and thought it would be a good idea for us to meet and compare notes."

"What is your specialty?" Jana watched as he took his time answering the question. The man was deciding if he was going to reveal or conceal some fact. He finally made his decision.

"I'm an anti-corruption specialist. There are all kinds of official misconduct involved in human trafficking. Too much money changes hands. So they sent me."

Jana thought he was telling some of the truth, but not all of it. "Does that mean you are investigating members of your own government? Do they have their crooked hands in the meat pie that Koba and his group have baked?"

"It would seem so."

"Not unusual for Russia."

"Nor Slovakia."

"Our people sell out cheaper."

They both smiled.

The elevator doors opened, and they stepped out into the first basement. The door that blocked the ascending stairs looked firmly locked. Levitin studied it for a moment.

"It looks like an easy lock."

"My turn," Jana insisted. She pulled on the handle to the door, and it opened. "Russians always think of doing it the hard way first." Levitin winced. Score for the Slovaks, thought Jana, as they walked up the stairs. The door at the top was locked. Jana looked to Levitin. "No key; no lockpick?"

"A master key. I added more money to my bribe to get it."

"Then why the hesitation at the first basement door?"

"I wanted to see what the Slovak would do." He shrugged in apology. "Time now for us to stop testing each other."

"Good idea."

"I accept that as an offer of a friendship pact."

Levitin opened the door, and they both entered the stairwell. Building security officers and a French policeman were securing the scene of the murder.

Jana did the only thing possible under the circumstances, transforming herself into a senior homicide investigator at a murder scene. She used her command voice and a few loud words to order everyone else out. "Laisse-moi tranquille! Tout le monde, depeche-toi! En avant marche!"

She went over to the body, crouching down to examine it.

Levitin followed her lead. Only his way was softer, and his French impeccable, as he herded them out the door, apologizing for his minatory tone of voice, explaining they needed privacy to begin their work. He eased the last man out, telling him to guard the door, then shut it behind him.

He joined Jana by the body. "You have found your niche as the head of the French homicide police." He knelt next to her. "But your French accent needs improvement."

"If one comes anywhere near the accent, and says the words loudly enough, stress prevents the people on the receiving end from hearing the difference."

She tilted the head of the corpse back. Moving its neck took effort. "Rigor mortis is well set in. He's been dead for some time."

She looked at the dead man's shoes, one of which was almost off. She checked the heels on the shoes, then looked behind her and pointed. "A drag mark, from the door leading to the basement. There's a parking area further down."

"Brought to the building already dead. No way to carry

him through the lobby." He began checking out the rest of the area. "Why make the effort to transport him here?"

"It's a statement. The one who stabbed Foch wanted everyone to know what he had done. To induce fear. What better place to make a statement than in this building? The Council of Europe. Everyone will hear about it." She pointed at the object in his eye. "An ice pick driven up to the handle through the left eye. Koba. He is known to use these. A nice terror weapon."

"Not too good to have Koba as your enemy, is it? In Russia he burned people. Molotov cocktails were his favorite."

"My automobile 'accident' victims may have met him on a very cold road one freezing night." She started going through Foch's pockets. "If Foch was an enemy who needed to be killed by Koba, and we did not know about Foch's connection to Koba, then Foch was keeping it a secret from law enforcement."

"Maybe we should pay our public officials more? That way they won't have to turn to lives of crime."

"Pay them more, they'd just want more. Maybe that's the mistake that Foch made." Foch's inside pocket produced a small address book. She tossed it to Levitin. "Something to start with."

Foch's left arm was wedged behind him. Jana straightened up, indicating that Levitin was to pull the arm out. When it emerged, it revealed the left hand was missing its ring finger. The finger had been neatly severed at its base.

Levitin examined the hand closely. "Cut off very cleanly. Maybe a saw with fine teeth."

Jana checked Foch's wrists. Bruising and abrasions on both of them. She examined his neck more closely. There were some of the same marks around the sides of the throat.

She then pulled both pant legs up. There were abrasions around both ankles.

"His wrists, legs, and neck were bound."

"Tortured?"

"Maybe. With the Foch I knew, you wouldn't have to torture him long to get the information you wanted. The man was not strong-willed."

Levitin stood back to get a last look at the Frenchman. "Nothing about his face is unusual."

"If there were bruising or lacerations, the rigor of advanced death and the swelling of the body might conceal it."

Levitin walked to the basement door. "Time to leave. The real homicide gendarmerie will be here soon."

They walked out, closing the door behind them very quietly.

Chapter 20

That evening they met with Moira and Jeremy in a small *winstub* whose menu for the evening recommended its *Choucroute* and *Baeckeoffe* dishes. Only Levitin ordered the *Choucroute*. When the tureen arrived at the table, it proved to have enough sauerkraut, pork, and sausage to feed three ordinary men, but Levitin began forking it into his mouth with such gusto, it was apparent that he was going to relish eating the entire dish by himself. The day's events had not deprived him of his appetite.

The other three ate lightly, Jeremy selecting a *Bouchée a la Reine* and both women opting for a nondescript white fish in a butter-and-caper sauce. Jana and Jeremy picked at their meals. Moira did not eat a bite. There was not much conversation, with Moira staring into her own private distance, only coming out of it when the dishes were removed. She finally began to talk, speaking very softly. The others had to strain to catch her words.

"He should not have died this way." She looked, in turn, to each of them as if fearing that they would disagree. "He had problems. We all have issues that we can't address and which create difficulties with others, but he was murdered, brutally murdered. Inhuman!" She looked at Jana. "You must keep abreast of the investigation; you must tell me if they identify the madman who did this. I want to be kept posted every step of the way."

"I'm not a member of the French police. They don't have to talk to me. They probably won't."

Moira put both of her hands deep into her hair, grabbing fistsful, pulling as if attempting to snatch herself bald. Afraid she would injure herself, Jeremy tried to pull her hands away.

"No reason to punish yourself, Moira."

Moira pursed her lips. "I have a headache. I need to do this. It relieves the pressure." She continued to move her hands through her hair, repeating the procedure. "Foch had a jaundiced view of the world, but it came out in humor. Not malice. The person who did this to him was terribly malicious."

Jana felt that at least she had to say a few words to let Moira know they were there for her in her grief. "No one deserves what was done to Foch."

Moira focused on Jana. "I was married to Foch at one time."

The admission startled both Jana and Levitin.

Jeremy patted Moira on the hand, trying to calm her while speaking to Jana and Levitin. "I knew that Moira and Foch had been married. So did a number of other people. It's no secret. When it ended, Moira and Foch remained friends."

"That's a good word: friends. We were always friends. But our marriage didn't work. It just didn't work."

"Why didn't it work?" asked Jana.

Jeremy winced. "Let's allow the lady her privacy on that subject, Jana."

"I don't mind answering," Moira assured Jeremy. "We didn't make love. He liked to entertain young men at home. Some of them were *very* young. He couldn't stay away from them. And he was afraid that if I stayed with him, and we were still married, it would hurt me, hurt my career, hurt my social life. He urged me over and over again to get a divorce, so I did." Tears started falling onto her cheeks. She made no effort to wipe them away.

The waiter appeared and began to run through the dessert selection. No one had any appetite. They paid their bill and the group broke up. Jana watched as Jeremy gave Moira Simmons his arm, trying to lend her support as they walked away. Jana and Levitin went back to their hotel together.

"I was not prepared for that," admitted Levitin. "Ordinarily I would place her on my list of suspects, if I had any, except that she is not Koba."

"Who or what is the Koba of today: Male? Female? Who is in the game he plays, who is not?"

"You are the homicide detective. You tell me."

"When I can, I will." They walked through the hotel lobby, stopping at the desk for messages. There was one for Jana from Trokan. She called him when she got back to her room.

He told her one of her cats was sick. Trokan had brought them home to care for them, and one cat had some sort of convulsive seizure. The seizures had stopped. But, to be sure the cat was okay, Trokan had left him with a veterinarian. Trokan apologized. Like Trokan, maybe the cat didn't care for his wife.

Jana laughed.

Everything would be okay, she told herself.

It didn't work. She couldn't sleep.

Chapter 21

For the sake of convenience, the conference organizers had booked all the participants into the same hotel. However, it was still a surprise when Moira Simmons knocked on Jana's door after midnight. It was a soft knock, hesitant, unsure. Jana pulled on her clothes. When she opened the door Moira Simmons was there looking like a little girl, her hair unkempt, her eyes big and pleading, her shoulders sagging. Jana stepped aside to let her in without asking why she had come. Her face was enough to tell Jana that she needed help.

Moira walked to the bed and, completely clothed except for her shoes, crawled under the covers. She lay there without talking, her eyes closed, her lips moving, soft, rhythmic sounds emerging. From what Jana could pick up, it sounded unlike any language she had ever heard. After some minutes, the woman opened her eyes, looking like she had experienced a nightmare and was pleading with Jana, with anyone, to stop her horrific visions.

Moira's voice was childlike. "I pray in Gaelic for the bad spirits to go away. Even though I pray and pray, I'm still as frightened as I ever was. I'm lost. Seven years old. No! Please tell me I'm an adult. Please tell me I'm safe."

Jana pulled the room's only chair closer to the bed. "Foch's death has taken a little of the adult in you away. Death, death of a close person, always does. To everyone. It's part of what grief is."

"I'm angry at him, dying like that on me."

"If he'd had a choice, he would rather not have died at all." Jana pulled her chair even closer. "People have a nasty habit of leaving us without our permission."

Moira closed her eyes again. This time she lay so still for so long that Jana thought she had gone into an emotion-induced coma. Then her eyes popped open.

"I keep seeing him, the way he was killed, with that thing in his eye." She turned her head, to look directly at Jana. "In my own apartment, all the while I am there, I watch the front door, afraid to look away. I think the door will be quietly opened without my noticing and a man will be there to kill me. I don't want to die like that."

Her voice had dropped in volume, and Jana was forced to lean over her to hear. She waited until she was sure that Moira was finished, then asked, "Who is this man who comes to kill you?"

"His name was Grosjean in Holland; Langlois in Belgium; Macht in Germany; Goncherov in Belarus. Many of them, all mixed into one face, one body, all of them in a single monster come to kill me."

"You have not mentioned our Koba."

"He is them, they are him, no matter what the name. The names I gave you are my older names, the monsters I first knew about. They're the ones who haunt me in my dreams. I can't sleep. I'm afraid to. That's when they will come."

Jana did not need to be a psychiatrist to realize that the woman was on the edge of a personal abyss. "You must think you are very important to these people for them to come after you. How do you threaten them? Is it enough to make them want to destroy Moira Simmons?"

"Foch couldn't hurt them. Yet, look what they did to him. Poor, silly Foch."

"We don't know yet why Foch was killed. It is different now, tonight. Why do you think this might happen to you? What evidence do we have that they are coming after Moira Simmons?"

"I'm trying to stop them. That's all they need to know."

Jana thought about Moira's rationale. "I think there is something else. You described monsters emerging from earlier in your life. When? How early?"

Moira reverted to her silent state. Then her right arm came up, pointing at the ceiling. "You see that spot? I will tell you a secret. I have the same spot, always there, like that spot on the plaster. Only my spot is much bigger. I cannot make it go away. I cannot lessen it, no matter how much I scrub my mind, no matter what I accomplish."

She sat up in bed, pulling up the sheet and blanket, gathering them around her in a crumpled heap which she wrapped as closely as she could around her body. She ended up hugging the bedclothes to her like a lost little girl. Then she told her story.

"My mother was a working girl in a house of prostitution. They used the term 'working girl' instead of 'whore.' She worked for one of those men. His name was Walsh. First she worked in the house, then later, when she got older and couldn't compete with the younger girls, on the street. Then Walsh found out about me. He had my mother bring me to the house to work.

"I was thirteen, just thirteen years old. She didn't think much of me, did she, to take me there? To make me a whore like her." Simmons laughed, an ugly laugh that came from deep in her throat.

"What did I know about men? About sex? Nothing. I was raped four or five times a night. They couldn't wait to get their dicks in a young girl. For five weeks. It went on for five weeks, six days a week.

"Then I found a knife on one of my *customers*. He also ran the place. Walsh used me like the clients, except he did not have to pay. He had fallen asleep. It was a bread knife that he had honed so it was very slim and very sharp. When the house closed that night, the bouncers left." She laughed again. "Then I walked up to him, casually, and stuck it into him. Just like they stuck it to me. Not just once. Maybe ten or fifteen times. He bled far more than I had bled."

Her arms tightened around the blankets. "The psychiatrists in the court hearing said the number of knife wounds was typical of a rage killing. They said I was not responsible for my actions. I was not convicted of anything, not even prostitution. They wanted to help me. They placed me in a treatment facility. It wasn't good enough. How could they help me after what I'd been through?"

Moira was panting for air. Jana waited until she had calmed herself. Jana could not find words with which to soothe the woman, so she asked a question, hoping that the right words would eventually come to her. "Walsh. You didn't mention Walsh as one of the people coming for you. Why?"

"He's dead. I killed him. He can't come back. I'm safe from him."

"Where did you get the other names?" Jana asked her.

"When I came to work here, I tried to put an end to the sex trade. I read and reread volumes of reports; I talked to the women who were sold and enslaved. The names of those men would come up. Other names, too. They are all still out there. Only Walsh got the death sentence he deserved." The ugly laugh came again. "They know I'm after them. They want to get me first." Her voice was becoming faint. She curled up in a fetal position, a little girl ready for sleep.

"Please, don't leave. I need to rest. If you go, they'll come back. Will you stay?" she asked.

Jana could not bring herself to refuse. "Not a problem. I've slept in chairs before. If those men dare to come back, I'll beat them off."

Moira smiled. "Yes, you would drive them away. We'll work together to beat them." Her breathing became more even, slowing until she slept.

After making sure she was asleep, Jana went to the closet and took down the spare pillow and blanket, tucking herself into the suite's large armchair. She wondered if Trokan would think it was part of police work to stand guard against the phantoms in someone else's mind. She rather thought he would, given the nature of these phantoms.

Chapter 22

In the morning, aching from being compressed into awk-ward postures all night by the chair, Jana pulled her clothes from the closet, took a quick look at Moira Simmons, who was still sleeping like a child, then slipped into the bath-room to sponge-bathe and put on fresh clothes, a pair of Eastern European knockoff Levis, a heavy blue cotton blouse and, after a moment's hesitation, the jacket from her suit. The only jarring note was her clumpy police shoes.

To hell with convention, she thought. I've given them my best imitation of a delegate. I am now going to be comfortable.

She returned to the bedroom. In the short time it had taken her to wash and dress, Moira Simmons had left.

Jana was relieved. The woman seemed half crazed, and Jana didn't want to deal with Moira's fearful past and neu-rotic present now. The woman needed professional help, and Jana was a cop, not a therapist. She decided to call Seges and deal with a more familiar source of stress: the busy morning telephone lines to Slovakia.

Seges was irritated when she finally got him on the line. He complained about the caseload building up while she was in Strasbourg. Seges never liked doing more than what he considered his share. He liked it even less when Jana told him to call the Irish police and have them pull the files they had on the killing of a man named Walsh and the person who had killed him. She carefully spelled out Moira Simmons's name, making sure that he correctly spelled it back to her.

Most important for Jana were the cases that she had left behind. Their investigations had to continue on the right path, so they discussed the most urgent. A procurator was demanding additional investigation; she told Seges to do it. He had interviewed the niece of the man who'd killed his son. The niece had observed the son hit the father on at least two occasions, so maybe this was not such a cut-and-dried murder after all. Jana told him to put the niece on the witness list, and she would interview her when she got back to Bratislava. A new case had come in: A customer had apparently gone berserk in a bar and killed two people, both the owner and the bartender. Jana told Seges to check the killer's background to determine if there was any intimation that he was employed in the business "protection" rackets so endemic in Slovakia.

Seges saved the most interesting item until last. The wine store owned by the "pimp" had burned to the ground. There were no immediate signs of arson, but the fire inspectors were combing the wreckage. They were searching for the bald thug. The address the man gave them had been vacated; no one there had seen him for months. Apparently he had some hidden bolt-hole which he'd crawled into.

The book with the codes, Jana reminded Seges. He told her that an expert in Slovakia had been recommended and they were going to give it to him. He was currently out of the country. Jana told Seges to make a copy for the Slovak expert and also to give it to the FBI's agent in their Prague office. To tell them it was important, and that if the Americans needed to know how important, one of their embassy officers from Paris would talk to them. She gave Seges Jeremy's name, smiling. She would have to remember to tell Jeremy that he might receive a surprise phone call from the FBI in Prague.

Jana was about to terminate her discussion with Seges when he remembered that she'd had a call from Ukraine, from Mikhail Gruschov. Gruschov had additional information, and she was to phone him between three and four that afternoon, his time. It was about a man who was a witness to one of the murders that had been committed in Slovakia.

"Which one?" asked Jana.

"He didn't say," replied Seges. "I didn't ask, because he wanted you, not me." Fine, Jana thought. For a change, Seges had surprised her: He was attending to business, and remembering to keep her appropriately apprised of events. On the other hand, there were other cases, and Jana couldn't stifle the thought that he had probably botched one or two of them and simply wasn't mentioning it. She finally thrust this worry out of her mind.

That left the matter of the tall Russian police officer with the large head, Levitin. She told Seges to inform Trokan that she had met the Russian cop. He seemed all right, but she wanted Trokan to obtain his dossier. The man was holding something back, and she didn't want any future shocks when whatever it was ultimately came out.

Seges added a last comment. He'd had heard that one of her cats was sick and he was sorry the poor little thing was in pain. Jana was glad to end the call.

As she hung up, Jana noticed a note on hotel stationery which had been left on the chair she had slept in. Moira Simmons thanked her for her assistance last night, and informed her that the meeting previously scheduled for that day would be moved forward. It would start at 10:30.

Jana reflected on the note. Simple and precise. Perhaps even cold. Jana put it down to the break in Moira Simmons's defenses. After last night, Moira had gone back to the formality that had previously characterized her. Jana guessed she had to, to keep her demons at bay.

Chapter 23

The room was half empty when the meeting began. Whether it was the murder of Foch, or the presence of the extra police officers in the lobby, or the taped and roped-off stairway and the guard outside their conference room, or just a fear of being the next victim, a number of the participants had stayed away. It could also have been because two French investigators were going to ask questions at the session. There is always a certain nervousness about responding to the whims of police officers. This was France, the home of love, and a number of delegates might not have wanted to answer the traditional question: "And where were you that night, the night when Foch was killed?" Tutungian, the turncoat gangster who was scheduled to speak, was conspicuous by his absence. Even his nameplate was gone.

Moira Simmons introduced the two police officers, then glumly sat back in her seat as they took over her meeting. They asked the other traditional question first: "Does anyone have any information which might reflect on the reasons for the death of Mr. Foch?" Not even Moira, with her belief that men were after her because of her work, made any comment.

More general questions followed, all of them predictable: Had they seen Foch the previous morning? Had any of them seen him the night before? At dinner? Every question the cops posed was met by indifferent silence. In fact, all anyone would say was they had not seen Foch since he had left the meeting on the day before his murder.

The police informed everyone that they might interview them individually in the future, thanked them for their cooperation, and then asked to see Jana and Levitin outside the meeting room.

The French cops were lean and muscular men with receding hairlines. They were tense with the angry impatience that all police have with anyone perceived as interfering with their work, particularly police from another jurisdiction. They both voiced that anger in no uncertain terms.

The police guarding Foch's body had described two people, a man and a woman, who had come upon the sealed-off area where the body was found, pretended they were the investigators, and demanded that everyone step outside while they examined the body. The description of the two, a man and a woman, fit Jana and Levitin, particularly Levitin, who would be very difficult to forget. Did they realize that the impersonation of a police officer was a criminal offense?

"Impersonation of a police officer?" Jana and Levitin were both offended. Of course, they were police officers in other countries, but they had never mentioned it to anyone there. "We never said we were police of any kind," Jana admonished. "I, for one, would never do such a thing." Levitin chimed in with his own denial: "A Russian knows his place in the world. This is France, not my country."

Both Jana and Levitin said that they had done nothing to disturb the scene; the reason they had appeared was merely to pay their respects to Foch.

The two Frenchmen were not happy with the answers but were even more unhappy with the possibility of having to take foreign "envoys" into custody, "envoys" who were in Strasbourg to attend a Europe-wide conference. Whether they believed it or not, after hearing that the two had merely prayed over the body, the two French officers took the path of least resistance. They issued a warning to obey all French laws in the future, and then left.

"I didn't know that police in Russia prayed," Jana observed to the Russian cop.

"When was the last time you prayed?" Levitin shot back.

Jana took the question seriously, surprised at her own response. "I pray for the dead; for the victims. I pray by doing my work well, so they know they are remembered. It's magical thinking. I like to believe I have eased their pain."

Levitin shrugged. "I commend you, Commander Matinova. Unfortunately, they still stay dead."

"Not while we work for them."

"Even more commendable. I will give this point to the Slovak, because of my regard for her empathy. Unfortunately, I am not sure if this is a good characteristic for a police officer."

"You might try it sometime."

"I promise to think about it."

They walked back into the conference room.

Chapter 24

O ne evening after Dano's departure, Jana realized that she had not taken a vacation in a year and a half. Conducting case investigations, making personnel evaluations of subordinates up for promotion, instructing at the academy, compiling departmental reviews—whatever the task, she'd felt compelled to accept and complete it. Everything consumed time, and maybe that's what she wanted. Yes, she wanted time to pass without quite noticing its passage. Filling up her hours brought less anxiety, fewer concerns about her mother's illness, less apprehension about dealing with an absentee father for Katka, and Jana's submerged but still very present fear about what was happening, or was going to happen, to Dano.

She had not seen her husband since he had left the house with instructions to her that they could not see each other. For Katka, waking in the morning to find her father gone had not immediately brought about the catastrophe that Jana anticipated. Jana and her mother pretended that Dano had found a job in Brno and had been forced to leave without saying good-bye to Katka. He had left a short note, telling Katka to be good, to listen to Jana and her grandmother in all things, and to remember that he loved her and always would.

"He will be back when he has earned the necessary money. It is not forever." Jana wondered if she were lying to herself as well. "He promised to come home."

Jana's mother had wanted to tear up Dano's note before Katka saw it, an "I told you so" look in her eyes when Katka had became upset upon reading the last lines. "Let his leaving be a desertion, as abrupt as possible," she had advised Jana. "It will speed the emotional break; sever the ties between father and daughter. It's best."

Jana had refused. "What comes will come naturally. We don't need to help it along. We are not going to be criminals, stealing her love from him."

"Who said anything about stealing?" her mother persisted. "We're not taking it for ourselves. It's to help her. When you have an animal that may come prowling around again, you make sure that the food he needs is not available any more. Then it won't come back."

"I don't like that kind of thinking!" Jana became angry at her mother, her voice taking on a flinty tone. "We are all trying to survive, including Dano. You can't change the fact that Dano is, and always will be, her father."

Jana's mother pursed her lips and blew, creating a vibration that sounded similar to a human passing gas. Jana's level of anger rose accordingly. She was afraid she would lose control of her own temper with the next escalation of the argument, so she left the kitchen. She and her mother did not talk for several days after that, and for weeks afterward communicated only in the briefest of sentences.

Katka continued to bring up her father's absence, most frequently in the first several months after he had gone, and in later months with less intensity, and then only on those events, like school holidays, when Dano would ordinarily have taken her to the park or to a café for a dessert treat. Once in a while, in the evening, Katka would still come over to Jana with the plaintive "When is Daddy coming back?" or "Why doesn't he write?" or "Doesn't he like us any more?"

Even that began to lessen as she accepted that Dano was in that unknown void, "out there."

With her mother becoming progressively more ill, suffering from congestive heart failure, her life force ebbing more each week, Jana finally decided it was time for a vacation. She walked into Trokan's office to get his permission.

"Vacation granted," he announced without a moment's hesitation. He asked her to sit and talk for a while. Jana was not in the mood and tried to avoid a discussion by edging toward the door. "If I'm going on vacation, I need to get as much casework done as possible."

"I didn't say you could leave," Trokan barked, very much her superior. "Sit!" he commanded.

Jana sat, uncomfortable, aware instinctively that Trokan was going to bring up Dano.

"Where are you planning to go?" he wanted to know, making conversation as he watched her, looking for something.

"The Tatras." Her answers were going to be as short as possible so she could get out of his office. "The mountains are peaceful."

"Lovely place, the Tatras. I would go, except my wife doesn't like walking up hills."

"What does she like?"

Trokan grimaced. "Nothing. I have concluded that my wife likes nothing and no one, particularly me."

"You have considered divorce?"

"I'm glad you brought that up. It is the topic I wanted to discuss. Not my divorce. Yours. Have you thought about a divorce?"

Jana had opened the door to the topic she wanted most to avoid. "I haven't recently."

"Think about it then."

"Why?"

"Because the wrong people bring it up with me very often. 'Has she severed all her ties to him?' they ask. I remind them that you are a good police officer, and you don't need watching. I don't have to tell you how they react." He shrugged as if to say, what can I do? "For all I know, they might be watching you now." His voice became more matter-of-fact. "They probably are."

"Divorce is a private matter."

"Not for a police officer in this country."

"To put your mind at ease, I will *think* about it."

"Good." He pulled a manila folder from his desk drawer, opening it on his desk to reveal several sheets of paper within it. "Papers. All folders contain papers which must be read by me. You see this stripe?" He pointed to a thin red stripe along the edge of the open side of the folder. "It means I have to read these first under penalty of being called color-blind by the Secret Police. That is a severe accusation, so I read these immediately, just in case."

He read a little of the facing page as if to satisfy himself that he was referring to the correct folder. "A number of items are in here which might most certainly affect you in the future. Let me see. . . ." His voice trailed off as he read a few more sentences, humming out loud as he read. Then he closed the folder as if slamming a door.

"I forgot. I can't talk to you about any of this. It is marked 'Highest Secret.' Sorry."

He stood. "I am going to the W.C. I will be gone, let us say, exactly five minutes. It is now fourteen hundred. Remember, although I am leaving this material here," he patted the file, "a file which some idiot has labeled secret, it should not be touched by you. That is too bad, considering the fact that the person who would most benefit by it can't peruse it." He walked out of the office, closing the door very quietly behind himself.

Jana wasted no time in opening the folder and laying the papers side by side on Trokan's desk. It was a report on the investigation of the Democratic Party of the Revolution, the DPR. The members of this "counterrevolutionary group" had been holding secret meetings throughout Czechoslovakia. According to the reports, all their meetings had called for actual armed rebellion against the state. The person who was most active in this call for action was Dano, her husband. Part of his last speech was printed verbatim in the report:

We are not here to discuss abstract issues. We are not here to evaluate the economics of poverty, disease, or starvation. We are here to discuss those processes that oppress the mind and sicken and starve the spirit in the most concrete way: We must be allowed to work, to train for what we and we alone want to do, to be promoted for our excellence and not on someone's whim. Why must we be prevented from talking to each other about the simplest of political needs: the questions that have come into our minds about our governing officers and their institutions? We cannot speak about our simplest needs as citizens.

What are we allowed to do? Watch our minds and spirits starve? Walk about like burglars in the night, concerned about making noises that the owner of the store, or the house, might hear? Remember, you don't own the house; you don't own the store. You don't own the country. They do! And they will always stop you from trying to own even a part of it. Under this government we will always be thieves in the night, afraid!

End the fear. Take the country back. It is our country, not theirs!!

Jana could see Dano in the light at the clandestine meeting, his hair tousled with passion, everyone enthralled by the drama of the moment, including Dano himself. She could see everyone coming to their feet, applauding every comma and period of the talk, including the police informants both in the audience and on the stage with Dano.

This time Dano and his DPR friends had fled before the police arrived, but there had been other arrests and other meetings. All this activity was succinctly summarized by the warrants that had been issued for his arrest for criminal acts against the state, listed on the last page of the report. They were hunting Dano.

She carefully replaced the pages in the folder and sat back down across from Trokan's desk. A moment later Trokan returned, pretending he had no notion that she had reviewed the folder.

"Sorry you couldn't read these." His voice was full of good cheer. Then the *bonhomie* was replaced by a slightly sour look. "Do what you have to, but stay away from him. I will not be able to save you this time if you don't. Understand?"

"Yes, Colonel."

"Good." He paused, trying to remember something. "Your vacation. In the Tatras. Enjoy it." He went back to his work as she left the office.

Chapter 25

A week later, Jana, her mother, and Katka were in Stary Smokovec, in the High Tatras, at the Grand Hotel. The hotel had seen better days. Now it offered bargain prices and a genteel poverty that reflected the way life had been three decades ago. Jana and her parents had vacationed there when Jana was a child. The country was still very green, none of the city noises or smells intruding, and aside from the one-too-many tourists, it was how Jana wanted it. Yet problems had followed them.

Jana's mother had had a very bad night, coughing, her breathing labored, forced to sit up to ease her lungs. Jana ordered food to be sent up for her mother and Katka, who insisted on staying with her grandmother during breakfast. She was still the little take-charge girl.

Feeling guilty about being more comfortable and less pressured away from her mother, Jana went down to the dining room and sat at a small table near a window. The window was slightly open, and through it a cool breeze came to refresh her neck and arms. She idly looked at the card that served as a menu, then looked up at the waiter to order.

The waiter was Dano.

Jana sat paralyzed, not knowing what to do. Dano the lover, Dano the husband and father, Dano the revolutionary had taken on a new role: Dano the waiter.

He placed the typical Slovak meat-and-cheese plate

breakfast in front of her, than asked if she wanted coffee or tea, finally deciding to give her tea when she did not respond. He nodded, smiling as a waiter should, asked for her room number so the meal would go on Jana's room bill, then went back into the kitchen as if he and Jana had never seen each other before.

Jana carried on with the motions of eating, then casually walked into the lobby, pretended to read the flyers advertising local events that the tourists could attend, while she unobtrusively checked the dining and desk areas, and then walked out onto the porch, deeply inhaling the mountain's pine scent, all the while trying to determine whether Trokan's intimation that she was being watched was true.

With the ebb and flow of tourists, and with the possibility that hotel functionaries were in the employ of the Secret Police, all of them watching her, she determined not to go back into the dining room to see Dano again in his incarnation as a waiter. Nor could she go into the kitchen to see him. Everyone would wonder why a guest was in that area. It was better for Dano not to look for her, but now that he was aware that she was at the hotel, Jana knew he would come to find her.

Jana wanted to see him and she didn't want to see him. If she was observed with him, the authorities would never believe that it was a chance meeting. They would place Jana at the hub of the outlaw activity that they were hunting Dano for, and, without a doubt, the case against her would be provable. The Procurator General would point out that she had never made a move to denounce Dano. Ergo, as a police officer and a citizen of the SSR, she had acted against the state's interest. At this very moment, simply by not doing anything, she was committing a crime.

Katka and her mother were upstairs. Jana knew Dano. He would visit Katka, daring people to recognize him. Even more worrisome, Katka would take enormous joy in seeing her father, and would waste no time in telling the world that her papa was back. No amount of cajoling or swearing her to secrecy would work. She was a little girl, and secrets were hard to keep. Katka would go to school, see her friends, and within days, a week at the most, everyone would know about it. Then someone's parents would denounce her.

Jana took several steps toward the telephone in the lobby, an inner voice urging her to call Trokan, to have the Secret Police come and pick Dano up. It was a simple, conceal-able act, an act that would forever remain locked away. Who would suspect her of denouncing Dano?

Instead, Jana went to the stairs, sprinting up them as fast as she could climb. There was another way: Get them all out of the place, out of the Grand Hotel, out of the Tatras. She rehearsed her lines as she ascended: "I've had an emergency call from Colonel Trokan. The minister has ordered me back to Bratislava to take personal charge of an investigation, an investigation of the highest priority. I could not refuse such an order, so we must leave at once."

A good plan. They would all be disappointed, but it would get them away from Dano.

When Jana opened the door to the hotel room, the plan vanished. Katka, distressed, met her at the door to inform her that Grandma was having a problem. Katka had tried to help, but Grandma became worse. She couldn't speak.

Jana's mother's condition had deteriorated dramatically. She was semi-comatose, her mouth open, a trickle of saliva running down her chin. She was inhaling with labored, suck-ing noises, as if she were not getting enough air. Jana tried to wake her, but she did not respond to either voice commands or a gentle shaking. Jana quickly gave up and called the desk to request an ambulance.

When it arrived an hour later, the ambulance took them all to the small hospital in Poprad. The doctors asked Jana for a quick history of her mother's ailment, then began working on her. The family could not stay in the emergency area, so Jana and Katka sat in the badly lit corridor outside the room where her mother had been placed. They settled in for the wait.

"She is very sick," Katka announced with great solemnity.

"They will save her," Jana replied, not at all sure they would.

"It's possible she will die." Katka patted her mother on the hand, then took it into hers, trying to give comfort to Jana.

"Doctors know what to do. They will give her things which will help her body fight. She will get stronger."

"Good," Katka declared. "But in case she does not, you have me, so you won't be alone."

"We have each other," Jana promised her.

"Always?" asked Katka.

"Always!"

A woman from the admissions office came into the hall and walked up to them. "The hospital director wants to see you at the front." She leaned close to Jana, whispering in her ear. "He wants to see you without the little girl."

The woman sat on the other side of Katka. "I'll stay with you while your mother attends to things."

Jana walked to the admissions desk. The duty person recognized her, pointing to a room with a closed door. Jana went through the door, knowing Dano was inside.

The small room was sparsely furnished, even by Slovak hospital standards, containing just a torn sofa and a pair of rickety old wooden chairs. Dano sat on the chair that stood against the far wall; Jana closed the door behind her and took the chair nearest to her and to the door. Picturing it in her mind later, they could have been two boxers in their corners waiting for the bell to ring to begin the fight, except that neither one of them really wanted a fight, both of them fearful that an all-out war was what this meeting would lead to.

For the first time Jana, noticed Dano was wearing glasses, and just below the left lens there was a small red scar on his cheek indicating a recent injury. Dano looked haggard and older: aged in a haunted way. As if he had just remembered needing to fulfill a duty, Dano reached into his jacket pocket to pull out an official-looking document.

"I have this for you."

He slid off his chair, stooping as if the ceiling were too low to allow him to stand erect, then took the two steps between them and handed her the paper. Without waiting for her to read it, he stepped back and sat again.

Jana opened the paper: a decree from the state granting a divorce to Dano and Jana Matinova, with all rights attendant thereto.

Jana ran her fingers over the seal on the document. Real enough. So was the rest of the paper. Except that she had never heard about any divorce action. This had to be a forgery.

"I didn't get any notification of this; I didn't appear. It can't be valid." The shock of receiving the document was in her voice. She shook her head, repeating herself. "It can't be valid."

"It was done in Prague. Today, you can buy the world and all its oceans in Prague. Not to worry, I did it right. I had a friend stand in for you. There was a lawyer and everything. Now my friend goes around telling everyone she used to be married to me." He saw Jana's lips tighten, angry at the joke. He stayed quiet for a moment. "It's good, unless you say it's no good."

"Why did you do it, Dano?" Jana folded the paper, then folded it half again, wishing it were not in her hands but also glad that it was. "Your reason, please?"

"They are after me. Better to close off all the points they might use to connect us." He gestured nervously with his hands, his face now registering fear. "I hide well, but not well enough that they won't sniff me out one of these weeks."

"Leave the country, Dano. Anywhere but here."

"Why must I go?"

"You don't need my answer to that, Dano."

"Why should I leave my home to them? No! It's clear, I shouldn't. So, I stay." He paused to regroup, to change the subject. "I am sorry your mother is ill. When did it start?"

"We first noticed serious problems a year ago."

"And Katka? I caught a glimpse of her when you left in the ambulance. She's wonderfully beautiful, isn't she?"

"Of course." Jana thought about the morning. "When you saw me at breakfast, did you have to stop yourself from coming to our room to see her?"

"Yes. And then, again, when the ambulance came. And now."

"What has stopped you?"

"You would have been angry."

"It would have made me afraid for all of us. Thank you for not giving in and coming to see her anyway."

"Has she started having boys come around?"

"No."

"So I'm still her only boyfriend." He stopped, realizing he had to wind their meeting down. "Almost time." He began patting his hair down with his palms, an old nervous gesture Jana recognized. He always made it just before he went on stage.

"Jana, things are going to heat up a bit more in the future. I want to warn you."

She raised a hand to stop him. "Dano, I don't want to hear what you are going to do. If I know that, and it is truly a criminal act, I would have to stop you."

"Not to worry. I'm through speaking."

She stood up; he stood up. He walked toward Jana as if he were going to kiss her on the mouth, then thought better of it, brushing his lips lightly across her cheek.

Close up, they looked at each other, each a little sad.

"You haven't changed at all."

Jana smiled at the lie.

"You have glasses," she pointed out. "They are becoming."

Her turn to lie.

"I can't read my speeches now without them."

"And the little scar."

"A tree branch."

Another lie.

"The branch had been made into a club," she suggested.

"It was very hard wood," he acknowledged.

"Good-bye," she said.

He walked out. She looked at the room: an ugly place, even too ugly for what had just gone on.

Chapter 26

Jana had missed her call from Kiev, from Mikhail. He'd had to respond to a police emergency, leaving a message that he would call back. Worse, the meeting chaired by Moira Simmons was still sputtering on. Given the catastrophic beginning to the conference, perhaps it was inevitable that the glitches in scheduling and presentation would be larger than normal. Speakers failed to appear, or arrived long after they were due; speeches would go on and on, way over schedule; audience participation was minimal, translations were inadequate; until the second half of the day when Moira Simmons decided to junk the agenda.

As the Chair, she declared that the participants would now interact directly on a number of issues. A freewheeling debate on the actions that should be taken and the recommendations they should promulgate for the EU would take place. She herself had generated a list of priorities and offered them for the delegates to discuss.

Jana watched Moira produce success from disaster. The woman cajoled, browbeat, insisted, gave ground when necessary, advanced when the opportunity presented itself, argued brilliantly, challenged national policies, skewered individuals, nagged, and finally cobbled together an agreed-upon set of principles, a timetable for goals and objectives to forward those principles, and, finally, a ringing call for immediate action.

The meeting lasted until four in the afternoon, with the last item the formulation of a press release that everyone could agree upon, not an easy task considering the egos and sensitivities involved. With that, the meeting was concluded.

Jana had made a few suggestions; Levitin had sat, Jana could swear, without blinking or uttering a word all day. But Jana came away from the session with a feeling of pleasure at Jeremy's participation. Her son-in-law was quite intelligent. He had made several contributions to the final resolutions of the group.

Jeremy begged off joining Jana for dinner because of a prior commitment, but promised to see her in the morning before he flew to Nice. She set out, not particularly wanting to talk to Moira Simmons. But Moira caught her eye, even while engaged in a five-way conversation encircled by other delegates, and beckoned Jana over. Moira stepped out of the circle, meeting her halfway, looking a little abashed.

"I want to thank you again for last night."

"If I helped, then I'm delighted."

"One thing: Please don't tell anyone about our 'meeting' in your room. It would be perceived as a weakness if it got out. People would wonder about my competence to handle emotional stress. So, please?"

"I understand." Moira was shoring up her defensive wall. "It's not my nature to gossip."

"Great. You'll keep me apprised of developments with the Foch case?"

"If I can keep up with them myself." Odd, thought Jana, how Simmons compartmentalized. Her ex-husband's death had now become the impersonal "Foch case."

"You should keep in mind that this is a French jurisdiction, not Slovak. They will be the investigators," Jana reminded her.

"Naturally." Moira now looked as if she was contemplating who the next person was whom she had to meet. "Goodbye." She walked back to the circle of people she had left, immediately jumping into the conversation, the most insistent voice in the group.

"Odd," thought Jana, feeling as if she had been pushed away. Moira had been instrumental in bringing Jana to this meeting, in placing her in the middle of the larger investigation of the Koba group, had cancelled Jana's talk with the group just before it was to have begun, and now appeared to have only the most passing interest in Jana or in Foch's death.

Jana searched the room for Levitin. He was leaning against the wall by the door, clearly waiting for her.

"Dinner?" he suggested.

"Business first."

"I'm hungry." He patted his stomach. "The barking dog has to be fed."

"Do you still have Foch's address book?" They walked out, going toward the elevator. "It's more interesting than food."

Levitin handed it to her. Jana flipped through the pages as the elevator carried them down. "Mr. Foch wanted his very important address book returned to him if it was lost. On the inside front cover is his Vienna UN address; in France, he has listed his home. It's in Alsace; we're in Alsace. We could be there very quickly."

"I will be thinking of food all the time it takes us to get there."

"The longer we wait to go, the more likely someone else may find what we want. They might even destroy it."

"And what do we want?"

Levitin was starting to waiver from his "food first" approach, but his stomach didn't want to surrender its claims.

"We want to know why anyone would murder the sweet, lovable, charming man Moira Simmons told us Foch was."

"If you promise to feed me after we go to . . ."—he checked the address—". . . Ribeauvillé. Yes, I've always wanted to go there." It was obvious that Levitin had not the slightest notion where the town was. "I am sure I will have the appropriate map in my car."

They crossed the lobby, going toward the front door of the hotel.

"Why do you have a car here?" Jana asked.

"I rented it. I saw the same address noted in Foch's book. If you had not insisted on going there, I would have—but after eating, naturally."

"Maybe the Russians sent us a good detective after all, Levitin."

"I would hope so, Commander Matinova."

They walked toward the car.

Chapter 27

They drove down the Route de Vin, about twenty kilometers from Strasbourg, then went south toward
Colmar, stopping northwest of that city in the small village
of Ribeauvillé. It was nestled in a green valley. Overhanging
houses lined the narrow streets. Several grand châteaus over-
looked the town, and they passed at least two ruined castles.
The area had to be filled with tourists in the summer; it was
too quaint to be missed.

The drive to the village had been an easy one, Levitin
proving he had a Russian's typical lead foot. He would only
talk in monosyllables while he drove, so Jana could not get
much from him about his background except that he worked
directly under a minister. That boosted Levitin's stock. You
don't need to send an official who works for a minister unless
the stakes are high. Trokan would ferret out the details.
There was probably a fax with the information she'd requested
waiting for her at the hotel.

They asked directions from a local *chocolatier*, and, at the slight
cost of a few expensive pieces of marzipan to soothe Levitin's
empty stomach, they were directed to a very large château on
the top of one of the nearby low-rising hills.

The château was even bigger close up, a sprawling mansion with a Palladian-pillared front. Unlike a number of the
other houses in the area, it was beautifully preserved, an

eighteenth-century icon lovingly refurbished and gardened into twenty-first-century splendor.

They parked outside the gate. There was no bell, so the two walked into the front yard, crossed to the large entry doors, and used the satyr-headed knocker to announce themselves. They repeated the knock after waiting, then walked around the building to determine if anyone, even a gardener, was there.

No lights inside, no noise, no voices. Jana decided that Foch, in life, had had such a sense of hospitality that he would have given them the run of the house. So he would not mind very much as she used her elbow to break a pane in one of the French doors and reached through to unlock the portal.

Inside, the house was lovingly furnished with Louis Quinze antiques, expensive rugs, and, to Jana's untrained eye, expensive art on the walls.

"I think I like Mr. Foch's taste," was Levitin's laconic comment.

They began wandering through the rest of the house. The first thing that caught Jana's eye was the collection of photographs scattered throughout the rooms. They included a number of the ex-Mrs. Foch, Moira Simmons, arm in arm with Foch. There was a small group photo that particularly caught Jana's attention. It showed three couples, obviously at a dinner party. One of the couples was unknown to her. Foch was with Moira Simmons, Jeremy with Katka. The picture of Katka was the first that Jana had seen in years, and, judging from the way Jeremy and the others looked, it had been taken fairly recently. Scrawled at the bottom of the photograph, in ink, was "Welcome to nice Nice, Jeremy and Katka."

Jana slipped the photo out of the frame; to Levitin's cocked eyebrow, she merely said, "Evidence."

The upstairs, particularly the master bedroom, was the next surprise. As beautifully furnished as the other rooms, it boasted a massive four-poster bed set on a pedestal in the middle of the room. There was an even larger collection of framed photos around the room, all of them of the ex-Mrs. Foch in various poses.

"Foch seemed to have been in love with the lady despite the divorce," Jana commented, amazed at the sheer number of pictures of Moira. It was more than just love. It was a worshiper's display. "He kept this place like a shrine to his goddess. Foch may have liked little boys, but he never gave up loving Ms. Simmons."

Levitin stepped up onto the platform that supported the bed. "Commander Matinova, please come up here."

Jana took the step up, immediately realizing where Foch had been sent off to his last sleep. The pillows were bloody. Ropes hung down from the posts, apparently the bonds used to secure Foch by his wrists and ankles. Foch may have loved Moira Simmons and loved his house, but he certainly couldn't have loved the last few minutes of life he'd had there.

"There should be a bedspread. It's gone."

"Used to carry the body away?" suggested Levitin.

"Probably. No blood on the carpet. A heavy bedspread would keep it off. Not much bleeding from the wound in the eye. Death was immediate, so no heart action to pump the blood out."

They left the bed forensics to the French police. An anonymous phone call when they got back to Strasbourg would alert the gendarmes to this location.

The two searched the rest of the house. In the back of the dressing room closet off the master bath was a floor safe. It was open, and bank books were scattered around a small case that stood near it. Twenty thousand Euros, still wrapped, sat on the lip of the safe. Foch had been interrupted while he was packing.

Levitin rubbed his forehead, puzzling the events out. "Our murderer doesn't need money. So, not a burglar."

Jana leafed through the bankbooks. Foch had been depositing huge sums of money. One of the accounts, a Swiss bank in Lucerne, contained 690,000 Euros.

"He was either an amazing businessman, incredibly well-budgeted when it came to spending money, or a very corrupt diplomat. What do you think, Levitin?" She tossed the books back onto the floor for the police to find.

"Maybe he won the National Lottery?"

"Doubtful."

"That was a joke."

"I know."

They walked down the stairs, Jana heading for the back yard.

"Where are we going?" Levitin asked as he followed her out the back door. "Our car is in front."

"They cut off his finger."

"'They'?"

"Very difficult to carry a dead man by yourself. Foch wasn't big, but he was substantial enough to cause a lone murderer problems. And when a person has just been killed, all the parts move unpredictably every time the body is shifted. Very awkward, which makes it even harder. And where did they cut off the finger?"

She walked purposefully toward a small toolshed half hidden by trees. "My guess is they used one of the tools in there." The door was slightly ajar, so the two walked inside. She switched an overhead light on. There was a bandsaw on the small worktable. Levitin and Jana examined it.

"Yes, here." Levitin ran his finger parallel to the blade,

indicating flecks of blood and bone. "The fine teeth on the saw would make the clean cut we saw."

"The killer had a plan. He wanted to make sure his message got through to whoever it was aimed at."

"It got through to me," acknowledged Levitin.

"These people are not very pleasant."

"They did not succeed in making my stomach less hungry." Levitin patted his belly.

They drove off with the aim of finding a local restaurant to get Levitin's stomach the meal it wanted.

Chapter 28

Jana met Jeremy early the next morning for a *petit dejeuner* at a small café a short distance from the hotel. Jana had eaten too much the night before, so she confined herself to a small pastry with large sprinkles of sugar on the top, and coffee. She watched as Jeremy carefully spread apricot jam on a hot croissant, then bit into it, relishing every crumb.

Between bites, Jeremy studied the photograph Jana had taken from Foch's house. "I remember this one. Foch liked to take photographs of his friends. Then he'd give the photos to them. He used to laugh and called it his biggest calling card. People naturally like to see pictures of themselves, so everyone welcomed Foch and his camera."

"This one was taken by someone else," Jana reminded him.

"I outfoxed Foch. There was a woman walking around taking photos. Foch didn't expect to be on the receiving end. 'Click,' there he was, in the photo. He had me write the inscription on it."

"Katka looked very well."

"It was just after she'd had the baby. Katka was still a little plump and working very hard at dieting the weight off."

"The extra weight looks good." Jana looked at the photograph, studying her daughter. "She was always too thin."

"I agree." He smiled ruefully. "I made a mistake. I once told her I liked skinny women and now she refuses to put on weight. Once she makes up her mind, there's no way to change it."

"Stubborn, like her father." Jana felt a sudden pang of anguish, thinking of Dano. She forced herself back to the reality of the photograph and the couple she did not recognize. "Who were these other two?"

"Pavel Rencko and his lady." He took the photograph back from Jana, scrutinizing the man. "He was a low-level diplomat from the Czech Republic. Got involved in smuggling things via diplomatic pouches, or in his car, or whatever. The police couldn't search him because of immunity. He couldn't resist the easy bucks."

"Where is he now?"

"Dead. His own people did for him. He was working with a group out of South Africa transporting all kinds of contraband. When the Czechs caught on, they recalled him. Instead of driving off into the sunset in disgrace, Rencko did a perfect half-gainer out of a fifth-floor window."

"And the wife?"

"She turned out not to be his wife. A Russian woman. She was window dressing, kind of a permanent escort for him. Surprised everyone."

"She was his mistress?"

"I guess so. It wasn't my business, so I did the diplomatic corps thing: I stayed away."

Jana went on to the person in the photograph they had not yet discussed. "How long have you known Moira Simmons?"

Jeremy eyed Jana, wondering what she was getting at. He finally decided she was being his concerned mother-in-law. "I am a good and faithful husband. No worries about that, Jana."

Jana smiled. "I assumed so, Jeremy."

"Good." He appeared mollified, taking another bite out of his croissant. "She came with Foch. We were all in the same field, we had interests in common. We met, I think, at a conference in Nice. Everybody likes to hold meetings in Nice. It has sun and beaches, and people can walk between the small raindrops when the sky decides to weep." He smiled at his attempt to be humorous. "Then there's Cannes on one side and Monaco on the other, so you throw a meeting in Nice and everyone scrambles to attend."

He tried to characterize Moira Simmons for Jana. "She has a dark side. She kind of hides in a corner when whatever it is comes over her. But Ms. Simmons is a very competent person, so you forgive her moods."

"And Foch?"

"He's dead. Ugh. What a way to go."

Jana persisted. "Had you heard any rumors about Foch's private life?"

Jeremy's eyebrows went up again. "Like, anything wrong with it?"

"Yes."

"I stay away from that stuff. Rumors run through the consulates and embassies like a dirty sewer that carries nothing but bad odors and garbage. I tune them out."

"Did Foch and Simmons see each other after they divorced?"

"Playing police officer again, are we?" He wagged a cautionary finger at her. "Better to stay out now, rather than dig deeper. The French cops are a pain if they think you're invading their territory. And I'm from the wrong embassy, so I can't be a hero on a white horse if they come down on you."

Jana shrugged. "I'm not 'playing' police officer; I *am* one." She decided to switch topics, sliding over into the area they had both been avoiding. "Can we talk about Katka and me?"

"Certainly."

"All I want is an hour to see her and the baby."

Jeremy looked down at the tablecloth, absentmindedly

brushing at crumbs, trying to think of a way to give Jana some shred of hope.

He finally looked up from the tablecloth. "If I can do it, I will. I'll try to be as persuasive as I can. I'll be persistent, I will promise her a luxurious life, sweet cakes and honey for her meals. But we both know how intractable she is." He took a breath, hoping he had not made Jana feel worse. "We will keep our fingers crossed, okay?"

"Okay."

"For the next couple of days, hang loose. Stay at the same hotel, so I can leave you a message. If she says you can come see her in Nice, I will call you."

Jana nodded. All she could do was hope.

Chapter 29

The very tanned man filled up an extraordinary amount of space. It was not that he was so large. His presence alone managed to substitute for volume. As he stood next to the shop window watching the reflections from across the street, the pedestrians gave him a wide berth. It was not because he appeared fearsome, but because he was "*formidable*," as the French might say, someone with whom you would not trifle.

The man had picked this window deliberately. It even had a mirror in one segment of its display case, which fit his needs better than the other windows on the street. He had been standing on the same spot for an hour, actually enjoying the show that passed by.

He viewed people as if they were in a performance being staged just for him. Some were good actors; some were bad actors. He would, in time, remove the bad actors from his stage. After all, they were just objects to amuse him, to please him, to do his bidding. If they didn't, he would make sure that they could no longer act on his stage. It was all very simple.

The man would occasionally move his head slightly, catching different reflective angles. One of his slight turns caught her coming down the street. He knew her at once, the description and the small picture sent to him fitting her like a stencil.

She was not too tall or short and carried herself well, shoulders back and head erect, without looking masculine. She had an overall air of confidence without losing her femininity. A good combination for a woman police officer. He would have to think carefully about his approach to the problem she presented.

She went into her hotel, and almost immediately the man saw Tutungian. A new element in the play. The watcher was momentarily angry with himself for not taking into account that the policewoman might be followed.

He shifted his feet, angling for a different view of the reflections in the window, irritated that he might have given himself away. He had moved too quickly. Moving objects are perceived more readily than stationary ones. The movement catches the eye, particularly the eyes of those who are anxious about their own safety. Tutungian was one of them.

The man quickly shed his anger. He was rarely angry at himself, and seldom stayed angry at others. Anger is a wasteful emotion that only drains you. Besides, everyone was an object, and who could get angry over objects? Tutungian, though, was a man who suffered deep angers and nurtured longterm revenge. Too bad for Tutungian, not to understand and use his time in a wiser way.

He watched even more closely. No reaction from Tutungian. Good. Tutungian had *not* seen him. He was pleased. If the man had been in Tutungian's place, he would have discovered the watcher. One of the major differences between himself and people like Tutungian.

Tutungian walked past the hotel, loitered for a while, then went inside. The tanned man did not have to see Tutungian's actions to know what he was doing. He had waited until the policewoman cleared the lobby, then gone inside to book a room at the same hotel, on the floor where the woman was staying. Tutungian would already have her room number. He'd make an excuse as to why he wanted the particular floor she was staying on without mentioning her name. Some silly excuse would do: superstition, lucky number, anything would be acceptable to the room clerk. Then, a false passport when he registered, as he explained why his bags would arrive later.

The man thought for a moment, the thought pleasing him. He made a small wager with himself that he was right: The false name that Tutungian was using would begin with an A for his given name and a T for his surname. One of the consistent mistakes that Tutungian made was the egotism that drove him to wear monogrammed shirts. Therefore, his passport and his registration required the initials A.T., matching the shirt. Otherwise the clerk might notice the difference.

There was a positive aspect to this, the man granted Tutungian: A matching monogram always eased the methodical minds of desk clerks. No man would go through the trouble of having a falsely monogrammed shirt. Ergo, he had to be the real A.T.

Twenty minutes later, Tutungian left the hotel, time enough for him to have checked in, gone up to his room to avoid leaving the hotel immediately after checking in, then come down through the lobby. He headed down the block, no cares, not paying any real attention to people on the street. He was no longer following the policewoman. Tutungian's defenses would be down. He was the stalker, not the quarry.

Tutungian never saw the tanned, healthy-looking man fall in behind him. Even if he had been alert, he would not have seen him. The man was too adroit at losing himself on a street through years of practice undergone through necessity. Tutungian's unawareness simply made it easier for the man to keep company with him, and easier for him to remove this actor from the stage. It was merely a question of how and when.

Chapter 30

The fax was waiting for Jana at the desk when she picked up her key. It was from Trokan, two pages, including a caution that it was not to be shared with anyone except Levitin. She read it through, than called Levitin's room, asking him to come down to her room.

Everything one does revolves around motivation, she thought. Fanatics have a warped abundance of it; businessmen, the most successful of them, have nearly as much as fanatics; nations have it as the sum total of their people's desires, often skewed badly through the centuries, so they devour and conquer other peoples. For individuals, it varied. She read the fax again and wondered how Levitin's motivation might have warped him.

Jana heard the knock and admitted Levitin. He sat on the easy chair, slouching, trying to stretch out his long legs.

"I'm still tired. Jet lag is catching up with me." He yawned. "I called you for breakfast, but you were out."

"I saw my son-in-law."

"So, will you now get to see your daughter and grandchild in Nice?"

Jana's mouth immediately became dry, her teeth involuntarily clamping together. She stifled a retort, angry at his invasion of her private space. Levitin, on the other hand, made himself even more comfortable, stretching out farther, giving out an audible groan of pleasure. She snapped out a command: "Take your shoes off if you are going to put those large feet of yours on my bed!!"

Levitin showed no emotional response to Jana's irritation, merely wiggling out of his shoes, dropping them to the floor. She noticed that he was wearing athletic socks, rather incongruous with his formal attire of suit and tie.

"And you need to wear dark socks to coordinate with your other clothes." Her commanding tone softened and dropped down a notch, losing its edge.

"You are not my mother," Levitin pointed out.

"Why white socks? You are generally fairly careful about your dress." Before he answered her, Jana came up with it. "You are allergic to the miserable dyes in Russian socks, so you wear white. Or, your feet are allergic to artificial fibers, so you wear cotton."

"You are still being my mother," he reminded her. "And you are being irritable with me because I checked your background and picked up something you don't want people to know about."

"You're right." Jana wet her finger and ticked the air, scoring one for the Russian. "Now, am I right about the socks?"

He ticked the air, giving her a point. "Right on, in your entire analysis."

"Feet have to be taken care of."

"And the eyes and teeth. My mother, now you."

"And what part did your sister play in teaching you?"

This time it was Levitin's turn to respond, his face tightening, his lips thinning.

"Researching me this time."

"I apologize. We have both been slightly uncivil. I needed answers. I knew you were holding back. So I checked."

"My exact reason for checking on you."

The edge in Jana's voice came back. "My hope of seeing

my daughter and granddaughter has nothing to do with this case."

"Your son-in-law may."

"How did you reach that conclusion?"

"He's in the middle of everyone involved. He knows all the participants. He even knows the people in the photograph you stole from Foch's house."

Jana had considered Jeremy's connections to all of these people. Only, her thoughts had not reached the category of possible criminality and a need to investigate him.

"You want to consider him as a possible suspect?" She wondered if Levitin had established a hard connection between Jeremy and Koba. "Evidence, please. What concrete items do you have?"

"None. Just that we have to think of all the possibilities so we don't overlook any."

"Agreed." Jana decided to get all the problematic areas laid out. "I received a fax about your sister. And about you. Your sister first. So, tell me about her."

Levitin had prepared himself for Jana's questions. He sank even deeper in the chair so that he was almost horizontal. He hesitated, not sure where to begin, than decided to start with the worst.

"My sister, like all young women who now grow up in Moscow, was exposed to cocaine at a party. She used it again, and again. And so became addicted."

"You tried to help," Jana guessed. "Your family tried to help. The authorities tried to help. Nothing worked. She disappeared."

"Worse." Levitin pursed his lips, hurting, thinking about it. "We knew she went into prostitution. We knew that she was on the street. I looked for her, my mother looked for her, my uncle looked for her. Nothing."

"Your uncle is the minister who sent you here?"

"Families take care of each other." His somber mood was broken by an embarrassed giggle. "How do you think I rose so fast in my profession? I'm smart, but nobody is that smart." He scratched a foot, then put it back on the bed. "I talked to the minister, my uncle, and he sent me here."

"Why here?"

"We know my sister left Moscow. She saw a woman who was an old school chum before she went. The friend told me that Alexandra, my sister, told her she was coming to France. This conference, then, was the perfect cover for me. I have come, on the surface, to attend this meeting, not to look for my sister." He scratched the other foot. "Then I found you were a delegate, and I recognized a possible ally."

Jana came to a rather sad conclusion: Neither of them had come any closer to what they really wanted. She studied Levitin. There was still something awry. Levitin's face betrayed too much satisfaction. One item, she thought, at least one item in his head he had not told her about: a witness, a piece of evidence he hadn't revealed, something. Jana decided to push him.

"You found something in Strasbourg?" His expression changed enough to reinforce her belief. "What is it?"

He tried to look blank.

"Levitin, I don't have time to pretend. You have found some small item."

He tried to deepen the look of innocence. It only succeeded in making him appear vacuous.

"Levitin, you have made me tired enough." She kicked at his chair, moving it enough so that he landed on the floor with a small thump. He looked up at her with wide eyes as if to say, "What did I do?"

"Time to give it up, Levitin."

He thought about her demand and finally nodded. "You have it."

It was her turn to look blank.

"You have it with you," he insisted.

"I have it now?"

"Yes."

Jana went over all the aspects of the case, everything she had done in Ukraine, at the conference. Then she realized the answer. Jana went to her purse, found the photograph she had taken from Foch's house, the one with her daughter and Jeremy and the others and looked at it closely. No doubt. It was there. She pointed to the woman on the arm of the Czech diplomat who had committed suicide. The facial resemblance was now clear.

"Your sister!"

"My sister," he acknowledged. Levitin stared at the photograph, happy at seeing her, unhappy at seeing her there.

Ambivalence is a part of human nature.

Chapter 31

Tutungian carefully applied pomade to his hair, not too much or it would look greasy, a larger amount on the sides to give his face a slimmer look. When he finished, he stepped back from the mirror for a longer view, then capped the tube and carried it with him into the living room, slipping it into his shaving kit.

Tutungian had already shipped his luggage off; the room looked as empty as when he had arrived. He checked his jacket side pocket. The gloves were still there. He patted his inside breast pocket. Yes, the thin wire with ends attached to the small bar-handles was neatly coiled within. The handles were important. Tutungian had once garroted a rival gangster without using handles and the garrote had cut into his palms when he tightened the wire around the man's throat. No reason to let that happen again.

There was a knock at the door, and he heard the landlady calling for him. "Monsieur Tillo. *Le taxi est arrivé*." He enjoyed hearing her use the name he had given her when he rented the small apartment.

"*Merci*, Madame." He exhausted most of his small knowledge of French with his use of the minimal "oui," "non," and "merci." Tutungian was uncomfortable here. He was always uneasy when he was forced to leave his country. He had no desire to be here; but until his business was concluded, he had no choice if he wanted to return home eventually. His employer did not react positively to independent conduct or mistakes.

Tutungian took a last look around. Satisfied upon his second examination that he had left nothing, Tutungian walked to the door and, with his usual caution, opened it, stepping to the side, ready for whoever might be waiting out there for him. Nothing. He stepped into the hall, then relaxed. It was always the most dangerous time, coming out of an apartment. You could never be assured there was no one lying in wait until you actually took the first step.

Comfortable now, he walked to the front door of the house, placed his key on a small table next to the door, and again used his customary caution in walking outside. The taxi was not there.

Tutungian walked the short distance to the street, looking for the cab. The street was narrow, cars were double-parked, making it difficult to see without his moving to the center of the street. Still no taxi. The stupid driver had probably been forced to drive off because he was blocking traffic. Tutungian made himself less unhappy by resolving not to give the driver a tip when he drove back around the block to pick up his fare and took him to his destination.

Rather than stand outside, a target for anyone, Tutungian walked back to the house. He would stand just inside the door, and when the taxi came he could quickly move to the vehicle.

Tutungian abruptly realized he had left the key to the door on the table inside, and the door locked automatically when it was shut. He tapped on the door for the landlady to let him in. Then, as a possibility, he turned the door knob. Miracle of miracles, the door opened. Tutungian stepped inside, never seeing the man who waited there for him.

An hour later, the police received a call from a woman

whose hysteria at first prevented them from comprehending what she was babbling into the phone. When they finally understood, they sent two cars to seal off the scene. When the first unit arrived, the woman was incongruously sitting on the ground in front of her building. She was wailing, several neighbors trying to comfort her. The woman adamantly refused to get to her feet or to stop wailing, even when the police tried to get her up.

One of the cops kneeled to talk to her; the other police officer walked to the open front door and cautiously stepped inside. He saw a man sitting in a chair, his back to him.

Because of the report they'd received, the cop slid his gun out of its holster, walking a wide circle around the chair. The man was dead, his face puffy and red, his eyes protruding. There was a wire around his neck, so tight it had cut his throat. A considerable amount of blood had spilled down his front. At the back of his neck a pair of wooden handles dangled from the ends of the wire.

Nestled in his lap, palms up, the man's hands contained an object. The police officer took a closer look, then almost gagged when he realized what it was: the dead man was holding his tongue in his hands, a small amount of blood pooling onto his fingers.

If he had been alive, Tutungian would have appreciated one thing: His hair was still slicked back, in the exact way he had combed it, not a single strand disturbed.

Chapter 32

Jana called Seges while she and Levitin sat in the lobby, nursing a glass of wine, waiting for the airport shuttle to arrive. Seges immediately began moaning about his caseload. Jana eventually snapped at him, getting Seges's mind turned in the direction she wanted.

There was no additional word from Mikhail in Ukraine, and Seges still hadn't the faintest clue as to what Mikhail had called her about.

The code book was now with the FBI in Washington, and they were making noises about sending it over to the CIA or NSA for them to decode, claiming those were the agencies that had the equipment that would enable them to decipher it quickly. Everyone was now waiting for an executive decision on whether they would send it and whether it would be accepted. Seges, as directed, had also sent a copy to the man in the Czech Republic who had written a book about codes.

Jana thought for a moment, then asked Seges to hold on while she talked to Levitin. "Do you know anyone who is good with numbers?" she asked him.

He tapped his temple with a forefinger, pleased with himself. "I am great with numbers, in any configuration. I never forget them. It helps me to investigate corruption at home." A grin crept into the corners of his mouth. "My uncle, the minister, didn't get me promoted *just* because I'm his nephew."

"Do you know anything about codes?"

"Not formally. Not even informally. There are code experts in my country."

"I know." Jana decided to keep the book out of Russia. The Russians were capricious. If she left it in their hands, they might decide to keep the work for themselves, and she would never be informed of their results.

Jana went back to the phone. Seges asked if she wanted to talk to Trokan. Jana had Seges transfer her.

"How are you doing?" Trokan's voice had a grumbling quality. "Are the French feeding you well?"

"They feed all visitors well. And how is my sick blind cat doing at the veterinarian?" Trokan's grumble this time was not so pronounced. The cat had been declared well enough by the doctor to allow Trokan to take the "poor little thing" home.

"One tiny tidbit," Trokan confided, his voice taking on a smile. "My wife now likes taking care of the cats. You may have a hard time getting them back from her."

"Her interests are transient," Jana reminded him. "She will be yelling for you to return them in another few days."

"Assuredly." Trokan lost the smile in his voice. "But meanwhile I am at peace. Are you getting along with Levitin?"

"More or less. Mostly more."

"Success?"

"Not yet." She took a breath. "I believe we will have to go to Nice." She waited for the explosion of disapproval that never came. "So . . . ?"

"To see our daughter?"

"No. To see *my* daughter," she corrected him, as she always did.

The smile came back into his voice. "To see your daughter," he amended.

"There is a lead that Levitin and I want to follow. We have to go there to do it."

"My wife wants to go there. It is very warm. Palm trees. The blue sea. When she hears you have gone, she will like you even less."

"Does this mean I have permission to go?"

"I want daily reports."

"Every few days."

"Daily!" insisted Trokan.

He hung up on her.

She held out the phone to Levitin. "Do you need to call for approval?"

Levitin still had that look of self-satisfaction which had appeared when he had told her about his ability with numbers. "You forget, it's my uncle. No problem."

They rose as the shuttle bus pulled up to the front of the hotel. Jana and Levitin picked up their baggage, walking outside with the other passengers waiting to board. The sun was hidden behind the clouds over Strasbourg. It was going to rain. When it did, it would be cold. Even when there was nothing but sunshine in this city, Jana decided, it seemed like it was cold.

They boarded the bus, the bus driver reading a newspaper as he waited for all the passengers to embark. The headline and the accompanying picture caught her eye. Jana stood behind the driver, reading over his shoulder. The driver finally realized what she was doing.

"You want to read the paper?" he asked, in English.

"Yes," she answered.

"I thought only the Americans read over other people's shoulders." He thrust the paper at her, and started the engine. "Don't forget to return it," he barked as she walked back to the empty seat next to Levitin.

The front-page photograph showed a body being carried away. A man had been murdered. Registered under a false name, he had been identified as Aram Tutungian, a delegate to a conference that had just been concluded in Strasbourg. Although the paper gave very few details about the killing, it was apparent that it had been a particularly nasty murder.

She passed the paper over to Levitin, no doubt in her mind that Koba and the killing were intimately connected. There was also no doubt in her mind that Koba, if he was still in Strasbourg, would soon be in Nice, the city they were now traveling to. She wondered if she would be able to identify him when he came after her.

Chapter 33

Sasha took the chance of walking down the Promenade des Anglais because she loved the Baie des Anges. Angels had to live here; the blue of the water, the beaches, the palm trees, everything about Nice and the Cote d'Azur was so different from Russia. Even at the end of January the temperature was mild; it was slightly overcast, but she could walk outside wearing a light jacket. Yes, it was worth a little risk to walk, inhaling the sea air, after spending almost all of her days inside to avoid being discovered.

Occasionally, Sasha would hug the jacket closer to her body, not because of the weather, but because she liked the comfort of the soft wool. It had been a casual gift from Pavel. They had walked by a store window, Sasha commenting on how pretty it looked, even on a window mannequin. Pavel had immediately gone in and bought it for her. It was not the rich-looking fur coat Pavel had later given her. However, her new life required a different look, and she was safer wearing wool.

Her naturally light brown hair had been dyed, not blonde as she first intended, but an even darker brown-black. Blondes attract too much attention, and Sasha could not afford that. All her clothes had been left behind in their suite of apartments as soon as she heard that her protector had gone out of the window. The event itself had told her she had to run. They would be coming after her next. There was no chance that Pavel Rencko had killed himself. He loved life too much, and no matter what crime they were accusing him of, he would have fought back, kicking and screaming, rather than take a suicide leap.

The old Russian couple who worked at the Queen Victoria had rented a room for her for a few days in their name so she could avoid registering. It was necessary. People leave their names in too many inconvenient places where other people can access them. Sasha had thought of leaving Nice, running to another city. Not a good idea, she had decided. She spoke imperfect French, and a Russian woman who traveled would leave a trail that was easily visible. In Nice, at least, she knew people, she knew the city. Her only real opportunity to escape was to become an invisible person, surviving until they gave up searching. Then, maybe Marseille, an easier, bigger city to hide in, but with the same light and sun she now enjoyed so much, might be the place for her.

Damn the overcast. Sasha wanted the full, blinding light of the sun after submerging herself in the place she'd found. She'd been fortunate. A developer had put up an apartment complex in the old quarter of the city where Sasha could rent by the week or month. It was owned by an absentee landlord, so there was no need to register, but also no postal designation and no telephone. Other than that, the place was fully furnished. The tourists would flock back to the complex once the season started at the end of March; but with all the vacancies they currently had, the rental agency had been only too happy to let her take it at an off-season rate, no questions asked. Only she missed Pavel.

Pavel had been fun. It was a business arrangement, yes. Yet it didn't matter to him that she'd been a whore, an addict who would provide any sexual favor for a fix. He'd truly become her lover rather than the keeper of a "do-it-for-me blow-up doll." He'd put himself on the line for her, telling the others to stay away. And he was enough of a threat to force them to back off. Then he'd helped her get the drugs out of her system.

A trio of teenagers rollerbladed past her. There were two girls being teased by a tall boy. The boy would skate up to them, gently shove one of them, then they'd both chase him while he skated ahead, or back, leaving them to scream at him. It was all love play. Sasha wondered which one of the girls was going to end up with the boy. It was obvious they both liked him, and were playing at the game, while playing him.

There were people on the *plage:* a pair of joggers, a circle of men kicking and heading a football. It was not like the beach would be in the summer, when it would be jammed, a place to stay away from. Her eyes drifted away from the beach, across the boulevard. It was then that she saw the dark Rolls-Royce with the blacked-out passenger windows and the pencil-thin red stripe down the side drive up to the front of the Negresco. She immediately felt acid in the back of her throat, forced up by the fear in her stomach.

Sasha bent, as if adjusting her shoe, to lower her profile and half-hide behind a small car. She pulled her neck scarf off, tying it around her head babushka-style, to change her appearance even more. She managed this while keeping her eye on the Rolls.

The chauffeur went to the trunk, pulling out luggage, as bellmen from the hotel ran to the car and the chauffeur handed them the bags. The driver then walked to the passenger door and opened it.

The passengers didn't immediately leave the car. They took their time, then made a leisurely exit. They had been finishing their drinks. One of the men handed the chauffeur his glass. The three passengers then walked up the hotel steps.

Sasha recognized all three of them. The one she could not take her eyes off was the Manager. Again, here, in Nice. The Manager was supposed to have gone far away from Nice, so Sasha had felt safe again. Now the trembling started in her legs, and traveled in waves up her body. She tried to slow her breathing, to calm the feeling that her head was bobbing so hard that it might snap from her neck.

No question, if the Manager was here, they would be discussing emergency measures, and she would be among the major items to be discussed. She was a large loose end they had to clip off. Pavel Rencko had used her for his errands, confided in her, given her access to his papers, made her an integral part of the business, and they knew it.

Knowledge is safety, Pavel had told her. They can't hurt you because they don't know what you've done with the knowledge, where you've put it in storage, and how incriminating to them it is. They will want you to keep on living, Pavel said, until they know. Pavel was wise about these things. He had comforted her, pulling her close. "If you die," he'd whispered in her ear, "someone they can't control may obtain what you know. They can't let that happen. So, you see, you are now safe."

Only they had killed poor Pavel. He was wrong: His knowledge hadn't protected him. And it wouldn't protect her.

Sasha waited until the Rolls drove off and she was sure none of the three who had gone into the hotel were suddenly going to emerge before she'd walked a safe distance away down the Promenade. She tried to hum a song to keep her spirits up, but all she could think of was the Russian national anthem. It gave her courage. Strange, she hadn't sung it since childhood.

Sasha picked up her pace. The clouds passed, the sun came

out, washing the street with its light. Everyone on the water-front responded, becoming more animated, more cheerful. Except Sasha, who no longer noticed.

No reason to hurry, Sasha repeated to herself like a mantra. Keep calm. She still had her hole to hide in. They would not find her today. She put tomorrow out of her mind.

Chapter 34

On the plane ride to Nice, Levitin had immediately gone to sleep. Jana admired the facility with which certain people, no matter what the circumstances, could curl themselves up, put reality behind them, and rest. Jana tried, then gave up, instead using the time to go over the phone numbers in Foch's address book one more time. The telephone numbers stared back at her. Most she failed to recognize, while others like Jeremy's and Moira Simmons's waved at her in recognition. When she had the time, Jana would probably have to call the unknown numbers, one by one, perhaps see some of the owners, doing the one-step-after-another drudge work so much a part of solving cases. She then pulled out a copy of the coded book she and Seges had found taped to the underside of the couch in the dead pimp's apartment. She browsed through it, hoping to see an item, a number, anything that would have make sense to her.

Each of the pages had a different number on the right side, each number written as if it were a continuation of the name corresponding with the telephone number first entered at the top of the page. But the numbers on each of the pages were not in order and did not correspond to the correct page in the book. On the left side of the page, again corresponding with the first name on the page, appearing to be the beginning of a name, but, written smaller than the other letters in the name, there was a letter. Again, they were not in alphabetical order, but like the numbers, did not repeat themselves, and did not appear to reflect a page number.

On the lower portion of each page, again on the same line as the last name and telephone number, the process was repeated, letter on one side, number on the other, each of them not corresponding to a page or to each other, and not in any order. They did not repeat the same patterns at the tops of the pages.

Jana tried to make sense of the letters and numbers placed as they were. She spent time going over them backward and forward, up and down, crossing the pages, letter to letter and number to number. They did not relate to the entries they were juxtaposed with. No logical relationship presented itself, either internally or externally.

The numbers, words, letters had to have a meaning, not necessarily with each other but by reference to an object outside themselves. Codes had to have a method that could be used to decipher them, a program, an Enigma decryption machine, a decoding book. The man who wrote the book found in the apartment would need a key in order to write in code, and so others in the organization would be able to decode it. It would be easy to decipher the book if you had the key. Unfortunately, if you were untrained, and didn't have the key, you might never be able to do it.

There was a key somewhere, a Rosetta stone allowing the message to be read. Names? Dates? Left to right? Front to back? Where did you start? On even days one set; on odd days the other? The key would tell her.

She snapped the book shut. Now a code expert had to work on what they had, without a key. Maybe the Slovak code expert or the Americans could do it. Or maybe even Levitin, who'd boasted of his gift for numbers. She'd have to think about that.

She tucked the book away, trying to doze, unable to stop mulling over the subject. She was sure that whoever had planted it in the apartment had wanted it found. Why? To suggest that the pimp was part of a large, complex organization? If so, who were the other people? A rival gang? A part of the organization the person who killed the pimp wanted to destroy? Was it evidence that could be used against them? Again, why? To have the field to himself? More conjecture without any real hope of reaching an accurate conclusion.

She tried to make herself comfortable, concluding that airline seats give a promise of comfort that they never keep. She was forced to put a pillow behind the small of her back, and sit upright. Again, no rest. She began picking at the facts in the case.

Foch? What part did he play in this series of events? Foch had been in Vienna, which was close to Bratislava. Was Foch involved directly in the murder of the pimp? Was Foch a member of the organization to be destroyed? Or a destroyer?

Dead Tutungian of the slicked-back hair, the "reformed" gangster who was to give testimony at the meeting. Obviously he had not been reformed enough to prevent himself from being murdered. Was it because of his pending testimony?

Jana was still thinking about Tutungian when she finally fell asleep. Not even the jarring of the aircraft when it landed at the Nice airport woke her. Her sleep was so deep that Levitin had to shake her awake.

Chapter 35

Mikhail Gruschov hailed a taxi. The taxi driver shocked Mikhail when he pulled over. The driver wore a wolf's mask that covered half his face, a jovial wolf who was laughing at his own appearance when he beckoned Mikhail inside. Were French cab drivers crazy? Mikhail wondered what kind of lunacy he had gotten himself into.

Even as he kept the driver at arm's length, Mikhail pointed at a small map he had picked up. Using gestures, grunts, vivid exclamations, and muttered imprecations, they reached an understanding that Mikhail wanted to be dropped off at Chemin du Bois. When they arrived, Mikhail pulled out a handful of Euros, holding them out, allowing the driver to pick through the money to pay for his services. Better to remain safe, far away from the man's teeth. The amount the driver counted out for himself seemed reasonably related to what the meter read, so Mikhail pocketed the rest and gladly eased his bulk out of the taxi, into the street, taking his small bag from the driver.

Mikhail wore his wool winter suit. The mild climate of Nice generated uncomfortable warmth, and he wished that he had listened to Adriana and worn light clothes. The radical change of geography, and its weather, was still hard for him to credit. In less than one day he had come from zero-Centigrade ice and snow to a climate where plants were green and flowering.

Despite his relief that the driver was gone, the taxi's departure left Mikhail feeling deserted. Mikhail was like Yuri Gagarin coming in from outer space and landing on the wrong planet. He pushed his feeling of alienation away and studied the building before him. Unlike the rest of the city, it was one of a cluster of high-rise flats, concrete slabs displaying little French flair or design sensibility. It might have looked sleek and new at one time, but Mikhail doubted it.

The occupants' washing hung out to dry on every one of the balconies that ran up the sides of the buildings, just like in ugly Ukrainian high-rises. Mikhail decided the buildings in France, like those in Kiev, must have been designed by local communists who had struggled to build at the lowest possible level of human habitation. Their dreary construction truly represented the proletariat.

Mikhail walked toward the entrance of the building. The kids playing in front were awed at his enormous bulk. Some of them wore outlandish masks and partial costumes.

"Are you here for Carnival?" one of them yelled. Mikhail couldn't understand them, so he ignored the question, walking on. Not a French giant, the kids concluded. Maybe a freak on leave from a circus? Clothes too drab to be French, his hair tousled, not in the careful uncombed look of the French males, he must be from some other place where style did not mean anything. A foreigner. They watched until he was inside, making unkind comments that it was fortunate Mikhail did not understand.

He checked the mailboxes inside the vestibule. Boyar, his cousin, was listed; Mikhail pressed the bell for admittance. He waited for a voice to demand his name. No response. Mikhail eyed the confines of the little hall, wondering how to get to Boyar's apartment. He thought of ringing another bell. That would never work. He spoke no French, and sign language would be an absurdity over a building intercom.

A good ten minutes later, a little old lady walking a tiny dog on a leash came through the inner door. Mikhail stopped the door from closing, his huge arm reaching like a bridge over the woman's head. Her little dog yipped once, rolling its eyes so you could see the whites, a warning to Mikhail to watch where he stepped. The woman, never noticing that Mikhail had stopped the door from closing, continued on her mission: allowing her dog to relieve itself by fouling the sidewalk with its waste.

Mikhail went to the door marked *ascenseur* and, miracle of miracles, it worked, creaking its objections to the weight it carried all the way to the eighth floor. Mikhail stepped out, checking apartment numbers until he came to 809, then knocked. As expected, there was no answer. His cousin had had the bad grace to be out when Mikhail arrived. Boyar, as Mikhail remembered, had never been a considerate man.

There was no choice. Mikhail sat down on the welcome mat, his back braced against the door, leaning an elbow on his knee, his head on his hand. With his massive head and shoulders he looked remarkably like Rodin's *The Thinker*, except he was not stone, and, unlike the statue, he was truly thinking.

Mikhail had to get to Jana, and get to her quickly. She had gone to Strasbourg, and he had made an attempt to contact her by calling her department. Then he'd become fearful about trying again. The telephone lines were suspect and the police were corrupt. Mikhail himself was one of the prime examples.

Adriana and he had argued when he had told her about his concern for Jana's safety. Jana was too smart, too dedicated. When she went to Strasbourg, she would soon realize she had to go on to Nice. The others would become aware of her arrival; they would then make her disappear. A magician with a wand would put her in a box, and poof, the lady vanishes!

A small skiff, a fishing boat would put out to sea, and the captain of the boat would suddenly have new equipment, maybe even a new boat, one that he had always wanted. *C'est la vie*, he would shrug. He had a family to support, and the fish needed to be fed. So did his children. The box he would put overboard? Who cared what it contained?

Adriana had listened to Mikhail's tale of his own corruption, the car they now had, the apartment they now owned, the jobs for his brothers. When she called him to task for being so weak, he had agreed. The organization had made it so easy for him, and for the others. Mikhail had not counted on Jana being put at risk. He finally went to Adriana: Give me your advice. What shall I do?

His wife had hesitated only for a moment, then handed him the phone to call Jana's department. Which was why he loved her. He had her trust. She was his moral compass, and always had been. She made his life worth all its problems. It was decided: When the call to the Slovaks failed, he had to do what he most wanted to do when he first became a police officer: save lives, make the world better, keep the lions from eating the lambs.

As long as Adriana thought he was okay, that was all Mikhail needed. She would continue to love him. His private world was safe. Everyone believed in him. It made everything he did, and had to do, so much easier. And here he was, waiting for his cousin.

Chapter 36

The events of the last few years had required Jana to compartmentalize. Initially, after the formal end of her marriage, she tried to keep focused on the successes she'd had at work, her unique ability to see things that others missed in cases that brought her departmental acclaim. That was the plus for her. Then the others, the minuses, began to mount again. Her mother finally died. That was a hard blow. Jana had come home at noon when her mother failed to answer her cell phone. Her mother had been feeling better that last week, even taking a walk through the neighborhood, chatting with a few old friends. That morning her breathing, always labored now, had appeared to soften and ease; her mother's energy level went up and she had looked forward to the day. So death was unexpected, though expected. Then who really believes your parents are going to die?

She found her mother sitting in front of the window, a book on the floor beside her. Nothing spectacular in her death, not like so many of the deaths Jana investigated. She could be thankful it wasn't one of those. On the other hand, there was a basic difference in the two types of mortality. This one was also emotionally different from those that were work-related. Jana had learned to steel herself against those public horrors she encountered at work; this one she felt.

Jana and Katka, and the few old friends her mother had left, attended a brief service, and her mother was buried in a small rocky grave. Jana had cried during the ceremony; Katka had been dry-eyed. It was later that Katka became despondent.

Katka had been rejected by those near and dear. She had obviously failed to live up to their expectations. Her father had left her, which meant she had not pleased him enough for him to stay at home. With Katka's grandmother, the same pattern had developed. To make up for her father's loss, Katka turned to her grandmother. She had made sure the old woman took her medications, forced her to eat, cleaned the house. She had done all the little things for the old woman.

Katka and her grandmother had tiffs, her grandmother cranky because of her semi-invalid status. Katka let it all roll off her back, even enjoying the little arguments. When her grandmother "left," as Katka put it, the emotional trauma Katka suffered from her grandmother's death mixed with what she'd suffered from Dano's departure. She withdrew from her friends and from Jana. She began to hate Slovakia, to dream of going to America and never returning home.

Katka threw herself into learning English, dedicating herself to speaking without an accent. She searched every magazine stand and library for the few English-language magazines allowed in Slovakia, and some that weren't. American movies, even though most were way out of date, were high on her list. American singers were idolized, and smuggled records reached Katka's avid hands. She memorized lyrics and practiced in front of a mirror to get all the nuances of speech and idiomatic phrasing. It kept her sane. Then things got worse for Jana.

Dano became an outlaw. He was no longer wanted just for anti-state activities in the political arena; he had turned to hard crime to pay for those activities. Like Stalin before him, Dano supported his revolutionary activities through bank robbery.

Three armed men walked into a bank in Kosice in March and held it up. All wore masks, the leader of the group announcing to the customers that the Revolutionary Democratic Party had commenced the next phase of its activities against the government and urged them to join in overthrowing the current despotic regime.

The robbery was reported by the government-controlled media; the call to arms against the government was not. The case was assigned, on paper, to the local police. In reality, the Secret Police led the manhunt. Jana didn't find out about the call for a new national movement until Trokan summoned her. In his office were two Secret Police officers waiting to question her.

Trokan instructed her to cooperate with the Secret Police, to answer all their questions honestly. If she did not, he informed her, she would be dismissed from the force. When Jana and the officers walked out, her eyes met Trokan's. Enough passed between them for Jana to know that he was powerless to help her.

They led her to a conference room in another part of the building that had been set aside for her interrogation. A stenographer was already there, along with a uniformed officer operating a backup tape recorder. The two interrogators started in immediately, asking if she was Daniel's wife, and if they were living together. Jana replied that they had been married; they were now divorced. Where was he, they asked? Jana replied that she did not know. At that point, the two officers told her the whole story of the bank robbery, omitting nothing.

The histrionics of the chief robber in making his pronouncements were redolent of Dano at his theatrical best. No question: Despite the mask, in her heart Jana knew it was Dano. He had never wanted merely to act, if people on the street failed to recognize him.

The shock to Jana was palpable, physically startling, as if she had been backhanded across the face. The shock she felt was helpful, to a degree. There was no way to fake her physical response. The interrogators saw it; their attitudes became less threatening.

When had she last seen Daniel? they wanted to know.

"Four years ago." Her voice was barely audible. "He left. We were not getting along."

"Did you know he was going to commit this crime?"

"If I had known, I would have reported it."

"He is an enemy of the state, armed, dangerous to everyone."

"If he robbed a bank," Jana reluctantly agreed, "he is an enemy of the people."

The questions went on for two hours. Odd, thought Jana, they use the same interrogation techniques she had learned. The words droned in her ears, her answers becoming pure reflex. They went over Dano's past with her, their mutual friends, schoolmates he was still involved with, the theater people he associated with, every aspect of their public and private lives, including Jana's political beliefs.

"No," she told them. "I am not political. I am a police officer, and the only 'party' I belong to is law enforcement."

They finally concluded the questioning. To Jana's surprise, they excused her to go back to work. Even Trokan was amazed when she returned to her office for duty. No arrest? No reprimand? No suspension? The next time, she knew, would be different. And she knew there would be a next time.

That night Jana went directly home after work, waiting for Katka, who was with her English tutor. There was no question about what Jana had to do. The hunt for Dano would intensify; they would eventually suspend Jana from the force. Katka and she would be watched day and night. They would become nonpersons with the neighbors, who would be afraid of being seen with either her or her daughter. Katka's friends would shun her. Even the stores would discourage their patronage.

After her grandmother's death, being told that her father was a criminal would be too much. It would be like living in Hades for her daughter. Jana had to get her out of the country.

Katka came home. Jana sat her down over lemon tea and a few biscuits. Jana took an oblique approach: She told Katka that her study of English had progressed so well that Jana had decided Katka should be rewarded by a trip to America.

Katka was overjoyed. America was Katka's ultimate dream. Now she might get to really eat hamburgers in the United States of her fantasies. It would be difficult, Jana warned her, trying to calm her down. People would be jealous of her going, so they had to keep it between themselves, Jana cautioned her, while outlining her plan. It, she knew, depended upon everything going exactly right.

First, they needed to contact Jana's aunt, her mother's sister in America. The two sisters had not been close; they had not spoken in the last few years of her mother's life. Jana had sent her aunt a notice of her sister's death. There was only a brief response. No matter. Jana would call her that evening. The call had to be made quickly, before a tap was put on the line.

There was a good chance that her aunt would take Katka in when she arrived in America. Aside from the fact that Katka was her grandniece, the woman was a rabid anti-communist and would welcome the fact that Katka had fled Slovakia.

Katka would go to school there. Chicago and the surrounding area had lots of Slovaks who had immigrated, so there would be something of her own culture there for her. Jana knew of at least two instances where refugee status and travel permits had been arranged by the Slovak Benevolent Association. Their Chicago relatives belonged to it. The relatives might know American congressmen who would help. All Jana needed to do before these things could be arranged was to get Katka across the Austrian border.

That night, Jana made the call to Chicago, telling the telephone control authorities that she had to talk to her relatives about money for her mother's gravestone. Brief exchanges of carefully worded letters followed the phone call. With the help of the Benevolent Association, and of congressmen only too glad to aid their constituents in a matter like this, the U.S. State Department agreed to furnish the necessary papers when the time came.

Jana found a smuggler who helped people seeking asylum. Within two months Katka was gone, smuggled across the Danube on one of the coal barges that plowed the river. A brief phone call let her know that Katka had been deposited in Vienna, then quickly flown to Denmark. Ten days later, another call followed, from Chicago, telling her that the dishes had arrived, none of them damaged . . . and she knew Katka was safe.

Medical excuses can only work for so long. Jana knew that Katka would be reported absent from school, or some nosy neighbor would start inquiring about her daughter's whereabouts. There was only one course for Jana to take. The next day, she phoned Trokan and told him that her daughter had disappeared.

Trokan was silent, assessing what she had told him. Eventually he asked her for more detail. Jana informed him that Katka, well known in the neighborhood to be a rabid admirer of all things American, had probably slipped across the border to Austria.

Trokan listened, then told her that she had to write a report, then inform the Secret Police of what had happened. If she was not sure that Katka had gone over the border, maybe Jana might also include the possibility that the girl, loving her father as she did, might have made contact with him and had been persuaded to join the criminals.

Trokan was trying to be helpful. If Jana reported that her father had abducted Katka, the Secret Police might feel that Jana was a victim. They might then ease up on her. But Jana could not bring herself to add any more reasons for the state to pursue her ex-husband.

Jana sent her report to the Secret Police. Almost immediately she was suspended without pay, pending a decision of the minister. They had begun the process of making Jana into a nonperson. It was not a surprise. Jana had been there before. She could live with it. Better that Katka be safe and sound where her clouded future in Slovakia could not touch her.

How wrong she had been.

Chapter 37

The apartment Sasha had found to use as her safe house was really quite cheerful. The living room and bedroom were papered in yellow polka dots, covering walls and ceiling. Reproductions of flower paintings carried out the theme of the yellow wallpaper, adding touches of pale blue. Over the French doors there was a large half-moon insert of glass that let in more sun, keeping the flower paintings happy. It would be cheerful and pleasant for most people. But Sasha, who had come to hate the wallpaper, now thought the flowers were ugly and wanted to tape over the glass above the French doors.

Tourists coming for a week would have loved the apartment, a cheerful sanctuary, a place from which they would sally forth into the noise of the streets to buy a croissant at a boulangerie, sample a fish soup specialty in this town of seafood gourmets, browse the shops for souvenirs, or merely view the quaint old buildings. For Sasha, a prisoner in a town she could no longer even walk about in safely, the apartment had taken on a cell-like atmosphere redolent of a dungeon. To her, the apartment had become ugly.

She had no choice but to stay indoors after seeing the Manager yesterday. Since then, the streets were quarantined for her; the only place she could continue to exist was indoors. Where the Manager was, there were the legions of the organization.

They would be patrolling the streets, probing for her
whereabouts, showing photographs of her, telling everyone
they talked to one tale or another that would make them
sympathetic to helping to identify her. Or frightening people
into talking. Or paying people to find the lady with the
Russian accent who had never learned to talk French prop-
erly. She had a week at most, if she were lucky, before they
were led here. No matter how she made herself up, she was
too distinctive to disappear.

Sasha went to the refrigerator for the fifth time that day.
It had not changed: an opened jar of orange marmalade, two
small cups of plain yogurt, and a half-full bottle of Eau
Minerale open for too long. She ransacked the cupboards
again. The same story: a half box of brown sugar and one of
herbal tea purchased by a prior tenant. Sasha had been
brought up on real tea and hated the smell of the herbs in the
boxes' little teabags. On a sudden impulse, she grabbed the
tea box and stuffed it into the garbage where it belonged.

No question remained after she completed her latest survey. No food, and her belly was sounding alarms indicating
that it needed to be filled. Sasha had to find a market, quickly
purchase as many staples as she could, then slip back to the
apartment.

The idea of going out into the streets brought fear back
into her throat. Indoors, she could repress it for brief periods
of time, watch television, make up little stories for imaginary
children, think about the good times she had had with Pavel.
There was no way to stifle her fear when she went out. But
there was no choice now; no alternative. She had to go.

Sasha dressed as nondescriptly as she could. She had very
little to choose from in this place; most of her clothes had
been left behind when she fled. But she scoured up a drab

brown blouse and pants, and put her winter jacket on, not because it was cold enough to warrant it, but to make her upper body formless and lumpy, disguising her shape.

Her hair, which she had restyled three times that day to keep herself occupied, needed to be less sleek, so she tousled it enough to make its outlines fuzzier. Then she grabbed her purse, and was ready to go, when there was a knock at the door. Sasha died a little. So quick: Only a day, and the apartment prison was ready to become a coffin. They were here.

She thought about screaming, the neighbors coming to her rescue. Unlikely. The French maintained their distance and would put her shouts down to a domestic dispute which was none of their business. The police? It would take too long for them to arrive. She would be dead by then.

A thin, reedy voice speaking Russian came through the door. "Sasha, its Rachel Lermentov. Are you there?"

Rachel Lermentov was the old lady who, with her husband, had arranged for Sasha to stay a few days at the Hotel Victoria when she had first fled. Sasha walked to the door, leaning close to its wood paneling.

"Mrs. Lermentov? How are you?" Sasha did not open the door. "I hope you are well."

"I'm fine, Sasha. Are you going to let me in?"

Sasha thought about opening the door. It was Mrs. Lermentov's voice. She did not seem to be under pressure to get Sasha to open the door. There was *probably* no one with the old lady. It was not enough. Sasha could still not bring herself to open the door.

"Mrs. Lermentov, I'm not feeling too well. I think I have the flu. If you come inside, you might get it from me."

"We have not heard from you, so my husband told me to make sure you were okay."

"I'm fine, except for the cold." She thought about how sweet it was for Mrs. Lermentov to come all the way across town to see her.

She thought about it again. When she had left the Lermentovs at the hotel, Sasha had not told them where she was going to live.

"I really would like to see you, dear." Mrs. Lermentov's voice took on a wheedling tone. "If you are too sick to come out, I'll go to the store for you. But I need to go through your cupboards to make a list."

Sasha could not ask the woman standing outside how she had found her. If *they* were with Mrs. Lermentov, it would only alert them. Should she take the chance and let her in? If she did, and Mrs. Lermentov was alone, the old woman would go shopping for Sasha and she would not have to chance the streets. Sasha started to reach for the door lock.

No. There was no way for the old lady to have tracked Sasha. They had to be with her, right outside, poised to come at her as soon as the door swung open.

"All right, Mrs. Lermentov, give me a half-minute to put something on." Sasha crossed to the other side of the room, away from the front door, quietly opened the French doors below the arched window, and stepped out onto the small balcony. There was a ten-foot drop to the walk below, which led to steps that would take her in a direction out of the old quarter.

Sasha had been a gymnast when she was a child, her parents hoping she was going to be another wonder-girl in that long line of gymnasts Russia produces. Sasha hadn't come near championship caliber. It didn't matter. What she was about to do didn't require a champion's ability.

Once she made up her mind, she did not hesitate. Sasha bolted out of the French doors, used her hand on the railing to support her vault, landed on her feet on the walk, rolling to absorb the shock. She came up running, not looking back, taking the steps at full stride, traversing the sidewalk, running like a gazelle.

When the men finally kicked their way into the apartment, they were angry, smashing some of the furniture to vent their frustrations. They would have to start all over again to find her. The men checked the apartment, took everything they thought might help them find her, and then finished up by killing Mrs. Lermentov before they left.

Chapter 38

Carnival in Nice is a wonderful event. Virtually everything stops in preparation. Huge signs go up, streets are cordoned off, lights are strung, gigantic caricatures of the Carnival creatures and themes are hung in Place Messina, bleachers are erected to house the thousands who will watch the parades, traffic is redirected, and the welcoming air of delightful tension transforms everything into a frenetic crescendo building toward the arrival of King Carnival and the revels that follow.

The previous night, the five-story-tall papier-mâché construction of the king had been danced into Place Messina. The monster gargoyle, ruler of all he surveyed, blocked Jana and Levitin from taking anything except tiny steps forward in their investigation. They made their courtesy calls on the French police inspector they were referred to, were given a slim investigation file on Pavel Rencko's death, and had been politely shuffled off to a small room by a subordinate who gave them a look that said, "Please go away and don't bother us any more."

The file was thin: photographs, a diagram of the scene, a compendium of statements to the effect that Rencko had been seen plummeting from the window of an office building. There was no reason the police could find for Rencko being in the building, except that it was one of the highest in the city and Rencko might have selected it merely for the purpose of killing himself. The conclusion of the investigation was that no one had seen Rencko being given a helping hand over the window ledge; and that since the man had financial problems and faced possible criminal charges and dismissal from the consular staff by his country, they ruled it a suicide.

An attempt had been made to find his companion, a woman he had been living with named Sasha, "true surname unknown," but the earth had swallowed her. Case closed.

Jana and Levitin were frustrated, Levitin because he could not think of a route to finding his sister, Jana because she was so close to seeing her daughter and granddaughter, and yet so far.

They were eating sweet rolls and drinking strong coffee, both of them morose, when Levitin received a call on his cell phone. Jules Vachon, the inspector they had contacted to obtain the Rencko file, wanted to see them at a murder scene. His aide gave them an address in the old part of the city.

There was no problem finding the place. The police had cordoned off the area. The usual gawkers were gathered for Jana and Levitin to push through when they arrived. They asked a gendarme guarding the tape barrier for Vachon, and were soon inside the apartment where the killing had occurred. Vachon greeted them effusively, suddenly very glad to see them. He pointed to a couch that had been ripped up and pulled away from the wall. Behind the couch was the covered body of a woman.

Vachon pulled the cover off the woman. "Look, look! I would like your professional opinion." He pulled the couch even farther from the wall to allow them easier access. "The poor old mother was beaten quite badly, no?"

Jana crouched by the body. Levitin was satisfied to let her make the close examination. Jana checked the woman's head, then her neck, surprising Vachon by then checking the woman's teeth. The woman still wore a short coat. Jana opened it, then pulled up the woman's dress. She then checked the labels on her torn dress, blouse, and sweater. The woman's hands were the last thing she looked at. Finally she stood up.

"Well?" Vachon looked at her expectantly. "You have conclusions? She was killed there, of course." He pointed to a pool of blood on the floor at the center of the room. "Then dragged over here and thrown behind the couch."

"She was in the way where they killed her, so they dumped her here. They didn't want to have to keep walking over her." Jana looked around the rest of the room, checking the area where the actual killing had taken place. "A partial heel print in the blood," she pointed out.

Vachon nodded. "We have photographed it, taken measurements." He indicated the dead woman again. "Tell me what you think of her."

"An older woman. In her middle to late seventies. Her eyes were starting to fail her. She and her husband do not have much money, but they manage. She is good at repairing her clothes. They are not new. She may have been a seamstress at one time."

Jana walked around the room, looking at the opened refrigerator door, the cabinets ajar, the front door. "Excuse me a moment, Inspector." She went into the bedroom.

Vachon had a small smile on his face as he watched Jana leave the room. Then he gestured at Levitin. "Don't you want to check anything?"

"I'm not a homicide detective. It's better left to her."

"Is she as good as I think?"

"Who told you?"

"We checked her credentials. And I've drawn my own

conclusions. Why do you think I summoned you both here?" He paused, giving Levitin a wink. "If I had known you were not a homicide detective, I would only have asked her."

"We are not trying to interfere in your jurisdiction."

Vachon made a moue, indicating that he'd never had such thoughts. "I called; you came."

Jana left the bedroom and went into the bathroom. "I am almost done." Her voice echoed slightly, bouncing off the bathroom tiles. "Not a bad place to live."

Jana came back into the room. "We can talk now." She remembered to say, "I would like to see your reports when they are written."

"You will get them." He pointed to the woman. "Tell me about her." Very French, he opened his arms expansively to encompass the entire apartment. "And tell me what happened here."

Jana walked back to the dead woman for a last look, then to Levitin, pointing to the French doors. "I would think that the ground is a good three meters below."

Levitin walked to the doors, and through them, looking down, then returned to Jana and the inspector. "Three and a half meters."

"And dirt or grass below?"

"Both."

She thought about it for another moment, then began to talk, her eyes half closed as if internally reviewing what she said as she spoke.

"The woman, as I indicated, is in her middle to late seventies. Age-related eye trouble. She can't see colors well any more, so she applies too much lipstick and face powder. She is still vain enough not to wear glasses, so she was probably a beauty when she was young. She does her hair herself. The color is not applied well, and it's not well cut or professionally

styled. A vain woman who was a beauty when she was younger
would go to a professional stylist rather than do it herself. If
she had money."

"Poor, then?" guessed the inspector.

"Not poor-poor. Just above the poverty line, I would
think. She still has an engagement ring on. A small diamond,
not worth much, but it would have been sold if she were living in abject poverty." She paused, looking at Levitin. "And
she is from Eastern Europe. I think from Russia."

Levitin caught Jana's glance. "A woman from Russia? A
big Russian population here, Inspector?"

"The Russians have always liked Nice. We have enough
Russians that you will see that a number of our stores have
Cyrillic advertising on the windows. There are Russians
everywhere these days." The inspector looked from one to
the other. "What does another Russian woman have to do
with this?"

Jana held up her hand for him to wait. "Let's finish with
this one first."

"It's worth the wait. I am getting my Euro worth." The
inspector righted one of the overturned chairs, sitting.
"Better than I could have hoped."

Jana waited to gather her thoughts, then continued. "The
woman: from Russia, or one the former SSRs. She has several steel teeth in her mouth. That's how they capped or
replaced teeth in the SSRs in the old days. Her clothes, well,
she has kept them for a long time. No labels, but not
Western. They have been carefully mended in spots. And she
was a friend of the woman who lived here."

"We are looking for the rental agent, to find out who took
the lease on the apartment."

"A good move."

Levitin pulled one of the other chairs up, righting it to sit next to the inspector, both of them taking on the appearance of schoolboys listening to their teacher. "Go on, please," Levitin prodded her.

"There was one sweater left on the floor of the closet. Expensive. A style for a younger, more seductive woman. Too big for our murder victim." She walked over to the French doors, examining the latches. "These were opened, from the inside." She took several steps back toward the dead woman, pointing to the torn dress. "She still had her coat on. My belief is that she was coming in, not going out."

"The front door was forced." Jana walked back to look down at the body. "I think the men who broke in brought the old lady here. Her dress was torn, torn under a coat that was still buttoned. A new rip, or it would have already been repaired by the old woman. A rip that was made elsewhere, and she was not given an opportunity to change her dress before they came to this place."

"Why would they bring the old lady here?" the inspector demanded.

"The occupant of the apartment. My guess is they knew each other. Foreign expatriates cling together. The men probably wanted to use the old woman as a ruse to gain entry. It went wrong, and they kicked in the door."

"Did they get the woman who lived here?" Levitin's voice betrayed his worry.

"I don't think so." She indicated the French doors. "A way of escape." She turned to the inspector. "If you check the ground below the window, you should find new scuff marks, torn grass where she landed, maybe even a footprint."

"I'll be back." The inspector went outside to talk to his men about checking the ground.

Levitin used the opportunity to privately quiz Jana. "My sister Sasha? The woman who rented the apartment?"

"You heard the inspector. There are lots of Russians here. It could be another woman; but my instinct, yes, I think, maybe so." She gestured at the kitchen area. "The refrigerator is virtually empty. So are the food cupboards. The apartment is almost bare of personal effects. Its occupant was living from day to day. She knew she had to leave quickly. If you are going to stay longer, you fix a place up. This woman had no place to go, yet couldn't stay here very much longer."

Levitin looked to the window. "Sasha was an athlete. She could have made that jump."

Jana wanted to encourage Levitin's hope that his sister had escaped. "The furniture that is broken. No need for them to break it if they were just ransacking the apartment. They were angry. And they were angry because their intended target got away."

Vachon came into the apartment, excited. "Recent scuff marks below the window. The woman jumped." He went to the balcony, looking down. "A very courageous woman to jump that far."

Jana corrected him. "A very desperate woman."

Chapter 39

Boyar saw the huge man sitting in front of his door as soon as he got out of the elevator. He stopped in his tracks. His first impulse was to run. After all, a man as short as Boyar was always in danger of being squashed, particularly when he encountered someone as big as the man on the floor. His second impulse, which he followed, was to walk toward the man. What harm can a sitting giant do? As small as he was, Boyar could outrun the big man before he could get his legs under himself.

Boyar stopped a meter away from the giant, pointing to his door. "You are blocking the way into my apartment." Of course, Mikhail Gruschov could not understand French, but he had accessed an old picture of Boyar to look at before he came, and this person, small as he was, looked enough like him for Mikhail to reply in his friendliest Russian.

"Hello. We didn't have a telephone number, so I just came. You are Boyar?"

Boyar had forgotten much of his childhood Russian, but he heard his name, and could still speak enough to remember his manners. He switched to his imperfect Russian, waving his apartment key in front of the giant's face, inviting him inside. The giant proceeded to unfold himself from the floor, allowing Boyar to unlock the door and lead the way inside.

The apartment was one large artist's studio. A drop cloth spattered with paint drippings covered the floor; there were two easels, both with unfinished pieces on them; and the walls were lined with a hundred sketches and photos. A little kitchenette off to the side of the room was filled with jars and tubes of paint, and dirty dishes and paintbrushes. Scattered around the apartment floor were stacks of oil paintings, water-colors, wood and wire armatures, and bits of art constructions, all leaning against the walls or simply piled haphazardly, tak-ing up almost all the floor space. Boyar picked his way through the apartment, utilizing the narrow paths he had left to walk in. Gingerly, Mikhail followed him, afraid that any misstep of his would destroy a month's worth of work.

The bedroom was different, neat, a small dresser, bed, chair, and a small bottle of pastis standing near several empty glasses. Boyar quickly wiped the glasses out with a dish towel and, without asking, poured himself a generous glass of the pastis, measured Mikhail's bulk with his eyes, then poured him twice as much, handed it to Mikhail, and settled at the head of the bed.

"You have come to pose for me?" Boyar asked. "You saw my notice?"

For a moment Mikhail thought his cousin was crazy. Then he realized that Boyar had no idea who he was.

"I'm Mikhail. Your cousin. From Ukraine."

Boyar checked Mikhail's appearance. "The one I used to beat up when we were kids?"

"I used to beat you up."

"That isn't the way I remember it."

"Look at you and look at me. Then figure out who beat who up."

"You were slow, ugly, and stupid."

"Now I'm big, ugly, and only a little stupid, so I need your help."

The little man looked at Gruschov, the ill-fitting winter suit, the shoes that were scuffed. "I have no money to give you."

"I'm not here from Ukraine for money."

"All Ukrainians need money."

"I'm a policeman."

"They're the worst. Cops always have their hands out."

"Do you want money for your help? Is that what you are saying?"

"Painters don't need money. What would I do with it?"

They both sipped at the pastis, saying nothing, savoring the anise taste.

"Not bad," allowed Mikhail.

"Cheap but good," acknowledged Boyar. "Cousin, what do you need to come all the way to Nice for? Not to see me."

"I'm looking for a Slovak. A woman."

"In Nice?"

Mikhail allowed himself to become a little angry. He had deliberately strained to keep his voice low, to be friendly. He raised it a few decibels. "In this city. The one and only! The woman is in Nice! And I am asking your help in finding her. Clear?"

Boyar again took a quick sip of the pastis, telling himself not to be frightened. Maybe he had remembered wrong. Maybe his cousin had beat him up when they were children? He thought quickly. "Does she speak Russian?"

"Yes."

"There is a Russian center. They will hold a large party." He rustled through a sheaf of papers. His voice took on a surprised tone. "It's tonight. Maybe she will come. It's also a good place to pick up information."

Mikhail lowered his voice to a low growl. "That's a good thought, Cousin." He looked down at himself, patting his jacket, than looked inquiringly at Boyar. "I don't have another suit."

"You can't fit into my suits." He threw his hands wide apart. "You are too gross." Boyar knew his cousin no longer had plans to beat him up, so he relaxed again. "Is she a police officer, too? If she is, maybe the French flics know where she is. You could ask them."

"I can't go to the police."

"Corruption, eh? The two of you. Up to your necks. I thought so. That's why no French police. Right?"

Mikhail's voice went up in volume again. "I did the right thing when I was a child, beating you up. Maybe I should do it again? You want me to beat you up?"

Boyar smiled. The giant needed him. He was not going to be attacked. "Okay, so if it is corruption, it's none of my business. Does she any friends?"

"We can't go to them." Mikhail lowered his voice. "Okay, maybe we go to them as a last resort."

Boyar poured himself more pastis. "Courage is a valuable asset to have. Too bad I don't have any. You go; I stay."

His giant cousin started to get up, his voice rising again. "Now I remember you beating me up when we were kids. I don't speak French, dwarf. I need you with me. However, since you are not coming, I may as well get even." He towered over Boyar. "Stand up. I will only hit you once!"

Boyar had stretched it as far as he could. He retrenched hurriedly. "Wait! I have a solution. You pose for me."

"What?"

"At no charge. I don't pay, so I take you to the meeting or whatever as your fee for posing."

Gruschov looked at him suspiciously. "I don't take my clothes off for a man."

"I don't need to see your ugly body."

Mikhail refilled his own glass with a double shot. "I agree." He gave Boyar a last, grim look. "But any funny business, and I remember how miserable you were to me as a child."

He smacked his fist into the palm of his hand for emphasis.

Chapter 40

The man walked across the street without hurrying, unlike the other pedestrians. He was disappointed. A light sprinkle, barely enough to call a rain, had arrived to spoil his plans to sit for an hour at the seaside. He had become used to water reflecting the light.

The house had spoiled him. Walking down the steps to his cove, dropping his clothes without a care, then taking his daily swim to visit his Madonna of the Waters. No, not a Madonna. Madonnas had small babies. His lady was too sexual to be placed in a religious light. No, his was a woman who gave him a daily kiss to remind him how lovely it was to provocatively touch, and be touched by, a Venus, his "Siren of the Waters."

He'd had many women, too many to count, too many to remember. And all of them were a part of his Siren of the Waters. It was always the same. Like her, when he finished with touching them, he went away, never thinking of them again, never really caring until he needed another. At the beginning, even as it started with a new one, he knew he would walk away, sooner rather than later.

Objects, all of them. Actors on his stage. Ugly, beautiful, no matter. Some stayed longer; only one of them had stayed for years. They had not had a sexual relationship but they had enjoyed setting the stage together and now she, too, was gone from him.

The rain stopped. He looked up. Still overcast. Not a good

day. He walked on, into the old quarter, entering the small restaurant that served *socca*, a local dish he liked. The man took a seat, as was his custom, away from the windows, next to one of the walls, allowing him front and rear views. Then he motioned the waiter over, ordering a glass of red wine and the plate of *socca* he had come here for. While he was waiting, he reviewed what would happen this evening.

The Manager and friends would arrive at the party between 2000 and 2100 hours. The title Manager had not been used; but how vain and stupid to announce their arrival time giving their real names to the press. Hubris. They would mingle at the party, showing the world their trappings of wealth and privilege; then they would leave for the night taking the short trip to their "nests." They would confer among themselves; they would think they had arranged their futures. The man grimaced. Their plans were incomplete. He was here now.

The waiter brought the glass of wine, than came back a moment later with the *socca*. The man nodded his thanks, took a small piece of the *socca* with his fingers, glanced at it to make sure it was the right color, then fed himself.

Time enough to determine what he would do. It was never hard to find a way to kill. It was the drama of the situation that was difficult, the choreography that everyone would remember. Events like this should never be casual affronts. Death needed to be staged as an event, as in Shakespeare or Ibsen's plays.

He ate another bit of *socca*, then sipped at the wine. The police officers, they were another matter. Together they would present a problem, again not in killing them, but in the end result of the killing. What would the audience think if he removed these objects from the stage all at once? What would the public's reaction be to conjoining their killings with the killing of the Manager and the Manager's associates?

He ran the taste of the *socca* around his mouth. For some reason, the *socca* did not taste as good as he remembered. Unevenly fried? Too much oil? Well, it was a fast-food dish.

He laughed at himself. All these years, all that money, all that luxurious living, and he still liked the occasional taste of food that was barely out of the gutter.

He drank the last of the wine, laid the money to pay for his meal on the table before the waiter had time to even prepare the bill, then walked out.

The overcast was lifting. Good. Maybe there would still be some sun today? It would be a shame to waste the opportunity to sit in the warm sun for even a few minutes.

Chapter 41

Jana had tried to find work that would pay enough to support herself and then still have a little left over to send to America for her daughter's upkeep. They had not dismissed Jana from the police force. Instead, she had been suspended indefinitely pending a departmental hearing. Each time the hearing was scheduled, for one reason or another it was delayed again. Not that she minded. Any hearing would have a forgone conclusion: She would be terminated, her career ruined.

So she did not push for an adjudication. Rather, she hoped it would be delayed until a new regime came in. Perhaps then events would move in her favor. Jana did not have great hope, but she fastened on the only one she had. Jana did have one ally: Trokan. His hand had to have been at work in securing the continuances. Trokan was trying to buy time for her.

Jana worked in a bakery in the early morning hours and a tannery in the afternoon. She had entered the same informal hiring system that Dano had been in, lower wages for jobs already paying low wages, with no reports filed with the government. She earned enough to keep herself, and every month she sent money for Katka.

Katka had tried calling her mother from the United States until she finally understood, from her aunt and others, that Jana was under further threat every time one of those calls was made. They would be used against her. Eventually, they stopped coming.

On the other hand, Jana did not stop writing. When she sent money to Katka, she used a number of ways to have it delivered. Generally, people she trusted who were going to other countries carried it. They could mail it from outside the country. Once she had used an Austrian traveling through the country. She had even mailed money from Prague under the name of a person she'd picked out of a directory.

The letters she included with the money contained all kinds of information: a smattering of what Jana knew about what was happening with Katka's school chums, bits and pieces of news of the rising tide against the communists, encouragement of Katka in her school studies. All the things a mother wants to say . . . except news about her father. That would have been catastrophic for Katka.

Dano was on the run. His activism had gone sour for him, as Jana had known it would, ultimately culminating in a botched attempt to rob a truck carrying the payroll for the large steelworks in the north of the country. One of the drivers had been killed.

Before the disaster, Dano had had a small following and had ridden the general wave of dissatisfaction with the government. Everyone loves a Robin Hood. Dano's three prior successful robberies had all been followed by declarations that he and his group were taking the money not for themselves, but to foment revolution and to do away with an oppressive government. Moreover, he had made sure that some money was distributed to other groups, groups following more normal channels of democratic dissent. And Dano had not forgotten the impoverished, doling out sums to them with a soupçon of anti-government rhetoric. Then came the botched robbery.

The government apparatchiks went into high gear, exploiting the death of the driver. He'd had four children, and his wife and children were featured in the government media for weeks, all talking about how they had loved their father, how kind, generous, and caring he had been to them, how the dead man's mother had suffered a mental breakdown at the death of her only son and had been confined to a hospital.

Dano was vilified at every opportunity. A supposed mistress surfaced who, she claimed, Dano had forcibly taken from her boyfriend. Later, the woman recanted. There was a purported drunken brawl in which Dano had beaten up a teenager who supported the government. The government procurator claimed that the teenager was underage and should not be subjected to public scrutiny, so he was never produced to verify the facts. Then the usual government informants appeared and were pirouetted before audiences, all of them attesting to various public and private sins. Dano was termed everything from a sexual deviate to a homicidal maniac, capable of killing anyone, who would, if given any further chance, kill again.

A large reward was offered for Dano and his confederates. The circle of repression became more constrictive. Travel restrictions became more severe, roadblocks became routine, suspected dissidents were placed under house arrest or imprisoned. One by one, the few men whom Dano had recruited were seized. The ones who had participated in the robberies with Dano confessed publicly, naming Dano as the ringleader. All of them expressed remorse, all of them placed the blame for the killing on Dano. The fact that, according to the eyewitnesses, the actual killer of the driver did not fit Dano's physical description, but clearly fit that of one of the confederates who was screaming the loudest that Dano was the murderer, did not matter. The government had decided.

A small country became smaller and smaller for Dano. Where could he run? Where could he hide any more?

It had turned into morning, and Jana was coming from her job at the bakery when she realized there was a man up ahead, looking back at her. Dirty, grimy from cleaning out ovens, fatigued from working two separate jobs which resulted in broken sleep and no time for the personal matters that everyone needs, she was surprised, even at this distance, that anyone would take an interest in her.

When he began walking, also in the general direction of her home, she decided, making rude noises to herself under her breath, that she had come too close and he had lost interest. Jana had decided to walk to her house, just to take the fresh air into her lungs after working in the bakery where the air was always filled with the fine grains of flour. She was strolling, in no hurry.

She noticed the man had stopped again, nearer this time, allowing her to close the distance between them. She came within twenty meters before she recognized him. Dano had come home.

The police officer still in her struggled with the fact that he was a robber. No matter. She pushed the policewoman deeper inside herself, remembering that they were both outcasts. She took his arm, threading his fingers through hers. Two lonely people walking home.

They did not say a word as they walked. Dano seemed to be in a daze. Jana's instincts, and needs, told her to accept the moment for whatever it was. No one bothered them; no one seemed to notice their presence. The neighbors were filled a space in another part of the universe than the place the two of them shared.

When they got to Jana's front door, she unlocked it. Both were comfortable in the shelter of the house. Jana took off her coat. Dano looked around, no longer familiar with the house as he once had been. He took the changes in: Things were shabbier, the walls needed painting. He was bone-weary, not from working two jobs as Jana was, but from the burden of trying to create a world he wanted and couldn't have. Dano was lost; he was beaten. She finally led him to an armchair, gently pushing him down into it.

"I only have tea."

"Tea is good."

"Are you as hungry as you look?"

"A little hungry," he acknowledged.

She hustled into the kitchen, feeling eager, lighter than she had in years, quickly washing her face, neck, and arms in the sink, hoping he hadn't noticed how drab she looked. She put the kettle on for tea, then searched in the refrigerator. Not very good. It was filled with leftovers from half-eaten meals. There was a little hope: two eggs, not enough for a complete meal, but a start.

The cupboards were next, but they were so barren and disappointing that she had to restrain herself at the last moment from slamming the doors. There was a bag of flour. Thankful, she pulled out a mixing bowl, poured flour into it, cracked both eggs on top of the flour, added water, then mixed it well. A second later, she had put a pan on a high flame just to get it warm quickly. Then, when it was hot enough, she spooned butter in. She turned the flame lower, and then she set about brewing the tea.

Five minutes later, her hair now tidied up, Jana came out of the kitchen with pancakes on a large platter, a half jar of apricot jam rescued from the back of the refrigerator, and pre-sweetened tea the way Dano liked it. She set it in front of him to help himself.

He stared at the platter.

"It's all I have in the house." She was worried that he would blame her. "It will be good to see you eat."

"Just a taste." He took a forkful of pancake without the jam. Jana ladled jam on the remainder of the pancake. He looked at it, chewing slowly. "I think one may be enough." He took a sip of the tea. "You know, I've developed a taste for coffee." He set the cup down, staring into space.

Jana found that she was irritated. Her perceptions were that Dano needed food, but he didn't want what she had. He eventually agreed that he would take tea because it was the only beverage in the house; now he criticized it because it was not coffee.

"I have nothing else to give you, Dano," she said. He continued to sit, staring into space. Didn't he realize that she was hungry too? Maybe she should encourage him to eat by eating herself? She forked a piece of pancake into her mouth and chewed enthusiastically, then took a mouthful of tea. "It's good to have food in your belly." She took another forkful.

"I am sorry that you did not come with me." Dano did not look at her as he spoke. "It would have been easier."

Jana's irritation increased. "There was no possible way I would have come. None at all. You knew that; you told me to stay here. Why are you now saying I should have come?"

"We would have been together."

"You wanted to go on a mission. I read about you, heard about you. The new Messiah come to bring the idolaters and despoilers down." She did not like the direction the conversation was taking. However, her rising anger refused to allow her to stop, so she rushed on. "You were the one who left us. You were the one who had a daughter. She needed you here!"

Dano started to stir. His voice took on a sharp, edgy quality. "Could I let her be brought up in the conditions in this country? Would it have been better to let her see me rotting away, a little bit every day? No."

"Our family was not so badly off. We had a house. I had a good job. My mother was happy. The family was fine. Since you went on your selfish way, we now have Katka far away from her home being brought up by someone else, my job gone, my mother dead, and you a fugitive."

Dano finally looked directly at her. She had reached him. Jana got up and moved away. "I do not like this government. I do not like what they did to you." She corrected herself. "No, I do not like what they did to both of us. Did that mean I should run and hide?"

"I stood up. I didn't run and hide!"

"The actor stood up for his bow. That's what you did, played a role and waited for the applause. Who were you? Moses bringing the Ten Commandments to his people? Did they applaud when you came down from the mountain? If they applauded, I could not hear it."

Dano closed his eyes for a moment, waiting for some inner voice to tell him how to respond. Then he managed to open them as if afraid to see reality. "Did I do you an injury? Did I do my daughter an injury? It was a risk. I knew that; you knew that, when I left. I did not think I was playing a stage part. It was real. Realize something: I hated myself for leaving; I would have hated myself more if I had stayed."

"I stayed, Dano."

"I know." He shrank a little. "We both have been damaged. I wish it were not so."

"Dano, you became a bank robber."

"We needed the money to keep going. The Party needed it."

Jana's anger, which had started to abate, flared up again, stronger this time. "The Party needed it," she mimicked. "How many of you were there? Five or six people, that was your Party. It was not a political movement; it was an armed outlaw band."

"We had others. They needed the money to publish, to hold meetings, to fight the establishment in other ways."

"Fight the establishment? You sound like the establishment. The government. The Party. You became like them. Everything and anything for the Party." She was drained. She felt anguish for Dano, her lover, her husband, the father of her daughter. She felt it for herself.

Jana picked up the plate of uneaten pancakes to take them back into the kitchen. She turned to face him once more. "My god, a man died in one of your armed attacks, Dano. Think about that. He had not committed a crime."

"We knew there was risk."

"How dare you decide what he should risk? Did you ask him?"

"I didn't want him to die."

"That's what most robbers say." She walked into the kitchen with the plate, then heard the door open. It should not end on this note, she told herself, hurrying back to the front room.

Dano was standing at the open door, looking out. Then he stepped back inside, closing the door.

"They're here." He had a resigned look on his face. "They've come for their criminal."

Jana ran to the window, pushing the curtain aside. Police cars were parking, more were driving down the street. There were armed men everywhere. She let the curtain fall back.

Dano smiled, the captivating smile she remembered when they first began to go together. "It had to end."

She nodded, not knowing what she could say. "I'm sorry," was what came out.

"It isn't right. I brought them to this house." He quickly stepped over to her, kissing her on the cheek. "I'm going to wash up. I want to look clean for the photos they will take." He walked toward the back of the house. "Just let them in when they knock."

Jana heard footsteps on the front stair. There was a long pause. Maybe they were trying to decide whether to break in without demanding entry. Why have them damage the front door, she thought. Just open it, Jana. She was reaching for the doorknob when she heard the shot.

As if in a distorted dream, she watched herself opening the door. Trokan was standing there, alone. He stepped in, closing the door behind him.

"Where is he?" Trokan asked.

"In the back," she heard herself say.

Trokan walked to the back of the small house. Time stopped, she would swear afterward. Even the ticking of clocks was stilled. The air did not move. The sun was fixed in place. The world had stopped revolving. No pulse, no breath, no life.

Trokan came back, holding her service revolver by the barrel. He walked over to her, placing the butt of the gun in her hand, closing her fingers around it. "It is a good thing you shot the fugitive murderer, Matinova. Otherwise we would have to believe you were giving him shelter. That, of course, would mean prison." He walked to the door, opening it. "I'm calling the others in. Congratulations on your proving your loyalty to our country and our principles of justice."

He walked out. Three weeks later, a state hero, she was reinstated in the police force at her full rank.

Chapter 42

The old man was crying. Not carrying on, wailing, or beating his breast. He was quiet, with the exception of a sound like a stifled hiccup which escaped his flaccid mouth from time to time. Tears rolled down his cheeks, released from his eyes almost in synchronization with the hiccups, wiped away by the back of his hand only when they reached his white pencil-thin moustache. His hair was very thin, yellow-white with age, dulled instead of brightened by the cheap hair gel that had been applied, the sparse hair combed both across and back on his head.

Jana could not tell, as she and Levitin sat across from Mr. Lermentov at his desk, whether he was short or tall. Grief and age had shrunk him into himself. He was mourning his wife, mourning the ending of a part of his life he would never experience again.

Jana waited for Lermentov to collect himself. She used the gap in the conversation to look around the Russian Friends Committee office. It was one large, drafty room papered with posters of Russia, Russian celebrities, Russian cities, a tossed salad of Russian life in travel posters, pinned to the walls, all of them browning at the edges, the most recent ode to Russia at least five years old.

The woman volunteer at the other desk, Veronike, a heavyset lump with no neck and a vivid yellow wig that emphasized rather than concealed her attempts to combat the ravages of time, occasionally would look up from the papers strewn across her desktop to glare at the two intruders bothering her friend in his time of grief.

Jana eventually had enough of the glare. She turned to Lermentov, interrupting his mourning with a raised hand. The old man seemed to hold his breath, waiting for her to give him permission to proceed with his grief. He settled for answering questions.

"You were together a long time?"

"Very long," he nodded.

"When did the men come to talk to her?

"She called me here." He paused, trying to remember.

The woman in the ratty yellow wig raised her head to fix them with another stare, giving Jana her answer as an afterthought. "Nine thirty. She called then."

He nodded. "Yes, nine thirty."

There was another period of withdrawal, emphasized by hiccups and tears. Again, Jana held up her hand and Lermentov focused on it as if it were a vehicular stop sign, quieting himself.

"Did she tell you why she was going with the men?"

He nodded. "Money. I told her not to." He reflected on his warning to her. "Don't do this, I told her twice. She was whispering into the phone. She went to the bedroom to talk to me without them knowing. She understood the danger. She wanted the money. So she took them with her."

Levitin leaned over to come closer to Lermentov. "Did they tell your wife what they were after?"

Lermentov seemed surprised by the question. "They wanted the woman. She came to us for help. She was running and hiding. We knew that. We helped her. We got her a hotel room. Then she found another place. I didn't know where that was. She never told us."

"How did your wife know where the apartment was if Sasha didn't tell you?"

"They posted a notice here and at the club." He stood up, shaky, steadying himself with a hand on the desk, then shuffled over to a large cork bulletin board hanging at a slightly lopsided angle on the wall next to the front door. He pulled the pins from a small group of cards, then brought them back to the desk, selected the one he wanted and read it aloud. "We are anxious to find our dear niece Alexandra Levitin. Five hundred Euro reward for correct information. Leave message with answering service." He pointed to the card. "The phone number is here."

Levitin took the card from him. Lermentov seemed not to notice. "These were posted everywhere."

"Your wife saw it?"

"Yes." Lermentov looked into the distance. "She called all over town. To every *immoblier*. Sasha mentioned an acquaintance who worked in one. My wife could be very clever. She wheedled, begged, threatened, all of those things and more." He looked from Jana to Levitin, then back again. "You know, I could never make money. My wife, she pushed me. I should have done better." He thought about what he had said. "Not only me. She pushed everyone."

He had a series of hiccups, his tears coming faster. The woman at the other desk came over, glared at Levitin and Jana, and then handed Lermentov an embroidered handkerchief. "She was a good person at heart."

He nodded, wiping his tears away.

"A hard worker," the woman continued. "She helped others."

He nodded again.

"It was the money. Too much for anyone to resist." The woman glared at Jana and Levitin, daring them to correct her. "Money makes people turn against their friends." She walked back to her desk. "I have your tickets to the dinner-dance. Do you want them?" She held a small ticket envelope up in the air, waving it at Lermentov.

"Who can go to a celebration at a time like this?"

"What shall I do with them? They cost you money. All my friends have tickets, so I can't resell them."

Lermentov eyed Jana and Levitin, then blew into the handkerchief. His voice took on a wheedling tone, a sly look playing across his face, overriding his grief. "I am just an old man. No money. Terrible to be old and have empty pockets." He stood up, taking keys out of his pants, then pulling all of his pockets out, the linings hanging like limp white tongues.

"Nothing. You see, I have nothing." His voice took on a priest's tone. "And they that shall take from them their labors shall have unto them reward for their toil." He started to cry again. "Nothing. I have nothing." He bowed his head, slowly lifting it to look sorrowfully at the ceiling, as if calling on God. When God didn't answer, he brought his eyes back down to them. "Shall I just destroy these tickets, or can you find it in your hearts to repay their cost to me?"

The woman made loud shuffling noises with the papers on her desk, faulting Jana and Levitin for the problem with the tickets. "Terrible! A man should not be reduced to having so little." Her glare became even more ferocious, sweeping over both of the intruders. "Help this man. Buy his tickets from him."

Levitin was about to make a sarcastic retort. Jana put her hand out to stop him. "What are the tickets for?"

"The Russian community dinner fête tonight." The woman went back to work. "You don't have to attend, you know."

Jana got up. "Levitin, pay for the tickets." She turned to Lermentov, ignoring the woman. "I am sad for you, Mr. Lermentov." He made a whimpering noise. Jana waited for a few seconds. "I wish I could make it easier." The hiccups began coming faster. She nodded at him, then walked out of the room, into the hall. In the dim hall, waiting for Levitin, she studied the poster on the wall advertising the fête. "The Russian Community presents the event of the year," she read aloud. "Yes," she said to herself. "I think it will be an event that no self-respecting Slovak police officer should miss."

Levitin emerged, shaking the tickets at Jana. "Why did I have to pay for these?" He closed the door a little too hard, emphasizing his displeasure. "Why should we go to this idiotic ball?"

"Because of this." She pointed to the poster. "I want to mix with the Russian community." She smiled at him. "And you have a bigger budget than I have."

"Slovakia is no longer being subsidized by Moscow," he pointed out, reading the poster.

"Think of the ball. All the people," she said, starting down the hall. "We may meet someone we know. Perhaps the men who killed the old lady. Maybe even Koba."

"He's not Russian." He followed her. "It's for Russians."

"Don't count on it. You know how everyone loves parties. Besides, we're trying to find a Russian, the girl Mrs. Lermentov was so willing to betray, Alexandra Levitin. You know the name. So, we go to the Russians."

The mention of his sister quieted Levitin. "So, we go to the Russians." He grinned. "If it's a Russian party, it will probably be fun."

Jana thought about his comment.

"Probably not."

She smiled when she said it.

Chapter 43

Sasha stayed under the stands during most of the Carnival parade, watching the legs marching in unison, the wheels of the floats, the dancers' feet fast-stepping through their choreographed routines, the spaghetti streamers of Silly String piling up for the midnight street-sweepers. She was biding her time until she could slip out and get food. She considered an old Russian axiom, "There is no risk too great when it comes to filling an empty stomach." She had to eat.

The marching bands and the boom-boom of their bass drums could be felt in her spine, the vibrations making her slightly seasick. After Sasha witnessed a young woman with pink and purple hair and a rhinestone-studded nose relieve her wine-laden bladder a few meters from where she was hiding, she decided she'd had enough waiting. She walked past the pink and purple-haired woman, who mewed something unintelligible at her, then slipped under the bunting hung on the sides of the stands, onto the square.

The parade was still going on, a huge mockup of Uncle Sam waving dollar bills gliding past, the French taking the opportunity to howl at the Stars and Stripes for usurping their Gallic claim to being the world's leader in cultural affairs. Sasha scanned the stands. If they were there, she wanted to see them before they spotted her. She tried, and then gave up. The bleacher seats were too full of yowling humanity, the colors of their clothes, the movement, the streamers, the costumes, even the cacophony of sound, contributing to Sasha's inability to see anything but those individuals who were very close to her. Maybe it was not so bad, she thought. If she could not see them, maybe they would not see her, particularly if she stayed where large groups were clustered, at the foot of the stands.

People trotted down the aisles to purchase food from the vendors. She followed several of them with her eyes until they reached the vendor of their choice, a man with a cart working the periphery of a street group. Sasha decided she would not go to him. Vendors were too much of a focal point. Her approach would be to slide into the group, then work her way through to a position where the vendor would intersect her spot. Then, a quick transaction for food. She could see the prices on the vendor's cart, made sure she had the exact change to pay him for what she wanted. No waiting; just the food, and away.

Sasha edged into the crowd, aiming for the spot she'd selected, then paused before stepping out to give the vendor the chance to come to her. Her strategy seemed to work perfectly. Obtaining the Croque Monsieur took a few brief seconds, the can of Fanta even faster. Sasha quickly returned to the spot where she had emerged. Again, she bumped her way through the tightly packed group of revelers, munching on her sandwich, sipping at the orange soda. Everything seemed to be fine. Sasha almost finished her prize, wishing she had bought a second one, when she ran into the man.

It seemed like a coincidence. Her mouth was working on the last few bites. She was not paying attention to his face, as she stepped to her left to avoid him. The man moved with her, continuing to block her way. She shifted to the right. He matched her movement. Sasha finally focused on his face, still hoping it was a coincidence. A tall man with a tanned face and eyes the color of dirty ice looked back at her. There was no expression on his face: a man going about his business, going through the motions of being human without any humanity of his own showing through.

A cold chill worked its way up from her belly through her chest and into her throat. There was no place to run. No camouflage good enough to conceal her. No weapon she could use that would be effective. An immovable object fronted her, blocking her way to the rest of her life.

The man looked at her, appraising Sasha like a piece of meat. "Hello, Sasha. Nice to see you." It wasn't nice at all. "Follow me."

He turned, walking away, no doubt in his mind, even though his back was turned, that she would obey his order. Sasha toyed with the idea of running. If she bolted through the crowd, she might be able to lose him. A moment's reflection, and she gave up the idea. She knew the man; she had heard all the stories about him. There would be no escape by running. Sasha followed him. The ice, cold in her stomach, came with her.

The crowd parted in front of the man as he walked, just as the Red Sea had cleaved itself apart for another. The drunks, the little children, the crowd-control officers, had no concrete notion why they stepped aside; they just did. Sasha cringed inside. No one knows it is death that is passing; there is just enough sensation to perceive the need to try evading mortal consequences. Maybe, as with Sasha, his passing chilled the air so that some of them wondered how, on this lovely Nice evening, a chill had found its way into their celebration.

The man turned into a women's clothing boutique. It should have been closed, like all the other stores on the block. But, for him, the door was opened. A rather mousy-looking woman held it wide for him, shielding herself with the door as he passed by. As soon as they were both inside, the woman, handbag in the crook of her arm, walked out of the store, closing the door behind her. The man paid no attention to her departure. He walked to the rear, motioning Sasha to take a seat at a small counter.

"Were you sorry that Pavel died?"

Sasha nodded, trying not to look at the man.

"I knew Pavel was good to you. He was killed by an enemy of mine."

Even though she was not looking at him, she could feel the man examining her.

"You are not my enemy, are you?"

"No." She shook her head, hoping he believed her.

"My enemy is searching for you."

"I know."

The man began examining the clothes displayed on the racks, fingering the material, checking their design. Occasionally he would pick out a garment, set it aside, then subject the other clothes to the same careful inspection.

"What size are you?" He pulled out a dress that was suitable for evening wear. "I think this color would be good for you." He held it up, looking from the dress to her. "Yes, this is the style." He snapped at her, impatient. "Size!"

She managed to blurt out her size.

"Try it on." He tossed it over to her. Sasha was too frightened to even think of going into the dressing cubicle. She took off her clothes immediately and put on the dress. The man eyed her, twirling a finger to indicate that she was to turn around for him.

Sasha turned, showing off the dress, beginning to believe that she was not going to die. He was costuming her for something. "A nice dress," she got out.

"No. Not quite right. A little cheap-looking. Cheap clothes

makes a person look uneasy. I want you to look confident. Take it off."

Sasha took the dress off, standing in her panties, covering her breasts with her folded arms, not bothering to put her clothes back on. She would only have to take them off again as he selected more clothes for her.

The man pulled another dress from the rack. "This one, I think." He walked back to her, holding it before her. "No question." He handed it to Sasha, gesturing for her to put it on, again twirling his finger to have her turn and display it for him.

"Shoes next." He gestured toward a display of shoes. "Then one of the wraps." Sasha began trying on shoes, as the man tossed a long black leather coat edged in fur at her feet. "I think that coat. Pick a scarf for the neck."

Sasha settled on shoes, slipping them on, then went over to a display of silk scarves, quickly selecting one, putting it on, then the coat, over the dress. The man was at the jewelry counter, looking through the case.

"Here now!" His command was given in the same tone as a dog-handler uses in an obedience class. She moved to where he was standing. "Simple is the word in jewelry." He held up a string of pearls, then circled them around her neck, clasping them in back. "Yes." He viewed her again. "Hold your arms out."

Sasha held her arms out. "A jeweled watch on one wrist, a diamond bracelet on the other." There was a wall showcase which he tried to open. It was locked. Without any hesitation, the man used his forearm and elbow to smash the glass in the vitrine, reaching inside to pull out the watch he wanted. Then he smashed another case to select a bracelet.

Sasha had continued to hold her arms out, afraid to drop them until the man told her she could. He slipped the watch on one wrist, the bracelet on the other, then pushed her arms down to her sides.

"Good." He opened the coat, to look at the dress once more. "No brassiere. The breasts showing through gives you just the right touch of insouciance, don't you agree?"

Sasha nodded, agreeing for the sake of agreement.

The man bent over to lightly kiss her on the mouth. "You will now be my new Siren of the Waters." He walked to the door, stopping just short of opening it. "There is a room registered for you at the Negresco."

Fear swept through Sasha again. The Manager was staying at the Negresco. Words would not come out of her mouth. All she could do was shake her head, trying to convey her refusal. The man stared at Sasha.

"I will not repeat myself."

She nodded her assent.

"I know who is there."

She nodded again.

"I am glad you have agreed with me." His eyes examined her. "There will be a ticket at the desk waiting for you. It is for a party tonight. Go. A limousine will take you. Anything else you need, you can order at the hotel. It's all been arranged. After the party, go back to the hotel. Understood?"

Involuntarily, her head bobbed a continuing assent.

He opened the door. "The cash register has money in the drawer. If you want anything else in the store, take it." He walked out.

The man had come, and he'd found her. Now he was gone. Sasha still didn't quite believe she was alive, turning to look into one of the store's mirrors to make sure. Elegant dress, one wrist with a diamond watch, bracelet on the other. Yes, still alive. Luxuriously alive.

He liked her. That was it. Pavel had been killed. She was

Pavel's friend. Therefore, the man was her friend. He who is the enemy of my enemy is my friend. At least for now. What had he said? Sasha would be his new Siren of the Waters. A few minutes ago, she had been hiding under the stands, ready to take chances with her life merely to get a morsel to eat. Now she was wearing diamonds. Whose reflection was looking out at her from the mirror? Yes, the Siren of the Waters.

Chapter 44

The Musée des Beaux-Arts had been the grand mansion of a Russian princess who had arrived in Nice before the overthrow of the Tsar and the slaughter of the Russian aristocracy. She had stayed on to live in splendid comfort as the titular head of the Russian community. Her art collection, not the greatest in the world, but a tourist attraction when combined with the royal showcase of her home, was irresistible to the local politicians, who turned it into a museum when she died. Once a year, as provided by the princess's will, and as a condition of the bequest she had made, the city had to allow the Friends of Russia to hold a ball in it for the Russian community. Virtually the entire old-line Russian community would then descend on the palace in their finery.

Being Russians, of course, they invited friends, who invited other friends, and soon anyone who could afford the price of a ticket came. Who would turn down the opportunity of saying they had been guests of the last remnants of royalist Russia?

The highlight of the evening was the toast to the dead princess, followed by a toast to the Tsar. Then everyone could go home, having lived their fairy tale, floating on a dream enhanced by good vodka and better champagne.

Jana and Levitin were early. It was not that they were impatient. It was just good police work. They had to know the layout of the palace to assure themselves that they had tracked and identified all the guests they could, and, most of all, to get a lead on Sasha's current whereabouts. Too many roads led to the party. There would be linkages if they were able to read them.

Levitin had rented a tuxedo, looking quite comfortable in his shirt with studs and black bow tie. Jana had surprised herself by renting an evening gown at a shop off the Rue de Rivoli, a short distance from the palace. Now she was uncomfortable, constantly moving, trying to ease her discomfort, wishing she had had the courage to arrive in her business suit. Their budget prevented them from renting a limousine. Instead, they had taken a local taxi to the front stairway of the palace. The stairs were lined by a row of liveried servants carrying lit torches to escort the guests inside.

At the grand entrance doors, a footman checked their tickets, then passed them over to another even more resplendent servant who gave each of them the opportunity to take a tulip glass filled with champagne from a tray.

At this hour, the building was virtually empty of guests, so empty that Levitin was convinced the ball was going to be a failure. An hour later, it was filled to capacity. Jana and Levitin tried to waltz on a ballroom floor packed with women in ballgowns and medal-bedecked men. Levitin assured Jana that all the medals were fakes, part of the necessary costume for the party. Jana, remembering the freedom with which the Russians had given out medals in Slovakia, wasn't so sure.

"You see the duchess with the tall hairdo, dancing with the balding man in the general's uniform?" Jana led the slightly resistant Levitin, just enough so he was facing the couple.

"Men are supposed to guide when they dance with women," Levitin reminded her.

"I wanted you to see them."

"I see them," he grunted.

"I saw her standing on a corner on Rue de Rivoli. She didn't have the hair, and was selling toy bears that performed acrobatics. The bald man had a stall a short distance away. He had plastic spiders that he threw high up on a wall, where they stuck, working their way down to the ground inch by inch. The spiders were rather grotesque."

"Our toy-sellers have come up in the world," Levitin allowed. "No spiders; no dancing bears. No need to be on the street. They will find it hard to go back to the spiders and bears tomorrow."

"Tonight everybody is dreaming."

They danced away from the couple.

Levitin saw Mikhail first. He had never met the huge policeman before, but the sight of Mikhail dressed as a Cossack, towering above the crowd as he came into the ballroom, was enough to catch anyone's eye.

"I have just seen the largest Cossack in the history of the world," Levitin declared.

Jana turned to look, immediately recognizing Mikhail. "He's Ukrainian, not Cossack." She broke away from Levitin, walking toward Mikhail.

Levitin quickly caught up with her. "A performer in our play?"

"If that's what you want to call him, yes, a performer."

Mikhail saw Jana and made what was, for the huge "Cossack," a small gesture with his head indicating that she should follow him.

Mikhail walked out of the ballroom. Jana increased her speed to catch up with him, Levitin keeping pace.

They moved through the spectators at the edge of the floor, then out of the ballroom itself, to a marble statuary-lined grand staircase that ascended to the second story of the palace. Mikhail stood at the top, waiting for them. Unlike his usual openness, Mikhail was subdued, his face rueful. He was not happy with himself. He hugged Jana, but without much enthusiasm.

"Hello, Jana."

"It is always wonderful to see you, Mikhail, even though it is a surprise to see you here."

"I hope you don't dislike surprises too much, Jana. But I had to come."

Levitin tried to introduce himself. "I'm Levitin."

"I know who you are." Mikhail didn't take his eyes off Jana. "You're the Russian Jana is traveling with."

Jana looked down the stairs. A little man in paint-spattered overalls and a beret was looking up at them.

"My cousin," Mikhail identified him. "He's an artist. He brought me here."

"He needs a better costume," Levitin commented.

"He wouldn't put one on. Artistic integrity, he said. It would be false if he wore anything but his own clothes. I had to pose for him."

"Oh?" smiled Jana, an eyebrow raised.

"Not like that," assured Mikhail. "In my uniform."

"I'm glad it wasn't embarrassing." The tiny man and the huge Mikhail together presented a very humorous picture, particularly considering the possibility of Mikhail posing in the nude for the little artist.

"Nobody would ever think you would do anything embarrassing, even for the sake of art," Jana announced, trying to assuage Mikhail's fears. She glanced at Levitin, her warning look telling the Russian to shut up.

Mikhail shuffled his feet before coming to the point. "I have not told you the truth, Jana."

"I know, Mikhail." She sat down on the top step, patting

the spot next to her for him. He eased his huge body down beside her. "Remember, old friends forgive."

"Thank you, Jana."

"I know about the club."

"Vadym's?"

"The explosion that destroyed the club, you set it off."

"Yes."

"You had a device in your pocket, and when Grisko began to walk back to his club . . . boom!"

"I am ashamed, Jana." His lower lip quivered like a little boy's. "I had to do it."

"I know, Mikhail. You also tried to help me."

"Yes."

"You couldn't set it off when I was inside. You didn't want to kill anyone, so you made sure even the employees were warned to get out."

"You knew?"

"There was no one else who would bother to save me. And there was no one else who could have set the bomb off at the right time to make sure that even Grisko was not killed."

"It was hard to let him survive."

"Not a nice man. I don't blame you."

"I got in too deep, Jana."

"Your apartment, and the one downstairs. You own them both?"

"A police pension in Ukraine: a pittance. They let you starve when you get old."

"So you took graft. And bought the apartments."

"I took a little. Nothing huge. Just enough to buy them."

"The apartments now own you?"

He nodded.

"The grafters, the big ones, they held it over your head."

He nodded again. "Grisko was one of them. He was squeezing too hard. So I tried to scare him off. Koba gave me permission."

Levitin jumped at the mention of Koba's name. "Koba let you bomb the club?"

"He suggested it. Grisko is on the other side."

"There is another side? Two groups?"

Mikhail nodded. "I don't know much. Just that there is a conflict." His face fell even further. "And your friend, Mikhail, is now a gangster."

"Mikhail, you are too nice to be a true gangster." Jana patted his shoulder in reassurance. "I am glad you came to tell me."

He ran a huge hand through his hair. "I came for another reason."

"To warn me?"

He looked at her, surprised. "You know that, too."

"It would take a very strong reason to bring you all the way to Nice, Mikhail. You traveled here to help an old friend."

He nodded again.

"Thank you, Mikhail." She leaned over, stretching up to give him a kiss on the cheek. "Who has come here to kill me, Mikhail? Koba?"

"Not Koba. My wife told me to tell you that you were in danger; that I had to come. Then he called. He told me to warn you."

"Koba did?" Jana found it hard to digest that piece of information. "Why would he help me?"

"Not to help you." He gestured at Levitin. "To help him."

It was Levitin's turn to be surprised. "Why would he help me?"

"Apparently you are valuable."

"To Koba?"

"That was all he said."

"Mikhail, have you seen Koba?" Jana took his huge hand in hers. "It would be very helpful if we could identify him."

"I have never seen him, Jana."

"Then how do you know it's him?" Levitin demanded.

"Oh, I know," Mikhail smiled. "You always know it's Koba, even if it's just a phone call. If you talk to him, there is no doubt. There is never any doubt."

"And the warning, Mikhail? The warning that Koba gave you for us?"

"Watch out for the Manager. That was all that he said."

Levitin didn't quite understand. "The Manager?"

"Yes."

"Nothing else?

"That's all."

"Good. You must now go home, Mikhail," Jana patted him one more time. "Go home to Adriana."

"I should stay. I could try to protect you, Jana."

"Better to go home. That would please me, Mikhail."

"You are sure?"

"Absolutely." She pushed at him. "Now, Mikhail. Go, and give your wife my love."

The giant got to his feet, helping Jana up. "Thank you, Jana."

"My thanks to you, Mikhail."

They watched him walk down the steps. At the bottom, he was joined by the little man in paint-spattered coveralls and a beret. The two of them walked out of the building together.

Chapter 45

Sasha eased out of the limousine and walked up the stairs as if she were the Princess Kotschoubey returning to claim her palace. She had begun to come back to herself for the first time since Pavel had been killed. As ordered, she had checked into her suite at the Negresco without any problems, taken a wonderful bubble bath, had a massage, then a facial, and ordered a stylist sent to her room to do her hair. It was much better than sitting under the stands at the Carnival parade. And she had eaten. Oh, how she had eaten, ordering half of the menu from the hotel's storied restaurant, then desserts, enhancing everything with a choice of five or six wines from the cellar.

It was not that she ate and drank it all, or even a large portion. She nibbled: a bite of an appetizer, then a pick at the Beef Wellington or Salmon in Aspic. She tried a dark, rich chocolate cake with Grand Marnier-laced fudge frosting; then an ice-cream dish *flambée* she had no recollection of ordering. By the time she dressed, luxuriating in her stylish clothes, she had a lightheaded feeling from the wines, but a newfound confidence that there was now a chance, even though slight, that she might survive. The man whose name nobody wanted to speak was her sponsor, at least for the moment.

The liveried servants could see the poise of the masked, beautiful woman as she walked to the top of the stairs leading down into the ballroom. Perhaps they were feeling the spirit of the princess in the air; perhaps this was the princess herself come back to earth on ball night? Whatever it was, they jumped to escort her, were disappointed that she refused champagne but appreciated her graceful gesture when she rejected the glass, allowing one of them to remove her coat, then favored the man who took the coat with the slightest of smiles. When she moved among the crowd in the palace proper, her bearing showed that she fully expected women to curtsy and men to bow as she passed.

What we think we are, we are; the moment you believe will occur does. You cannot just wish it; it must be yours, firmly and without question. As Sasha passed her, a woman, perhaps playing a role as all of them were that evening, bent her knee in obeisance. Sasha acknowledged it with a slight nod. The woman's companion, a bearded hussar with a shako under his arm, perhaps to please his companion, bowed, too. Not to be outdone, others picked up the gesture. An aisle opened up for her to pass through, everyone genuflecting, others running up from all parts of the museum-cum-palace to enjoy this unexpected moment. The small orchestra went silent, then broke into the Tsarist national anthem, the musicians straining to catch a glimpse of royalty as they played.

Jana and Levitin had already descended and were watching, wondering who the woman was. As she approached the two of them, Levitin reacted to her presence with agitation. Jana saw his tension building. She put her hand on Levitin's arm to stop him from blocking the princess's progress through the aisle of her loyal subjects.

"It's Sasha," Levitin mumbled, as much to reassure himself as to give Jana information. "She has come back." He tried to pull away. Jana was now forced to hold him in check with both hands.

"Stay away from her, Levitin."

"She's my sister."

"She is at the party for a reason. Look at her, Levitin. Sasha is here to show herself; to show that she is not afraid. It is important to us for her to succeed. Leave her alone."

Reluctantly, Levitin watched her pass, aching to speak to her. Sasha's glance flitted past Jana and Levitin, never hesitating as she conquered the room. One of the liveried servants brought a high-backed chair to the dais at the end of the room, the dais supposed to be used later in the night by the master of ceremonies, and placed the chair on it. The chair became a throne as Sasha regally sat on it, comfortably assuming her proper place in the world.

The audience broke into spontaneous applause. Sasha looked down at the upturned, expectant faces, then raised a hand to the bandmaster. The small orchestra began to play again, more vigorously now, having been given the royal imprimatur. Reluctantly, the princess's subjects began to dance again. Sasha nodded approvingly, then looked to where Levitin and Jana stood, nodding to them as well.

Sasha had seen her brother.

Chapter 46

For the next hour, a steady stream of "courtiers" approached the stand. The liveried servants quickly brought red velvet ropes, which they hung on gold stanchions to guide the line of those wishing to pay respects to their new royalty. Levitin kept muttering uncomfortably, wondering how his sister was going to continue to keep them satisfied. Idolaters would chat with their "Princess" for no more than two minutes. Then, guided by some inner clock that governed protocol, they would make their smiling departure, now slightly more erect, more prestigious to themselves for having spoken to her.

Jana watched Sasha only intermittently; she was more interested in the crowd. There was no question in Jana's mind that Sasha was here for an event. No, Jana corrected herself, she was here to create an event by her presence. Whatever the event, Jana was determined not to let it escape her, hoping to take advantage of the circumstances. The least she hoped to get was information.

Levitin's cell phone rang. He pulled it from a tuxedo pocket, answered it briefly, and then handed it to a surprised Jana. "Trokan. For you."

"Having fun?" was Trokan's first question. "How much did it cost?" was his second. When she started to answer Trokan cut her off. "I couldn't reach you. Your cell phone is off."

"There's no room for a cell phone in what I'm wearing."

"Then you shouldn't be wearing a dress like that. It's probably sinful."

"Sin. Yes, something new and wonderful for me." The cell phone had static on the line, so along with the music and the crowd noise, it was difficult to hear Trokan. She slapped the cell phone, then held it tightly to her ear. "I'm having trouble with reception. Talk like you are yelling at a new cadet."

She stepped through tall glass doors and onto a nearby outdoor balcony to get away from the noise. Trokan's voice became louder. "Why do I always have to shout when I talk to you? Listen closer."

"I've been carefully listening for years."

"Then why does your beloved commanding officer think that you do not?"

"He is insecure?"

"Careful, Matinova."

"Always, Colonel."

"Seges has been trying to reach you. He gave me some information to forward. He contacted the Irish police. The file that they had on the murder of this man named Walsh was purged some years back. Too old to keep any more. The investigator on the case died of lung cancer a few years ago. So they have nothing for you."

Jana involuntarily winced. If there was anything more to Moira Simmons's trial for murder, she was not going to find out about it. Trokan rolled on, back on his favorite topic.

"The minister wants you back. Now! He thinks you are taking a vacation on Slovak funds. From what you tell me, I am beginning to believe it."

"We are close."

"To what?"

"To finding out what is happening."

"Matinova, come home."

"Two days, three days. If I'm wrong, I will let you deduct all the expenses from my salary, including my salary."

"Assuming you still have a job."

"Take it from my pension."

"We don't pay you enough pension money for you to reimburse us for the trip. So, are you coming back?"

"All flights are booked."

"Police officers are not supposed to lie."

"I'm learning to be dishonest."

There was a long silence on the phone.

" . . . Colonel?"

"I'm here. You are also there. Two to three days, you say?"

"Yes."

"That's all the time you have, Matinova!" His voice had taken on an official tone. This was her limit.

"Thank you, Colonel."

The phone went dead.

Jana looked out over the balcony railing, thinking that her time was running out. The colonel had given her his orders. She looked down. Directly below the balcony on which Jana stood, Moira Simmons was emerging from a limousine.

Jana walked back into the palace and over to Levitin, handing him the phone, waiting for Moira to make her grand entrance. When she appeared, there was another shock.

Moira Simmons entered first. Lagging slightly behind, so that Jana did not see her at first, was her daughter Katka. Jeremy walked behind them.

There was a second man, older, thick in the body, who trailed them, his eyes sweeping the room. He fixed on Levitin for a quick moment, then reached into his pocket for a cell phone, turning away to speak into it, turning back for an even briefer moment to say something to Katka, then leaving the way he'd come.

The others continued into the room. Both women wore gowns, Jeremy a tuxedo. They were offered glasses of champagne. The three of them smiled, clinking their glasses in a toast, sipping the wine, enjoying the moment. Jeremy leaned over Katka, his arms raised in dance position, asking her for a waltz. She shook her head. He exaggerated his dancing motion. Katka held her arms out in acquiescence. The two spun onto the dance floor, leaving Moira Simmons standing alone.

Jana watched Katka sweep around the dance floor in Jeremy's arms, looking beautiful in her long white dress, swirled around in the dance by her obviously adoring husband, both of them caught up in the pleasure of the moment. Jana was very anxious. She desperately wanted to talk to Katka, to embrace her daughter after such a long separation. She took a half step toward them, then stopped herself, remembering the last disastrous time when they had seen each other.

Chapter 47

Two great events had occurred almost simultaneously: the communists had finally fallen, and Katka had finished her undergraduate studies. Katka was coming home. Before she went on for an advanced degree, she was returning home to Bratislava. Katka had flown first to Prague, then taken another plane which would arrive in Bratislava at five P.M.

Jana was at the Bratislava airport almost an hour before time. She paced back and forth, fearful that some last-minute event, a slight mechanical problem, a storm, some terrible act of God would prevent them from embracing each other, mother and daughter finally reunited after so many years apart.

Jana had brought flowers. Dissatisfied with the size of the bouquet, she returned to the flower shop, doubling the number of flowers, hoping that in some way they would fill a void for Katka. They were the only soft, welcoming things Jana could think of to give Katka to show her love.

How does a mother prove to her daughter that she wishes it had been different? Forced to relinquish all those years of her daughter's youth, forced to miss all of Katka's emergence as a young woman, Jana had not been the mother she expected—no, wanted—to be. If those were Jana's expectations and disappointments about herself, what were her daughter's? Jana could never soothe them. No triumphs witnessed together; no ideals or aspirations shared between them.

No dreams they had dreamed together. What did they still have for each other?

Jana forcibly reminded herself: There was to be no sadness, no bitterness at the world for their separation and absence from each other's lives. This would be a time of celebration. They would pick up the fragments and rebuild their relationship, together again.

Trokan came ambling into the terminal, a huge box of chocolates in his hands.

"I came to see our daughter return home."

"*My* daughter." Their little ritual of claim and counterclaim was complete. No, it was not as satisfactory as it normally was. "I am very frightened," Jana admitted.

"Frightened? She is your daughter; she will always be your daughter. Katka knows that, so she will love you."

"Easy to say." Jana glanced through the glass windows at the runway. "Still no plane." She went back to brooding. "I could have kept her here. I didn't. I sent Katka to America. . . ." Her voice tapered off. "Will she resent my actions? Will she feel I abandoned her?" Jana's eyes pleaded with Trokan to tell her that she had done the right thing.

"Children think a lot of crazy things." Trokan shrugged, as if telling Jana that it was not within their ability to control Katka's emotions. "What you think, here and now, is more important. I remember those times very well. You had more courage than most mothers would have had under the circumstances."

"Thank you, Stephan."

"I knew what you did at the time. As your commanding officer I ignored it; as her once-removed 'father' I applauded." He smiled, a sly edge to his voice. "You took chances. You always take chances. If I had been 'officially' made aware of it, I would have arrested you and thrown away the key." His belly quivered as he chuckled. "But you did just enough to make sure I was not slapped in the face with it." He stopped laughing, nodding his approval. "You did well."

"You helped."

"Of course I helped. What are friends for? You gave me just enough to allow me to remain your friend."

"You saved me."

"You saved yourself. Maybe I just pushed you in the right direction. A little nudge here, a little nudge there. That was all that was needed. And if I lied a little to the *nomenclatura*, who cared? They lied enough to us."

The plane abruptly came into sight, landing just as quickly, taxiing down the tarmac, pulling to the front of the terminal. The airport technicians rolled the stairs to the rear of the plane for passengers to disembark.

"Our daughter will come out of the plane and will be looking for you. Don't you want to go onto the field to greet her?"

"Yes, and no. I will cry."

"You will also cry here."

"I'm not allowed on the field."

"You have a police badge."

"We shouldn't use our badges to get personal favors."

"Stop being sanctimonious. It's not like you." He hooked her arm into his. "Fortunately, I have no such qualms."

Trokan hauled her with him, then pulled his credential case from his jacket, flashing it at the airline employee who tried to stop them from going onto the field. As they reached the tarmac, the passengers began disembarking. Trokan pulled his arm out from beneath Jana's elbow, lagging slightly behind her as they approached the plane. Finally, a young American woman, fresh-faced, poised, came down the stairs. It was Katka.

When Katka got to the tarmac she immediately recognized

Jana. The two of them faced each other, neither one seeming to know what to do. Then they both moved at the same time, Jana's flowers crushed between them in their embrace. Katka was more reticent, a bit stiff, but Jana was crying, kissing Katka, laughing, then crying again. Each of them confessed that she'd missed the other. There was happiness, joy, their words interspersed with more hugs and tears from Jana.

Finally, Trokan moved up to the two woman. "Enough mush. I think it's time to go inside."

They paid no attention, so he spoke louder.

"I have candy for my adopted daughter."

"She's *my* daughter," Jana emphatically stated. "No one else's daughter." Katka laughed; Trokan laughed. The three of them finally moved to the terminal entrance. The conversation turned into small talk.

"Was it a good trip?"

"Easy."

"You must be tired."

"A little."

"Have you eaten?"

"Too much."

"I can't wait to show you Bratislava." Katka stopped walking; the other two waited.

"Mother, I just want to go home."

"Yes, home," agreed Jana.

The two held each other in long embrace, then walked into the terminal. Trokan wiped a tear from the corner of his eye, glad no one was watching him, then followed them inside.

Chapter 48

Moira Simmons glanced around the room as Katka and her husband took the dance floor, immediately noticing Sasha seated on her throne as she received her subjects on the reception line. Moira reached into her purse to pull out her cell phone, dialing rapidly, her eyes swiveling around the room as she appraised events. She noted Jana and Levitin in the sweep; her expression did not alter. Her eyes remained on them as she spoke, then listened. After a moment, she put the phone back into her pocket, then approached Jana and Levitin.

A smile appeared on her face. She seemed to be enjoying the moment.

"Good evening, Commander Matinova." She nodded at Levitin. "Investigator Levitin."

Jana nodded to her. Levitin, still mesmerized by his sister's appearance, barely mumbled a greeting.

"You meet the most unexpected people at the Russian Friends' Ball. Did you come all the way to Nice just to see it?"

"We're hunting." Levitin's attention was still on the stage. Reluctantly, he focused on Moira. "I got hungry for a bit of Russia."

"People who have a Russian relative, even a distant make-believe relative, come to the ball." She turned back to Jana. "They pretend that the Romanoffs were never shot by the Bolsheviks and still rule their world."

"What brings you here to Nice, Moira?"

"I have a place here. That's where I first met Jeremy and Katka, at a diplomatic party. And Carnival is a wonderful time to be in Nice. A time for fun. And any excuse to have fun is a good excuse." Moira glanced at Levitin. "This is a very odd place to go hunting, Levitin. All the animals in this room are tame."

Levitin, his eyes locked on Sasha and the reception line, did not hear her. Moira followed his gaze.

"A very beautiful woman, your sister."

Both Levitin and Jana were startled.

"You know she is Levitin's sister?" Jana spoke softly, covering her surprise. "Please tell me how."

"Pavel, her old boyfriend, the Czech who threw himself out of the window, once told me that Sasha had a brother who was a police officer in Russia. The way you were looking at her, and as I know her last name is the same as your last name, I put it together." She laughed. "Maybe I should apply to a police force to become a detective."

"You only knew her through Pavel?"

"Where else? When Pavel died, poor Foch and I lost track of her. I'm glad to see that she is in such good health and apparently able to take care of herself. I always used to feel that there was a childlike quality about her, that she needed to be taken care of. I think that was what Pavel responded to."

Jana pursued the issue. "Ms. Simmons, has the United Nations an interest in the ball, or are you hunting as well?"

There was a quizzical half-smile on Simmons's face. "There's no big game to hunt here. I want to have fun."

"Without an escort?"

"My escort is Russian. He had to leave. I stayed to view the people show." She turned back to the dancers and the stage. Jana followed her eyes. She was watching Sasha, and Sasha was watching her.

"The lady on the throne recognizes you," Jana informed Moira.

"We got along well when she was living with Pavel. And see how she has come up in the world, a princess dispensing grace to her subjects."

"Truly a princess," Levitin agreed.

"One would not know it from her fairly recent history," Moira Simmons murmured, just loud enough for Levitin to hear.

His mouth tightened, his voice took on a warning note. "She is my sister." His look was angry. "Careful what you say."

"I meant no harm." Moira finally took her eyes off Sasha, and glanced at the table where Katka and Jeremy were now seated. Katka took a quick sip of her champagne. Then Jeremy led Katka onto the dance floor again. They blended in with the other whirling dancers. "People look so graceful when they dance."

They watched the people gliding around the floor. Moira moved closer to Jana. "Your daughter is angry with you."

" . . . Yes."

"You have a lovely granddaughter."

" . . . I'm happy to hear that."

"I don't know if I can help moderate your daughter's feelings about you; but if you wish, ask me and I will try."

"It is between the two of us."

"As you wish."

The music ended for the moment, the dancers drifted off the floor. Katka and her husband were one of the last couples to leave.

Jana was overcome by the need to talk to her daughter; the urge to bridge the gap between them welled up inside her. It was impossible to wait any longer.

Jana barked an order at Levitin. "Stay here, please."

Moira Simmons was already moving toward the edge of the dance floor. Jana caught up to her in three steps. "She is my daughter. It's time I talked to her."

"I would wait," Moira advised.

Jana paid no attention. She had gotten within ten feet of her daughter when Katka saw her. Jeremy noticed Jana at the same time and took a tentative half-step forward as if to stop her.

"Katka, isn't it time for us to sit together, to finally talk again?" Jana blurted out.

Katka heard only sounds; she shut out the meaning of Jana's words.

"Stay away from me, Jana!"

"Katka, I did nothing to your father. I loved him."

Katka's husband stood mute, not moving a muscle.

"You are the criminal, Jana. You are a killer!" Katka spit out.

"Katka, just ten minutes together."

She tried to take her daughter's hand. Katka pulled away. The two woman formed a brief, silent tableau, one in a rage, the other in shock. Oh, God, thought Jana. *She hates me now far worse than she did before.*

Katka moved first, turning to the other people attending the ball, many of them already staring at the scene. Yelling as loud as she could, Katka forced everyone to pay attention. "Ladies and gentlemen, I would like to introduce all of you to my mother, the murderer. To save herself, she shot and killed her husband, my father."

She stepped close to Jana, flushed, an avenging angel. "See her in all her glory. A killer who, by her murderous act, maimed and destroyed a little of everyone dear to her!"

With that, she slapped Jana across the face as hard as she could. Everyone was watching. In the quiet ballroom, the sound of the blow carried to every cranny of the hall. The echo seemed to last forever.

Chapter 49

"It looks smaller," Katka murmured as they entered the house she had left so many years before.

"Everyone says that when they come home again. You were smaller; it looked larger to you then."

"It looks older," Katka kept repeating, walking from room to room.

"It needs a coat of paint," Jana explained, following her. "The furniture should be polished. And the rugs are worn."

Jana wondered if Katka thought she had failed to maintain her patrimony, had fallen down in her guardianship of the house. "Too much work in my job. You're right. I need to do more here. I did take care of the garden in back," Jana mentioned. She had placed small bouquets of garden flowers around the house hoping to make it cheery and welcoming. Katka paused to sniff at one of the bouquets, then passed on without comment.

Her daughter sat in the living room. She was breathing a little unevenly. However, aside from that, she appeared to be calm.

Odd, thought Jana, trying to examine her own emotions. She was feeling sad and happy at the same time. Jana could see the little girl inside the grown young woman, and felt tender and proud and loving and anxious, and a million other emotions. She was sure all of them were fighting for display across her face.

Katka's appearance, her face, her expression showed some of what Jana was feeling. Her daughter was having an inner dialogue between her past and her present, between love for the house and anger at a past that had been taken away from her. The feelings flickered across her face, brief frames from a faded film. Then they were gone.

"Why are we bound to the house we grew up in?" Katka's voice carried a subtext, as if to say that she didn't feel any ties. She pulled one of the flowers from a vase on the small end table by the couch, rubbing it on her cheek as if applying rouge. "All those expectations. It's disappointing to come back. Nothing could live up to what you want."

"Everything lives up to it. Here we are, Katka and Jana, mother and daughter."

"Is that good?" Katka asked. She did not seem to want an answer.

"For me, it's so good that you're here."

"Thank you."

Jana began to laugh.

Katka murmured, "Share it, if it's funny."

"You said everything looked smaller. Am I smaller?"

"No, bigger."

"Fatter?" asked Jana, worried.

"No, bigger. That's all."

"Maybe if I had seen you more when you were a child, you would think I was smaller now. I wish I could have seen you all the time, but there was no way. Grandma and Dano, they had to care for you."

Jana busied herself with making tea. Katka, hearing the water running, called out that she wanted coffee.

"Sorry. I only have tea." She heard an echo inside of her.

Jana realized she was apologizing, in one way or another, over and over again. She felt guilty for her inadequacies as a mother, for not being small enough, for the house, the rugs, and now for having tea and not coffee. She paused to regroup.

"I baked cookies, like Grandma's."

"Good," Katka approved. "When are we going to see Grandma's grave?"

"Whenever you want."

Katka stood, ready to go. "How about right now?"

Jana dried her hands. "The tea and the cookies?"

"We'll eat the cookies there."

"Okay." She put the dish towel on its rack, then pulled her coat off the hook. Things were not going according to plan. Jana had practiced saying certain things for weeks. She knew what words to use about her mother. She was going to talk about her police work. And she would certainly not forget to ask Katka about her life in America.

Now they were off to the cemetery without touching on so many things: most of all, Dano. As they walked out of the house, Jana felt uneasy at leaving the one place in the world where she thought the two of them might be comfortable with each other.

The trip to the cemetery was short. During the drive, Katka was silent, staring out the window, not volunteering a word until they were among the gravestones.

Jana had tried to draw her out. "I tracked down some of your old classmates."

"I'm sure we've all outgrown each other," Katka replied.

There were a few other people among the graves, cleaning them, arranging fresh flowers, leaving food. But Jana's mother's grave had no one near it. They sat there, apart from the rest of the people at the cemetery. Jana kissed her own fingers, then transferred the kiss to her mother by touching the small headstone with her fingertips. Katka pulled a cookie out of the sack, breaking it into several pieces.

"For you, Grandma." She spread the cookie pieces over the grave. "That's for all the cookies you baked me."

"The world is not fair," Katka announced, some of the little girl she had been in her voice. "If it were fair, we would all be munching on these together: You, me, Grandma, and Dad."

Jana nodded.

"Are you a fair person, Mother?"

"I hope so."

"We both hope so."

Katka's tone had changed. It was now accusatory.

"Where are we going with this, Katka?" Jana deliberately kept her voice soft and non-threatening.

"To a place we should have gone years ago, Mother. Are you an honest person?"

The questioning raised warning flags for Jana. She had the odd feeling that she was being interrogated.

"I have reason to believe you may not be as honest as you pretend to be, Jana," Katka went on.

An attack. Unmistakable, when she was addressed as "Jana" instead of "Mother."

"I'm not pretending anything, Katka." Jana waited for whatever would come next. Her daughter's pent-up emotions were about to erupt.

"You have been concealing something from me, Jana."

Whatever it was, was going to be bad.

"You murdered my father."

Jana felt the blow. *Murder.* Her daughter was accusing her of killing Dano. Her thoughts scuttled around inside her head like a frantic animal trying to find an escape.

Katka was relentless.

"You killed my father. You shot him." She launched the words like torpedoes, enjoying the explosions as they hit their target. "One shot, at close range. How could you do it?"

Jana tried. "No. I did not kill your father. And he was dead before any shot killed him."

Katka stood up. "You lie."

Jana thought about the statement. "I have never lied to you."

"I learned the truth from my great-aunt. No," she corrected herself, "my 'real' mother." She observed Jana's response. Satisfied with what she saw, she continued, "She housed me, she fed me, and she gave me all the news of Slovakia. The Slovak newspapers carried the details of your glorious deed. He came to you for rescue and you destroyed him instead." Katka took pleasure from the pain she was inflicting. She went on, "He fought the communists. He fought for democracy. And you killed him."

Jana stood, hurt, unsure what to say to heal herself, to heal Katka, to close the chasm that had appeared between them. "Katka, I loved Dano. We were divorced, but I still loved him. He had done terrible, stupid things, but I still cared. I would not do him any harm."

"More and more lies." Katka's words spilled out of her mouth. "He loved me; he loved you. He loved the whole world."

"Katka, how long have you lived with this idea? How long have you believed I killed Dano?"

"For years, Policewoman Jana Matinova. Everybody in the United States, the whole Slovak community, they knew. I lived with it, lived with all of them trying hard not to bring the subject up around me."

"And you waited to come home to tell me?"

"I waited to tell you what I knew over my grandmother's grave. I wanted to see how dirty, how ugly you were. I know it now. I hoped I was wrong. But I was not. You are not my mother. You were never my father's wife. You were just a communist police officer."

Katka walked away, leaving Jana, stunned, standing by her mother's grave. She took Jana's car back to the house, moved her things to a hotel, and left the car with the key still in the ignition on the street for the police to find. The next day she was on her way back to the United States.

Later, despite all the entreaties, the letters, the pleas sent by way of friends or relatives, Katka refused to see Jana again. With the new baby, there had been some hope of being allowed to see her new grandchild. It was short-lived. Jana received a note from Katka's husband, with one word underlined: "Impossible." Katka steadfastly refused to see Jana again.

Trokan was upset. "Tell the truth," he ordered Jana. "Blame Dano. He pulled the trigger. Unless she knows that, your relationship with Katka will be over."

"Have her find out that Dano killed himself? No. Not now; not ever," swore Jana. Katka had to have something to believe in. "Her father is her belief; her anchor in life. A good illusion is better to live with than an ugly truth. Fathers cannot rob banks; fathers cannot kill themselves."

"You have blinders on," grumbled Trokan. "She has blinders on," he added. "And neither one of you is interested in seeing anything except the black tunnel ahead."

Chapter 50

The ball dragged on interminably for Jana, only beginning to phase out around 2 A.M. A magnificent meal had been served on the grounds to the rear of the palace, then everyone drifted back inside anticipating Princess Sasha's toast, followed by the formal toast to the Tsar. Sasha had been eloquent. Levitin was amazed at her showmanship and audacity. Sasha was in another world, cocooned by the people flowing around her, all of them beaming love and affection at her in their mutual fantasy. She was living the life of royalty.

When the toasts ended with the crowd's roars of approval and the smashing of glasses, the more decadent phase of the party began. There was erotic dancing, sexual games in the corridors and on the stairways, behind the drapes and anywhere there was a nook where bodies could come together. No one was abashed enough to stop, and nobody was offended enough not to look on, to see if there was anything new to learn or be entertained by.

It was very late. The diehards who still refused to leave the ballroom floor were being serenaded by the remnants of the orchestra, three musicians whose notes creaked out of their instruments sounding even more fatigued than they were.

Jana continued to watch the proceedings from the stairs. Levitin leaned against the wall, his eyes never leaving Sasha. When Katka attacked Jana, Jeremy had frantically pulled his wife away, quieting her, making embarrassed gestures and noises at Jana, none of which made up for the terrible moment. The other ball guests attributed the scene to too much alcohol, and the event was passed over.

Jana retreated to the stairs. Moira ignored her. Jana continued looking at the table where Katka, Jeremy, and, particularly, Moira Simmons sat. There was an inconsistency in the personality the woman projected. Jana was aware of it now. It was the reason Jana had not taken her advice to stay away from Katka. In fact, it had goaded her on.

A picture kept coming back to Jana. Grisko had seen Koba kill a man by driving an ice pick through his eye. Grisko himself could do nothing, not even arrest Koba, after the event because, as he described it, a pretty woman had been holding a gun to his head.

Moira Simmons kept flashing through her thoughts. The pretty young woman holding the gun to Grisko's head? No evidence; just a feeling. People like Koba and the woman who had held the gun to Grisko's head always found each other.

Jana pushed the idea away. There was no proof at all. There was nothing about Moira Simmons that suggested the ability to commit terrible crimes and not feel a qualm. Koba's accomplice would have to be like that. The woman who had come to Jana's room, huddled in her bed, crying, was not like that. Although there was the story of her past. . . . Jana repressed her speculation about Moira. Now that she had destroyed the possibility of reconciling with her daughter, she was looking for someone else to blame. This was not right.

Katka and her husband were absorbed in quiet conversation at their table. Moira sat slightly apart from them. Abruptly, her cell phone rang, startling everyone.

It would have been muffled in the great press of people in the ballroom earlier in the evening, but now its theme song could be heard across the room. Moira listened briefly, then put the phone away. The three of them stood and walked out. The women had not even checked their appearance. The sudden departure after the call suggested to Jana that they had been given a signal to leave.

This was a cue for her and Levitin to depart as well. "Time for us to move."

Without responding to Jana, Levitin started toward Sasha, passing the few remaining dancers, stopping just short of the dais where Sasha was enthroned just as one of the liveried servants approached to hand her a small envelope.

Levitin talked to her while she was opening the envelope. "I've come to help, Sasha." He stopped, struggling with his voice, which threatened to break from too much emotion. "I am so glad you are alive and well. We have looked for you everywhere. I love you; everyone loves you." He stopped, shaking his head, trying to find words. When he began again his voice was husky, soft, a whispered plea. "We can go back. We will find you a secret place, a safe place. I beg you to forgive me, to forgive the family for what you think we may have done. All of us." He gathered himself. "No. I, particularly, want you to come home. Come back with your big brother."

Sasha finished reading the note, let Levitin finish his plea, then stepped down from the small platform to give him a kiss on the cheek.

"I love you, Brother. No matter what, I will always love you."

The orchestra used the princess's descent from the throne as the signal to stop playing. Management took the opportunity to blink the lights signaling the end of the evening. The ballroom took on a deep after-party hush. The ball was over.

Levitin tried to hug Sasha, but she held the envelope out, stopping him. He took the note and read it. "Go back to the Negresco. Levitin later."

"You were sweet to look for me, Brother. I remember all your kindnesses and all your affection. Now, you have to leave me."

"Sasha, come with me. You can't go on like this. We can protect you."

He tried to take her hand. She looked him in the eye for a brief second, then used her other hand to push his away.

"Obey the note." There was no questioning her tone. The matter was closed. Sasha walked off. A footman brought her coat and scarf, the last of the guests bowing to her, and with a majestic flourish, she swept out of the doors, the last of the royal Romanoffs.

Levitin stared after her, dejected, wondering what to do. Jana took the note from his hand. After she'd read it, she stuffed it in the breast pocket of his tuxedo.

"The note is clear. We meet her at the hotel, later. This is not the time to grieve."

Levitin stared at Jana blankly. Jana made a fist and punched him hard on the chest. He gasped, but his eyes focused on Jana.

"Later! She's still out there dangling like a piece of fruit for someone to pick. I think that's what he wants," Jana said.

"Who wants?"

"Koba wants to see who tries to pluck the lady. Then he plucks them. That's his game."

Levitin considered. "Is he expecting to pluck Moira Simmons?"

"Maybe; then again, maybe not. She kept staring at Sasha. That is something to conjecture about."

"I was too busy looking at Sasha myself to notice."

"Your sister is the one everybody seems to be hunting. She's the reason for the murder of the little old lady."

Levitin thought about his sister being in danger.

"Sasha's been through too much already in her life. How can we help?"

"We need to think. But I'm too tired to exercise my mind."

Jana looked toward the grand entrance to the ballroom. There were two large but nondescript men, dressed very unlike the celebrants, standing by the entrance. The men could have been hired for the night as bouncers to take charge of too-aggressive guests. Except that there was no reason for them to remain at the ball when virtually all of the celebrants had departed. Jana's police instincts stirred.

She led the way as she and Levitin walked into one of the anterooms. A champagne bottle was on the floor next to a pair of stockings. Levitin pointed to the stockings. "She'll wonder what happened to her silk hose in the morning."

"She'll know exactly what happened to them, and probably be very happy that it did." The French doors to a small balcony at the end of the chamber were open. The two of them stepped onto it.

"I think there is someone we don't wish to meet waiting for us at the main entrance," Jana suggested.

Levitin nodded agreement. "The two men at the front."

"You feel the same undercurrent I do?"

Levitin nodded.

"We'll leave a different way," Jana suggested.

She examined the wall at the end of the railing. A thick plastic-covered electrical conduit ran down the building. Jana removed her pumps, put them in the inside jacket pockets of Levitin's tuxedo, then climbed onto the balcony railing, grasped the conduit, and quickly, hand over hand, worked her way to the ground. Levitin was right behind her.

Chapter 51

The streets were empty. It was too late to be out even on a Carnival night except for the occasional drunk or the married man hurrying home from the wrong woman's bed. Vacant as it appeared, the city loomed as a single dark body, an uneasy, inhuman shape that was amorphously threatening. Directions were lost, north became south; there were no familiar landmarks, and all shadows were enemies. The two of them felt the urgent need to find even the smallest recognizable guidepost.

Jana and Levitin scurried along the Rue de la Buffa. The stores that had earlier been so full of life now were dead-eyed, closed. They finally passed a pair of glowering street cops who pointed the way to the Palais de Justice area and the approximate location of the nearest police station. Jana reasoned that there was nothing like a short stay in a police station to discourage even a persistent street thug. If necessary, under Inspector Vachon's aegis, they could remain until the late morning, then head over to the Negresco to find Sasha.

"We're going in the right direction."

"Why would they have men waiting for us at the main entrance?" Levitin asked Jana.

"I think we have been placed in the 'dangerous' category by one or more of the generals in this battle. Basically, they are all thugs. Thugs always respond the same way when they see a threat: Kill or maim."

"Maybe we misread those men at the ball?"

"It would be nice to be wrong about them. Unfortunately, there is a small part of my mind that keeps telling me to hurry and get to a safe place before they catch up with us."

Jana surveyed the area, no longer sure they had correctly followed the cops' directions to the police station. "I think we go down here."

Jana pointed; Levitin hesitated. "I don't know, so that way is as good as any," he concluded.

They trotted in the direction Jana had pointed.

"Multiple competitors are fighting over Koba, a corpse that may very well not be dead."

"Everyone is jockeying for position."

They reached Place Messina, and Levitin heaved a sigh of relief. "I know this place."

"The main Carnival area." They cut diagonally across the square.

"We have talked about the book that I took from the apartment in Bratislava that was hidden, but not really hidden, under a couch. Ask yourself one additional question: Whoever left the book wanted someone to find it. Why?"

"Must there be some logical answer?"

"Why us? We're the police. Why the police? Maybe we acted too quickly in Slovakia. Maybe it was left for one of these people to find."

"What for?"

"To mislead."

"He saw everyone as a possible enemy. He would never let anyone get close to the book."

"Remember, we may be dealing with Koba. He has reasons within reasons."

They had reached the Carnival structures. Now darkened for the night, huge cut-out figures loomed over the grandstands, squatting at the edge of the *Place*, waiting for something dreadful to begin. Then they saw the men. Four of them were spread out in a chain facing them.

As one, Jana and Levitin turned in the direction they'd come from. Three more men were coming up behind them, closing rapidly. Levitin reached down to his ankle, quickly unstrapping a very small automatic from its holster.

"Levitin, that pop-gun is not going to stop anyone. If they see you with it, they will kill you first." She looked around for instant aid, finding none, then saw Galeries Lafayette, the upscale department store, on the opposite corner. It reminded her that there was something she had always wanted do when confronted with opulence of that sort.

She lengthened her stride, grabbing one of the garbage cans for Carnival debris stacked on the corner. Jana threw it at the window of the store as hard as she could. The can bounced back, the window unbroken.

"They've made the panes extra-thick to stop hooligans like us. Shoot the window," she ordered Levitin.

He gaped at her.

"We need to weaken the window. That little pistol of yours can at least do that." He was still unsure. "Shoot the window, damn it!"

Levitin pointed the gun at the window, pulling the trigger four or five times, creating surprisingly tiny holes, even for such a small weapon.

"Grab a can," she yelled. The two of them smashed the cans against the window, which finally buckled as a sheet, crashing to the ground in a cascade of glass shards. At the same time, the burglar alarm attached to the window went off with a continuous clanging noise. Other alarms, apparently wired to the same window, added their cacophony to the din. The noise was deafening.

They checked out the thugs who had been coming after them. They were hesitating, no longer sure what to do. The wail of approaching sirens made their minds up very quickly. Almost as one, the men turned, bolting back into the darkness.

An hour later, they were in the police station they had been trying to find. Inspector Vachon was not elated about having to awaken from a deep sleep to get them out of a jail cell. Fortunately, his French sense of hospitality stopped him from showing his anger, and he had one of the other *flics* bring them both coffees in his office.

"You have caused a fair amount of damage."

"We were about to be either killed or kidnapped, Inspector," explained Levitin.

Vachon looked at the small automatic that had been taken from Levitin. "You are not supposed to have a gun in this country, Mr. Levitin."

"I know."

"We may charge you."

Levitin gave a very good imitation of a French shrug. "Unfortunate for me if you do."

"Convince me why I shouldn't keep you in jail."

Levitin thought about it. "For one thing, we have information on the Lermentov killing."

Vachon's eyes went from Levitin to Jana. "Ah, I sense you are about to avoid having charges filed against you."

Jana picked up where Levitin had left off.

"The men who were coming after us last night, I think they were the same men who killed Mrs. Lermentov."

"And who are they, Commander Matinova?"

"We don't know yet, Inspector."

Vachon had taken a small pad from his jacket pocket, prepared to write names in it. Disappointed, he laid the pad down. "So, we will have to sacrifice Mr. Levitin after all. Our jails in France are almost as bad as the jails in Russia, Mr. Levitin."

"By tomorrow, Inspector," Jana assured Vachon. "We will know then."

"Tomorrow," echoed Levitin, a note of hope in his voice. "You are both sure?"

Levitin nodded, Jana making a brief gesture of assent.

Vachon eased his pad back into his jacket pocket. "I cannot wait much longer. The store you damaged has influence in Nice. I have to show them I am working in their best interests."

"Tomorrow, Inspector." Levitin was trying to avoid jail.

Vachon focused on Jana. "Day or night, Commander?"

"Night, day, who knows. Tomorrow is all I can say."

Vachon sighed. "Don't upset me, Commander. Serve me up this meal as you have promised."

"With dessert," Jana added.

"Good."

He called an officer into the room, waving at his two guests. "Take them where they want to go."

The cop drove them to the Negresco, very impressed that they appeared to be able to afford a room in the most expensive hotel in Nice. Jana and Levitin didn't enlighten him. It takes a lot to impress a cop, and they didn't want to disillusion him.

They waved as he drove off.

Chapter 52

Jana and Levitin sat in the large oval reception room just off the main lobby of the hotel waiting for Sasha. They had offered to go up to her room, feeling they would all be more comfortable in the security of her suite, safe from possible attack, but Sasha had been insistent on coming down. Jana and Levitin had been waiting for an hour and Levitin was alternately apologetic and worried. They had to content themselves with viewing the wildly expensive but uneven and eccentric art collection that the owner of the hotel had scattered around the reception area and its environs.

"I don't care for the portraits," Levitin abruptly declared. "The people all look like they have bad indigestion and worse breath."

To make conversation more than anything else, Jana studied the art and indicated that she liked the sculptures, a number of them antic and playful, which elevated her somewhat somber mood. The events of last night with Katka had been ugly; their relationship appeared irreparable.

The only hope Jana had was the intervention of Katka's husband. But she had not stayed away as she had promised him, and he would probably think twice about trying to help her. Who wants to deal with a distraught mother, anyway? She feared she might never reconcile with her daughter.

Sasha finally walked through the arches that led into the room from the elevators. She loked refreshed and wore virtually no makeup. She was clear-eyed, dressed in clothes with simple lines that accented her body's contours without exaggerating them.

Levitin jumped up, ran over to her, kissed her on both cheeks, then pulled her into a bear hug. She worked her way loose, giving him a peck on the cheek, then came over to Jana, smiling in greeting. She seemed to be continuing her performance of the night before, her back straight and her head high. She held out her hand for Jana to take, then hooked her other arm into Levitin's.

"I'm so glad you have come to visit me. My rooms are now tidy. We can go up." Gazing up at Levitin, who was melting in the glow of his sister's affection, Sasha walked them both to the elevator and they rode upstairs to her floor.

"I've been hearing all about you this morning." She looked over at Levitin. "You have been doing very well for yourself. Everyone is impressed."

"I don't understand, Sasha." Levitin sounded confused. "Who has been telling you all about me?"

"Uncle Viktor, of course."

Levitin passed from confusion to astonishment. "Uncle Viktor is in Moscow!"

"No, he is here. He saw you at the party last night. But only for a moment. He decided not to stay."

Jana remembered the thickset man who had arrived with Katka's group. "Sasha, did your uncle arrive at the party last night with Moira Simmons? Was he the man who left just after he came in with her?"

Sasha smiled, her teeth even and white. "That was Uncle Viktor. He wants to speak to you both, but in private."

Jana lifted her eyebrow at Levitin. "Your uncle, the minister? The one who sent you? Is that Viktor?"

"Yes." Levitin's face took on the look of a man in peril. "There is only one Uncle Viktor," he finally got out.

They entered Sasha's suite. Like all suites in the Negresco, it was luxurious, fit for any millionaire or visiting dignitary, even for a bourgeois couple out to spend a huge sum of money on a once-in-a-lifetime fling.

Sasha led them each to a separate couch, seating herself next to her brother. She continued to cling to his arm.

Jana persisted with her questions. "What is the minister doing here?"

"He's engaged in his criminal activities, of course," Sasha explained, as if he were a merely a workman or any other kind of low-level drone. She moved away slightly, turning to face Levitin. "Did you know Uncle Viktor supplied me with drugs in Russia? And when I was unable to do without them, he exchanged sex for drugs with me on a regular basis until he was tired of my services and put me on the street to earn money?"

Sasha's ingenuous way of talking, her open face, was more telling than if she had cried or raged through her recital. However she disclosed it, it was clear to Jana that this was a woman who had been severely damaged and hadn't yet come to grips with what had been done to her. Her demeanor never changed; she remained a young lady describing her recent pastimes as she spoke, irrespective of her words' meaning.

"He's a terrible man," Sasha continued, her voice still devoid of emotion. "But I've survived him. Uncle Viktor couldn't get over how well I look. He has no conscience, you know."

"I never realized." Levitin tried to ingest her statement. "He was always my favorite uncle," he finally uttered in a bewildered tone.

Sasha studied him, a slightly quizzical look on her face.

Levitin saw the look. "Why didn't you come to me? I'm your brother."

The quizzical look remained. "You went to work for him.

To me, that meant you were allied with him. How could I come to you?"

"Sasha, I would never . . . I cannot believe you would think. . . ." His voice trailed off. "We are brother and sister."

Sasha took his hand, kissing the back of it. "It's all right," she whispered soothingly. "We are together now." She turned to Jana. "Uncle wants to talk to you." She checked the time on the watch that had been given to her the previous day. "Uncle Viktor should be here any minute."

Jana saw Levitin's anguish. He was feeling the same way she had last night when Katka abused her.

She focused on Sasha. "Is Uncle Viktor the man called Koba?"

Sasha looked surprised. "I've never heard that name." She nodded toward the entrance of the room, announcing his arrival. "Our Uncle Viktor."

Viktor walked into the room followed by two men, bodyguards who were burly enough to make four individuals. They stayed at the door, facing out rather than in. No one else was going to be allowed to enter the suite. Uncle Viktor wasn't afraid of the individuals inside.

Levitin's eyes were fixed on his uncle.

"I am Viktor Levitin," he announced to Jana. "My niece and I had a charming conversation together in which she was kind enough to refer me to you. It's about a ledger."

"Uncle," Levitin whispered. "You are a monster."

"No question, dear Nephew." Viktor took no offense at the characterization. "All of us are. I'm just luckier than most to realize it, and act on it." He pulled a chair over, sighing as he sat down heavily.

"How could you have mistreated my sister so badly?" Levitin was becoming angrier. "She is your brother's child. You abused her."

"I only gave her what she wanted, Nephew."

The animal growl that came out of Levitin's throat was a precursor to an attack. One of the bodyguards appeared, as if by magic, at Levitin's shoulder. A massive paw held him down in his chair.

"Nephew, you will have to sit still. Commander Matinova and I have to talk, and we cannot be interrupted." He eyed Jana. "I once thought my niece had the ledger I wanted. Now I have been told that you have it. Is that so, Commander Matinova?" He shifted his heavy bulk, the chair creaking in protest.

"What ledger, Minister?" Jana asked, as if she hadn't the vaguest notion what he was talking about.

A look of distaste appeared on the minister's face. He snapped his fingers for the second bodyguard, then pointed at Sasha. "Her!"

The bodyguard balled his hand into a fist and punched Sasha in the stomach. She let out a whoosh of air and slid off the couch to the floor, the shock of the blow paralyzing her. Levitin tried to get to Viktor, but the other bodyguard put a headlock on him, immobilizing him.

Viktor threw his hands up, palms out. "Since you do not know about the ledger, my niece obviously lied to me and has to be disciplined. We will have to keep on disciplining her until she tells us the truth." He nodded at the bodyguard, who promptly kicked Sasha in the ribs. A small moan came from the young woman.

Viktor smiled at Jana. "If my niece persists in lying, we will have to punish her even more severely. I think this time we'll break both her wrists."

"No!" The word popped out of Jana's mouth. "The ledger. It's in Slovakia."

Viktor sighed, a deep sound of contentment. "I'm so glad

my niece was not lying to me. But how terrible. You let her be punished for nothing." He looked down at Sasha. "I'm so glad you were telling the truth to your Uncle Viktor."

Jana bent to help Sasha, rolling her over. She was having trouble breathing. Jana spread Sasha's arms, hoping to give her more lung capacity. "Breathe in and out, slow breaths. Make them deep breaths if you can."

Sasha nodded, her eyes opening wider, her breathing steadying. She was in pain, but her eyes were clearing. She moved her head, first to one side, then the other, checking the muscle function of her neck. She held out one hand to Jana for help in rising, her arm held tightly to the ribs that had been kicked by the bodyguard. Jana gradually helped Sasha to get her legs under herself. Painfully, the young woman rose to her feet.

Sasha winked at Jana. The wink so surprised Jana that she stepped back, quickly becoming angry at herself for almost giving Levitin's sister away. The young woman had a plan. As gracefully as her sore ribs let her, Sasha sat once more in the same place. "The hurt will go away," she assured everyone, even Viktor.

Jana watched Sasha gradually recovering, astonished at the young woman's ability to continue as if what she had just gone through was the most natural process in the world. Jana turned back to Viktor.

Viktor motioned to the bodyguard who had a headlock on Levitin. "Nephew, my friend is going to release you. If you choose to commit a rash act, then it will go very badly for you." The bodyguard loosened his hold on Levitin, pulling him erect, allowing him to take full breaths again.

Levitin swayed, his face flushed, trying to get his bearings, then focused on his uncle, rage stiffening his posture. Sasha's surprisingly firm voice stopped him. "Brother, everything will turn out as it should. Listen to Viktor and me. Stay still!"

Levitin shook his head, a bull deciding whether to charge, looking at Jana, then back at Sasha. Gradually, Levitin contained his rage, deliberately cooling down. This was not the moment to take action.

"Good for you, Nephew," Viktor encouraged Levitin. "Wait a while. If you still want to come after me when I'm without my large friends, you can try. I wouldn't advise it, but you are notable for not taking good advice." Viktor shrugged.

"Now, Commander Matinova, I'm afraid I can't take a 'no' for your answer. You need to get me that ledger."

"Is it yours?"

"Of course it's mine. Not that I wrote it, but as the legitimate successor of the person who did."

"You are the legitimate successor to Koba?"

Viktor got up from his chair, amused by Jana's guess. "The ledger's author is of no significance. He's dead."

"Are you sure?"

Viktor's eyes and mouth took on the look of a man who had swallowed a very sour pill. "I have every reason to believe Koba is dead, dead, dead."

"Did you kill him?"

"Do I look like a murderer?"

"Yes."

The sour expression became worse. "If I had killed Koba, I would be the first one to brag about it." He walked to the door, followed by his bodyguards, one running ahead to open it, the other to check the corridor.

"Efficient; very efficient." He seemed to be complimenting himself rather than his men. Viktor turned back to the people he was leaving, planting his feet, giving them a last glower. "I don't demand the actual ledger. A copy will do."

He thought for a moment. "Have it in my hands by tomorrow, noon."

He started out of the door, turning just outside the doorjamb which framed him. "If you don't get me the ledger, then I will mourn your lack of intelligence, or generosity, as the case may be, and what happens to my nephew, my niece, and you, will all be on your head." He paused to make sure she understood the import of what he had said. "Good-bye."

A bodyguard closed the door behind him.

Levitin came over to his sister and gave her a soft, careful hug. "I couldn't do anything, again," he announced sadly. Levitin's hair had become disordered. Sasha patted it into place, comforting her brother.

Despite her pain, and to cheer the other two up, Sasha announced that she was hungry. "It is amazing what you can order in this place just by picking up the phone. What would you like?" She looked from one to the other, then dialed before they could answer. "I'm ordering for all of us." Room service answered. Sasha said, "I have guests for lunch. I want everything I had yesterday, only for three."

Jana watched her put the phone down. "Sasha, I would like an answer or two. Honest answers."

Sasha looked surprised. "I wouldn't hide anything from you. Since my brother trusts you, then so do I." She moved too quickly, uttering a startled gasp of pain, her hand going to her ribs. "I'd like to go to the bathroom first, okay?"

"Sure. If you need help, just call."

Levitin tried to assist his sister. She gently removed his hand, indicating that she didn't need help. Her head still high, she walked slowly to the bathroom, closing the door behind her. A moment later, they heard the shower.

Levitin was still feeling overwhelmed by the recent confrontation. It was not just his physical manhandling by the bodyguard, but the revelation of his uncle's degradation of his sister for years, and seeing her physically abused while unable to do anything about it, that had emotionally drained him. His uncle was a criminal, and a pervert, even when it came to his own family. Levitin was still trying to adjust to this reality.

"I am a baby, left alone by his parents, not sure if they will ever come home, and absolutely sure that there are demons ready to devour us." He sat, closed his eyes, and stretched his legs, elongating his back, not to get the kinks out, but to contain his fear without curling up into a ball and becoming a fetus. "I will have to kill my uncle."

"How will you do that without being arrested for murder?"

"It doesn't matter if I am arrested."

"How would you kill him?"

"I don't know."

"That's the difference between you and him. He would know just how to kill you in a dozen ways without thinking too much about it, and they would never connect him to any of them."

"So?"

"So, you are not capable of killing him. That's not what you're good at. His men would bring you down before you got within spitting distance."

There was a knock at the door to the suite, and a voice announced itself as room service.

"Come in," Levitin responded.

The door opened, and three waiters and a busboy entered, all of them rolling food carts. They began uncovering silver food warmers, bustling over their guests. They worked as a team, finding space on several tables to spoon and ladle out portions of the food into dishes, uncorking both a white and a red wine, forking various cheeses onto plates, laying out napkins and place mats, glasses and silverware. Finally, they stepped back.

The senior waiter flourished a hand. "Paillard de Veau, Beurre de Citron; Saumon Poché, Sauce Hollandaise; Supreme de Poulet en Croute de Sesame et Parmesan; Oeufs à la Niege."

Jana raised a hand to stop him. "We're fine by ourselves now."

The headwaiter handed her a bill and a pen. Not knowing what else to do, she signed the bill. The headwaiter bowed, and they trooped out, silently closing the door behind them.

The humor of the situation, with the waiters in their penguin uniforms, the huge number of gourmet dishes served while they contemplated murders and threats of more murder, made Jana laugh.

Her laughter had a hysterical quality to it. She tried to fight it, unsuccessfully. Finally, she used the only remedy she knew, pushing a fingernail as hard as she could into the back of her head, then focusing on the pain. The laughing finally stopped.

"Feeling better?" Levitin asked, a touch of mockery in his voice.

"No." She thought for a moment. "I'm frightened; you're frightened. The only one who does not appear frightened is Sasha." Jana thought about the young woman's strength. No one could be that strong. Jana had almost missed it. "Sasha, in the bathroom! She is in trouble!"

Jana ran to the bathroom. The door was locked. She yelled at Levitin, "Kick it in."

Levitin kicked the door, snapping the lock. The two of them darted inside. Sasha was sitting in the shower. The water cascading over her ran red. She had slit her wrists.

Chapter 53

An hour after they got her to the hospital, a nurse appeared to inform them that Sasha was in no danger. Another hour passed before a rather bored young emergency-room doctor found them, and between deep pulls on a cigarette, told them that the cuts on Sasha's wrists were not deep. He exhaled a steady stream of smoke as he related that the sutures had been put in the right places, there were no tendons involved, she had a full range of motion, and she needed to rest. They could go up and see her. He then strolled off, lighting another cigarette with the stub of the one he had just finished.

They walked up one flight and along the corridor to the room number the floor nurse had given them. Just before they got there, it was opened from the inside by a male attendant stationed in the room to make sure the patient didn't try to kill herself again.

Jana and Levitin pulled up chairs and sat next to Sasha on opposite sides of the bed. The attendant relaxed in a corner of the room, his face buried in *Le Monde*. Sasha's eyes stared at the ceiling; her wrists were bandaged, and both hands were strapped to the bed frame. Levitin tried to get her attention.

He patted her on the shoulder, whispering her name. She did not respond. He repeated her name, louder this time. Again, there was no response. Then he began talking to her, adoration apparent in his voice.

"The ball last night, it was a triumph. They worshiped you. We watched you enter the room, the people bowing and reaching out to touch your gown, all of them royalty themselves because you were there. Your bearing was that of a princess. You owned everyone in the building, myself included. You were more than a princess: you were a goddess."

He shifted uncomfortably in his seat, aware that he was not getting through to her, changing his approach, his tone now pleading. "You are that person, Sasha. The goddess. Not the one who was beaten by our uncle. He is not a man. Men do not do what he did. But you, you are a woman of strength, a woman with steel in her spine. Anyone who was there knew it. You must know it as I know it. Sasha, I know you are strong. Tell me I am right, Sasha. Tell me!"

A full minute passed before Sasha turned her head toward him. Her voice was soft, but clearly audible, with a throaty quality that Levitin had not heard before. "I killed Sasha. I had to. She had to go so I could come here."

Levitin looked shocked. "You are not dead, Sasha. We are talking, you and I, brother and sister, like we used to talk."

Sasha tried to raise her arms, abruptly becoming aware that they were strapped to the bed. "Why have they tied my arms?" She began to strain, attempting to twist her wrists free. Levitin held one arm down, Jana the other, trying to stop her from doing additional damage to herself.

"You have to stay still, Sasha." Levitin held her tighter as she continued to struggle. "Please stop, Sasha. You will only hurt yourself more."

She stopped. "I told you, I am not Sasha. Don't be afraid. It is not because of Uncle; it is not because of Sasha. It is because of me. For the other man; so he would like me. He could not like Sasha."

Jana walked around to Levitin's side of the bed, the side

Sasha had turned to. "Sasha, I think you are going to be all right."

Sasha shifted her eyes, focusing on Jana. "Sasha, yes, she is all right. She is fine where she is."

Jana tried to penetrate the closed circuit Sasha had created. "Please listen carefully. Try to help us. We don't understand: Where did Sasha go?"

"To heaven. God excused her from earth."

Levitin began to quietly weep, the tears rolling down his face. Jana watched him for a moment, deciding that he didn't need her immediate help, then turned back to Sasha.

"Would you like the straps taken off your arms?" Jana was now careful not to use Sasha's name.

"You can't take the straps off," Levitin mumbled. "It would be dangerous."

Jana didn't bother to answer him. She untied one of Sasha's arms, then went to the other side of the bed, ignoring Levitin's look of disbelief, untying the second strap.

The orderly in the corner looked over the top of his paper, then apparently decided he did not want to interfere. Sasha flexed her fingers, then lifted one arm close enough to examine the bandages on her wrist, then lifted the other arm, entwining the fingers of both hands, then stretching.

"Would you like help in sitting up?" Jana didn't wait for an answer, slipping an arm around Sasha's shoulders, and, with Sasha's silent cooperation, managed to bring her to a sitting position, then propped her up with pillows. "Better?"

Sasha nodded.

"Can you tell me who you are? Now that Sasha is gone, you must have a new name."

Sasha gave Jana a very solemn nod. "I'm the Siren of the Waters."

Jana smiled. "A very nice name."

"Thank you," Sasha responded, still very solemn. "Maybe we should thank him. He named me."

"Who is he?" Levitin tried to enter the conversation, Jana glared him back into silence.

"Forgive our friend. He is really a nice man most of the time. Generally he has better manners and doesn't interrupt."

"Sasha told me he was nice," the Siren of the Waters informed Jana. "He can be a good friend."

"I'm happy Sasha feels the way I do." Jana sat at the head of the bed next to Sasha. She indicated Levitin, whose face had softened on hearing that his sister liked him. "You see, Mr. Levitin feels better now that he knows you are not angry at him."

Sasha shook her head. "I'm not angry at him."

"That's very good." Jana though about her next words very carefully. "Sasha tried to kill herself. You won't try to kill the Siren of the Waters, will you?"

Sasha considered the question. "No. I couldn't. He wouldn't like that."

"I'm glad to hear that." Jana reviewed what Sasha had said. "The man who named you, the man who wouldn't like you to hurt yourself, who is he?"

The Siren of the Waters became even more solemn. "I think he is my angel."

Jana winced. The girl was sinking deeper into her dream world. Jana tried once more. "Does your angel have a name?"

"He is the emperor of the angels, God's will on Earth. He is the king of all he sees."

Jana continued to push for an answer. "His earthly name; tell us his earthly name, Siren of the Waters."

Sasha focused on the question. "He was once called. . . ." She tried to pull the answer out of her memory, but failed. "I can't remember." She brightened. "It doesn't matter. Angels can have any name they want." She lay back on the bed. "I'm tired. I think I need to sleep." She closed her eyes.

Levitin came out of his corner, walked to the bed, looking down at his sister, then kissed her on the forehead. "Have a nice journey, Sister."

Jana pushed him away. "Not now! Wait!" she hissed at him, frustration getting the better of her. "I need the answer to one more question."

"She's tired," Levitin grumbled.

"Too bad!!" Jana leaned over Sasha, clutching her shoulders, shaking her. "Siren," she commanded. "Open your eyes. One more question."

Sasha's breathing began to slow as she drifted into sleep. Jana shook her more forcefully, Sasha's head bobbing up and down. "I have one more question, and I will keep on shaking you until you give me the answer. Do you hear me, Siren of the Waters? I will keep on shaking you!" Jana became even more vigorous. "Who is the Manager?"

Jana abruptly slapped Sasha across the face, waited, then continued striking her. Levitin tried to pull her away, but Jana shrugged him off.

Sasha's eyes popped open.

Jana leaned closer, holding Sasha's face between her hands. "Sasha, Siren of the Waters, who is the Manager? Is it your Lord of the Angels?"

Sasha smiled sweetly. "How could he be the Manager when he's an angel?"

Jana could feel the frustration building inside her. "If he is not the Manager, then who is?"

"The other one." Sasha's eyes closed and she immediately fell asleep.

Jana let go of the girl. "Why would someone want the Siren of the Waters so badly?"

Levitin shook his head. "Right now, I have no idea. Worse, I'm no longer even sure who I am."

The attendant finally poked his head out from behind his paper. "Sometimes I feel like doing that to some of the patients."

"Well, don't," Jana warned him.

"I would never do it."

"Good," Jana approved.

"I haven't interfered, have I? I stay out of a patient's business," the attendant apologized.

"You haven't interfered," granted Levitin, pulling money out of his pocket, shoving it into the man's hands.

"I didn't ask for money." The attendant held it out for Levitin to take back. Levitin waved him off.

"Time to leave," the orderly suggested.

"Time to leave," Jana agreed, discouraged by how little information she had obtained. She walked to the door, reproaching herself for having used force against a girl who was bedridden and half-crazy. "Next time you have a patient whom someone is abusing, you are to stop it. Understand?"

The man retreated behind his paper.

Jana's voice took on an official warning tone. "I asked if you understood me."

"Yes," came from behind the paper.

"Take care of my sister," Levitin ordered, as both he and Jana walked out of the room.

The orderly waited a moment, then put the paper down and went over to the bed. He looked down at Sasha, and her eyes opened.

"Did I do well?" she asked.

He smiled down at her. "My Siren of the Waters could never do anything badly."

Chapter 54

They sat on a bench overlooking one of the beaches lining the bay. Neither Jana or Levitin had much to say. Both were brooding over the day's events. Levitin was depressed by his sister's suicide attempt and her flight from reality. Jana, involved in running over the events that began with the murders in Slovakia, paid little attention to his mood. They both ignored the occasional passerby, each focused on his and her own thoughts. Levitin, however, began conducting a vivid conversation with himself, interfering with Jana's reflections. She slapped him on the knee to bring him out of it.

"I can't hear myself with your gabbling."

"I didn't ask you to listen."

"How can I help it? You're sitting next to me."

"Okay, I'll watch it," he grumbled, shifting uneasily in his seat. The quiet lasted for a few seconds, then he said, "She was faking it."

"Sasha?"

"Yes."

"The cuts on her wrists were real."

"But not deep."

"Maybe it was a cry for help? People have all kinds of ways to signal. Some of the ways they choose are crazy. I've seen it before."

Levitin shook his head adamantly. "Not her, not after that performance at the ball."

"She wasn't beaten by your uncle at the ball. He did it the next day. It could have affected her."

"Yes," he reluctantly allowed.

"Perhaps?" she reflected.

"Make up your mind," he demanded.

"When I was slapping her to wake her up, my feeling was that she was not asleep."

"So, maybe I'm right."

"For her brother, you're awfully unsure of yourself."

"I've been wrong about her before." He lapsed into silence. Then, in a slightly stronger voice: "I still think she was faking it."

They watched the sea roll in, a last few hardy bathers being scattered by the tide. Jana got up, stepping to the iron railing on the concrete edge of the drop to the beach, leaning on it to watch the last of the sun go down. Levitin hesitated for a moment, than went over to stand next to her.

"Maybe you are right, Levitin."

"What's that mean?"

"The man in the corner of the room, the orderly. He had a tan."

"He likes to sunbathe?" Levitin suggested. "The man has a sunlamp at home? Maybe he goes to tanning salons?"

"They're all pasty-faced."

"Doctors, nurses, interns, the whole lot?" He thought about it. "There's always an oddball in the group."

"With wing-tip shoes on?"

"The orderly had dress shoes on?"

"Yes."

"My sister was faking it for the man in the corner?" He nodded. "She was putting on her performance at his instruction?"

"Yes."

"A new face in the game; one not hired by those we've already met."

"Maybe. At least not hired by them. There was no reason for her to put on that performance for them."

"You think the man was Koba?"

"The only things we know about that man are the shoes he wore and that he was tanned."

Levitin moved back to the bench and stood on it, then rotated slowly in a 360-degree arc until he faced Jana again.

"What are you doing, Levitin?"

He smiled down at her. "Getting a different perspective on things. It helps. The world looks different. Even colors change from the variation in the angle of the light. So you think differently. Join me." He held out his hand for her.

Jana jumped up on the bench, turning the same 360 degrees that Levitin had rotated.

"Yes, different," she agreed.

An old couple passing by, both with canes, stopped to look up at them, wondering if the two had joined a mutual insanity society, finally deciding they were not dangerous, and walked on.

"Let's talk," Jana suggested.

"We are talking."

"From your different perspective." Jana waved at the horizon. "Begin with the basic proposition that all the actors have taken the stage, and what we have to do is track back, using what we know of them, to verify the facts from our new perspective."

"Good. Start."

"Whether the orderly was or was not Koba, Koba wants us to stir the pot. Otherwise there is no reason to make even a brief appearance."

"How is our stirring the pot going to help him?"

"He's engaged in a war. He wants to make sure he has identified all the combatants and the sides they are on. Once he has, then he will take action."

"With Koba, that means killing people."

"Yes."

They paused to watch a small fishing boat chug across the bay, rounding the spit of land leading to the small port that serves Nice.

"It's got to be cold out there."

"Cold, but peaceful."

The boat disappeared around the point, a small wake all that was left. The sea birds were crying less, the city noise reduced to traffic and the occasional horn of an impatient driver.

Jana felt the night cold creeping in. "He knows who is against him. The more he baits the hook, the more the fish fight over it. Then, maybe they'll become cannibals, eating each other." She paused. "If they don't chew each other up, he will. I think he only wants to know one thing for sure, now. The name of one person."

"The Manager, the person who tried to kill him." Levitin suggested. He too felt the evening cold, rubbing his hands.

"Maybe there is more than one Manager?"

"Perhaps. But your sister seemed to say there is only one. I think Koba thinks he knows who it is, but wants to be absolutely certain before he acts. I think he has an emotional reason for wanting this."

"I don't think Koba can be emotional."

"Even the beasts in the forest feel emotion."

Jana wished she had a sweater. The small gusts of wind coming off the water made their perch colder than the interior of the city. "We have to go."

"Go where?"

"They all want the code book, and we're in the middle. I think we should give them the book."

Jana jumped down from the bench, Levitin following her lead, both of them walking to a crosswalk leading away from the sea.

"Your uncle thought Koba was dead."

"Yes."

"So he must know there was an attempt on Koba's life."

"By him or one of his associates, you think?"

"I think."

"All we have to do now is find the Manager."

"We will know soon."

She took a last look at the bay, the water now turned from dark green to black. Jana thought about the water and how it looked in the daylight, a beautiful cobalt blue. "I can see why people like Nice. I could get used to living here when the sun is shining."

They walked into town.

Chapter 55

Jana made the phone call, arranging a meeting, then had to persuade Levitin not to come with her or follow her. The Russian was adamant, and it took all of Jana's bag of threats, tricks, temper, and determination to finally wear him down. Only after insisting that she call him every half hour after she got there so he'd know she was safe, did he agree to let her go alone.

Jana sat at a small table outside a café on Garibaldi Square. A heat lamp near the table gave off a welcoming halo of warmth. Jana was thankful for its comfort on this windy day. She placed the brown bag she was carrying on top of the table, then ordered a double espresso and waited. Fifteen minutes later, Moira Simmons arrived. A Rolls-Royce with a thin red stripe along its side let her off at the curb.

There were two men in the car, both of whom gave Jana hard stares while surveying the area before they parked a few doors down. Neither of them left Jana with any doubt as to his profession. Moira Simmons took her security seriously.

Moira walked over to Jana's table, a smile on her face, and sat across from Jana, her eyes flicking to the bag, then coming back to Jana.

"I'm so glad you called me," Moira gushed. "I wanted to talk to you about what happened with your daughter last night. It must have been a terrible experience for you. I thought I might be able to help."

"That's very nice of you, Moira. I should have listened and not made an attempt to speak with her. Jeremy had warned me."

"We never think about being estranged from our children. It should never happen, but it does, over and over, for a whole dictionary full of reasons. I used to want children; then I saw how much trouble they got into in the world, and how much trouble their parents had either with them or trying to save them, so that I finally concluded, for me at least, that it was perhaps better that I never had any."

"I understand."

"So you agree: One should not have children."

"No, I disagree. If one can, one should have children."

"Even after what happened at the ball?"

"I still love my daughter. And, if I did not have a child, I would not have a grandchild."

"You are content to leave it that way?"

"I haven't given up. I just have to wait longer."

"Forever, maybe?"

"Maybe."

Moira hesitated. "Tell me how you got my phone number."

"Foch's address book. A legacy from his murder."

"Ah, yes. He would have had it. Poor Foch." She reflected on Foch for a very brief moment, then decided to come to the point of the meeting. "What do you want from me? You called me. Why?"

"I want to see Katka before I have to go back to Slovakia."

"Are you going back soon?"

Jana sipped her coffee. "As soon as I see my grandchild, get to meet her, cuddle her a little, and tell her I love her."

They sat in silence for a moment.

"You want my help in arranging a meeting with your grandchild?"

"I have seen how convincing you have been in the past. You are close to Katka. I think you might persuade her."

"And in return, what do I get? My payment?"

"My eternal thanks."

Simmons's face lost color, undergoing a transformation which changed the cast of her features to something bleak. She half-closed her eyes. "Nothing is free."

"The truly valuable things are free."

"Not so. Everything must be paid for, generally sooner than later." She indicated the brown bag on the table. "What do we have here? Is this a present for me?"

Jana drew the moment out, letting Moira anticipate what might be in the brown package.

"You should have something to eat first. A coffee and perhaps a small pastry."

"Is there a book in the bag?" Moira asked.

Jana pulled the brown bag closer to herself, resting her hand on it. "Maybe."

"My question is serious. Don't be coy, Matinova."

"It seems to me that you have toyed with me."

"Toyed? No. Everything I do has a reason. We all do what we need to for survival. I simply do it better than others."

"Who is the real Moira Simmons?"

"Whoever you want to think she is."

"When did you meet Koba?"

"Koba." Simmons mulled the name over. "I have heard that name. He uses other names as well." She looked at the brown bag. "I could have my people take the bag and its contents from you."

"You think the ledger is inside the brown bag?" Jana stared back at Moira without blinking, letting the woman know she was not frightened.

"You are on a road to disaster, Commander."

Jana let the words hang in the air before handing the
paper bag over. Moira ripped the book from the bag and read
the title on the cover. Then she opened the covers, riffling
through the pages, becoming more and more agitated. With
great effort, she quieted herself, gently laying the book on
the table.

"A volume of *Montaigne's Essays.*"

"He was a very wise man."

"Not what I expected."

"You want the ledger."

"The account book, the ledger, whatever you want to
call it."

"A few questions have to be answered first, and then I
need a favor."

"It depends upon the questions, and the favor."

"You say you have heard of Koba?"

"He is dead."

"If you say so."

"Some men I know killed him."

"On your orders?"

Moira stared at her without answering. The silence was
explicit enough to tell Jana what she wanted to know.

"Next question," Moira prompted.

"Are you the Manager?"

"If you want to call me that. My friends do not."

"Is that a 'yes'?"

"A yes or no, whatever you make of it. Enough questions.
What about the favor?"

"You already know it."

"You want me to persuade your daughter to let you see
your grandchild?" She relaxed, now in control. "Do you have
the ledger?"

"I have it."

Simmons took the torn bag that had contained the book of essays, writing an address on it.

"Call, and then deliver it to me."

"You'll have it . . . when you have persuaded my daughter to let me see my granddaughter, and it is confirmed to my satisfaction."

Moira smiled, a show of teeth rather than an expression of cheer.

"I will expect the book."

"Good." Jana pushed the volume of essays toward her. "Please take this one in the meantime. A small gesture of good faith."

Moira took the book, then rose from the table and walked to the Rolls. One of the men opened the door for her. She got in without looking back, and the car pulled away from the curb and out of the square.

Jana sipped her coffee. It had gotten cold. She laid down money for the bill, then walked to middle of the sidewalk and, glancing up and down the street, wondered where Koba was.

She saw no one she could identify as him. There were too many people about to single anyone out. But, as sure as the sun was in the sky, she knew Koba was there.

Jana walked out of the square.

A few minutes later, a tanned man seated in the café next to Jana's got up from his table and casually sauntered away. He was content, if not happy. He knew who all his enemies were.

Chapter 56

J ana had a hard night. She could usually sleep when she was investigating even the most serious cases, but tonight there were too many nightmares. People were chasing her daughter, then her granddaughter, intent on hurting them. And Jana was tied by a wire leash, unable to help, her hands bloody from trying to work herself loose from the embedded wire, her mouth sealed by a metal strip, prevented even from screaming for help. She was glad when the bedside phone rang, freeing her from her half-sleep.

She mumbled a "yes" into the phone. It was Trokan.

"What are you doing sleeping?"

"It's normal to sleep."

"I let you go to Nice to work on a case."

As she spoke to Trokan, Jana began to dress. "I'm working on the case."

"Not wearing an evening gown today?"

"I'm back to being an ugly police officer."

"I called to welcome you home."

"I'm not home yet."

"A friendly reminder. The deadline remains. There will be consequences if you are not back by the time we agreed upon. The French police have also told me you are not being as cooperative as they would like."

"I'm cooperating. They are just being French."

"The French say a lot of odd things."

"How are my blind cats?"

There was a long pause. Jana did not like the pause.

"Tell me," she ordered, knowing it was bad news.

"Both dead. They died yesterday. No real reason we could see. Just died. I thought about having a veterinarian perform an autopsy, but who ever heard of an autopsy on a cat in Slovakia?"

Jana was silent, trying to absorb the blow. She had grown to love the helpless little things.

"Jana," barked Trokan, sensing her emotion. "These things happen."

"I wish they didn't."

"We're adults. We know they do."

"Yes. Thank you for telling me."

"I debated whether I should or not. The truth, unfortunately, won out. What is happening there?"

Jana gave him a fairly detailed rundown of the events that had occurred over the last few days, then told him what she planned to do.

"You are sure?" Trokan muttered.

"No."

"Then why are you going to do it?"

"All of them have surfaced. Now we need to prompt the rest of their actions."

"You have no control over what they will do."

"The truth is, we never do."

"You sound angry about that fact."

"There are things we get angry about."

"Good. I consider anger to be a marvelous motivation for all my subordinates. Stay well."

He hung up.

Jana had breakfast in the hotel restaurant, then went back to her room, expecting a call. An hour later, Jeremy telephoned. He was quite cheerful, the bearer of good news for Jana. Their mutual friend Moira Simmons had talked to Katka. She had been incredibly caring and sympathetic. No, Katka would not come, but wonderful Moira had persuaded his wife to let Jana see her granddaughter. Jana could visit with her for an hour in the late afternoon at La Colline du Chateau, an old park with even older ruins on the top of a small mountain overlooking the Côte d'Azur.

The thought of seeing her granddaughter lifted her depression over the cats' deaths. Things might work out. At least she could hope they would. Now she would have to keep her end of the bargain.

Jana called the hotel business office for a messenger, then picked up the ledger, idly leafing through it. It was time to use it. Jana wrote carefully worded notes for Moira Simmons, Viktor Levitin, and Inspector Vachon. When the messenger arrived, Jana gave him the ledger with instructions to reproduce two copies, one for Moira and the other for the inspector, then handed over her three notes with explicit instructions on how to deliver them and the two copied ledgers.

The note to Moira Simmons read, "I have kept my end of the bargain." The note to Uncle Viktor was as terse. "Moira Simmons has obtained the ledger." The third note, to Inspector Vachon, read, "Here is the Koba ledger. You will hear more in a little while."

Then Jana decided she had to get out of the room for a walk. The remnants of Carnival were being cleared away, the stands disassembled. The lights that had been hung in celebration were being loaded onto trucks. The Niceans were very quick to clean up their city after Carnival and to welcome a return to sobriety.

Jana watched for a moment as a large papier-mâché lion's

head was set on the street for a moment before being picked up by a crane. Part of its face had been smashed in the dismantling. There was a sad-looking, lopsided grin on the beast now. It looked so woebegone that Jana had a sudden fleeting fantasy that it was still alive, but now forlorn, desolate that its brief span of life was nearly over.

She walked on, looking toward the area by the harbor. Dark gray clouds were moving in from the sea. There would be rain, brief but heavy from the look of it. The Boulevard Jean Jaures was emptier then usual. Perhaps people had anticipated the new storm moving across the city and decided to stay indoors.

For Jana, the breeze that was sweeping in over the water was cold, though not as cold as it had been in Slovakia. The fresh air felt delicious, redolent with the smells of the Mediterranean.

Then she saw the Rolls-Royce sailing down the boulevard. From its direction, Jana assumed its destination was the Negresco. Either Uncle Viktor or Moira Simmons must be behind the dark windows, one or both thinking that they might soon own the world.

They were in for a terrible surprise.

Koba, the legend, had not lasted as long as he had by being careless. Largess was not part of the man's makeup. He guarded the keys to his empire carefully. The ledger would not come free.

Jana eyed the dark clouds that were nearly overhead now. When it broke, the storm would be a big one.

Chapter 57

Late that afternoon, idly watching the rain from her hotel-room window, Jana received a phone call from Inspector Vachon, summoning her to the Negresco. There had been another crime, and the inspector wanted her opinion. Jana took a cab from the taxi stand near her hotel, riding through the pouring rain to the Negresco. Inspector Vachon's adjutant met her in the lobby, then accompanied her to a deluxe suite on an upper floor.

There were police, forensic personnel, and medical staff all over the huge suite. It was immediately clear that they were performing their assigned tasks in the investigation of a murder.

Jana was taken through the anteroom into the large living room. Levitin was seated in a wing chair, his tall body slumped in resignation, his face bleak. Across from him was Vachon, who looked up from his notes as Jana was led into the room.

A few meters behind the inspector was a plastic-blanket-covered body on the floor. From the foot and shoe that protruded, it was a man. No one was paying any attention to the corpse, so Jana assumed they were through with their preliminary examination. The inspector waved her to a nearby love seat.

"Coffee for Commander Matinova," he ordered a nervous hotel employee. The man quickly fixed a small silver tray with coffee and accompaniments and brought it to her. Levitin appeared to pay no attention, staring fixedly ahead, clearly miserable.

Jana sipped at her black coffee for a moment, waiting for the inspector, who had gone back to his notes. He finally looked up.

"Viktor Levitin was murdered."

She thought about it. "I do not think it will be a loss to the world."

"His two bodyguards were also killed."

"I have similar feelings about them."

"One of them is behind me, on the floor. The other is in the bedroom with Viktor. Investigator Levitin informs me that Viktor Levitin was his uncle."

"Not a kindly uncle."

Vachon waved a hand, as if to say "That's the way things are in the world." He thought for a moment.

"The person who killed him was not kind either. Whoever murdered Viktor Levitin also cut off his testicles and stuffed them in his mouth. Judging by the bleeding from this wound, he was probably alive at the time. A rather dreadful way to die, wouldn't you say?"

"In my experience, there is no pleasant way to die, Inspector."

Levitin finally looked up. "He liked beating up women. He was not a man. So his balls were superfluous."

"You didn't like your uncle?" Vachon asked.

"Once. Not now."

The inspector nodded. "Still and all, a bad death." He shifted uneasily in his seat, a thoughtful look on his face. "Whoever the murderer was, I do not think I would like to meet him in a lonely place without a pistol in my hand."

"I would suggest that you have a bullet in the chamber of

the gun with the safety off and the hammer of the weapon cocked as well," Jana interjected.

"Thank you for the good advice." The inspector darted another glance at his notes. "I understand you and Mr. Levitin, the murdered man's nephew, met him the other day?"

"Yes."

"Viktor Levitin was, as you have noted, a singularly vicious man. A sadist." To Dmitri: "Do you have any idea where Sasha Levitin, your sister, has gone? She was registered at this hotel. She checked out late last night."

Dmitri Levitin sighed, rolling his head on his neck as if working out sore muscles. "She was in the hospital when I saw her last. I went to visit her there. She had left. There was no address or other contact information."

Jana took another sip of her coffee, then set it aside and stood. "May I see the bodies, Inspector?"

"I always appreciate another professional's opinion, Commander Matinova." He pointed to the door people were going in and out of, the entry to the master bedroom.

Jana walked into the room, taking a brief moment to look around. One of the bodyguards was crumpled on the floor, his face against the wall, a pool of blood surrounding him. Viktor Levitin lay on the bed, his arms and legs tied to the bedposts, gagged. The man had been ugly in life; he was even worse in death.

Jana walked back into the living room and took her seat again, nodding to the inspector.

"Anything you care to tell me?" he asked.

"I think so. I saw a scene like this recently in the Strasbourg area. A mutilation was involved, although not this one. The killing took place in the man's house. His bedroom, in fact. I would check with the police there. There was also another murder in that city at about the same time, a man named

Tutungian. His tongue was cut out. That one is probably connected as well."

The inspector winced. That meant two more murders he had to investigate, along with old Mrs. Lermentov's death.

"And did you investigate those murders also, Commander Matinova?"

"I was an observer, Inspector."

"Mr. Levitin as well?"

"Yes," Levitin said. He straightened in his chair. "I think you should talk to Koba or Moira Simmons."

"The murderers?"

"Or the people who ordered the murders."

"Where can I find Moira Simmons?"

"I don't know," Levitin answered.

"Have you checked with the EU, Inspector?" Jana inquired. She did not mention Foch's diary, which contained Moira's phone number.

"I will check with them now. And also with this hotel, just in case." He gestured at the aide who had accompanied Jana. The man went to the room phone and dialed the desk.

"I will want a complete description of this woman."

"She worked for the EU. They will have it."

Vachon made another few notes on his pad.

"So?" he asked the aide.

"Viktor Levitin was registered at the hotel. Ms. Simmons was never a guest. They know nothing about her. The EU personnel department will get back to us. It will take a little time."

"I believe she has a local place," Jana interjected.

Vachon nodded at the aide, telling the man to follow up on this information.

Jana considered telling the inspector to call Katka and Jeremy, who probably knew how to reach Simmons; then thought better of it. She could not bring them into this, not just when she was about to meet her grandchild. If the inspector still needed it, she would ask the two for Moira Simmons's contact information, then give it to the inspector without involving them. As to her meeting with Moira, now was not the time to tell him about it. She would not say anything that might interfere with seeing Katka and little Daniela.

The inspector looked over to Levitin, the same question on his face. Levitin followed Jana's lead.

"I have no inkling of where this lady is hiding."

"You think she is in hiding?"

"If she has not committed these murders, I think she wouldn't like whoever did to find her." He slowly eased out of his chair. "I need to inform my country about my uncle's death. Then I have to call my relatives and let them know." He went to a corner of the room, using his cell phone to make the calls.

"Commander Matinova," the inspector began, "I think you are a good detective, and a very nice person, but you seem to have a close affinity to murderers and their victims. Personally, for my sake, and for that of the other police in this country, I'd like you out of this business."

"I'll think about your suggestion, Inspector."

"Thank you, Commander. When I get the information from the EU, I would like you to come down to the station for additional questions."

"I will answer any and all questions you have for me, Inspector."

His old smile flashed across his face.

"Thank you for being a professional. You're free to go, Commander."

Jana left. Levitin was still talking earnestly into his cell phone.

Chapter 58

Jana walked to the city's old quarter on the shore of the Baie des Anges. There was an elevator at the foot of the Colline du Chateau which would have taken her to the summit of the hill, but Jana decided to climb up the long flight of steps to the top. She had come early, and the physical activity helped suppress her anxiety at the prospect of meeting her granddaughter.

As she climbed, she paused to view the harbor. This time, the fabled blue of the sea did not excite her. In her mind's eye, the little girl looked like Katka before Jana had sent her out of Slovakia. Would she see her daughter in the little girl? Would there be love there?

By the time Jana reached the top, she was winded. She straightened her shoulders, took a last look at the view, then walked through the rock-strewn, almost shapeless ruins of the two old cathedrals in the flat area at the apex of the hill. There was nothing there for her, her thoughts all fixed on her meeting with her past, present, and, she hoped, her future family.

She took a seat on a park bench at the head of the road. When Jeremy drove up the hill with her granddaughter, Jana wanted to make sure that she saw them, and they her. As she waited, trying to relax, her other life, the facts of the case, began to course through her head.

There were two principals left, she thought: Moira

Simmons and Koba. Neither would be content until the other was dead. If Jana was right about Moira Simmons's past, she and Koba had been together once, probably as lovers, certainly partners in crime. But, whatever their entwined lives had been at one time, they were now deadly rivals.

She thought about the personalities of these two people. They each wanted to keep the world all for themselves, doling out small bits at their whim or caprice. That's what criminals did. They either gave the orders or they took them. And these people were two of a kind: Each had to give orders. And that meant a death.

She heard the sound of a car horn and looked downhill.

Jeremy's car swept by Jana. She quickly stepped into the middle of the street, waving to call attention to herself. The car finally stopped a hundred meters away.

Jana could see Jeremy and Katka through the windshield of their car. They were arguing, their words muffled, but it was clear that they were having a disagreement. Katka might be reneging, at the last minute refusing to share her daughter with Jana.

The driver's door opened, and Jeremy climbed out. He said something to Katka that sounded final, then reached into the back seat of the car, taking his daughter out of her safety seat. Jeremy carried Daniela, and a bag packed with her necessities, toward Jana.

Katka sat glowering in the front seat, not looking at Jana, unwilling to admit her into her life even for this brief moment. Jeremy's face was flushed; his voice when he spoke still carried a serrated edge of anger. As for Jana, she only had eyes for her granddaughter.

Blonde hair, large brown eyes, pale complexion, her nose was straight, her mouth not full but not thin either. Small ears. She was dressed neatly in a peaches-and-cream dress, a dainty little girl whose fingers clutched a small Raggedy Ann doll.

Daniela looked directly at Jana, her eyes unafraid, merely curious.

Jana's granddaughter did not look like Jana, nor Dano. She was a combination of her father and mother, Katka and Jeremy. A thought struck her. Yes, also Jana's mother. She was there in the face, the eyes, the hands. Looks sometimes skipped a generation or two. No doubt about it, she could see her own mother in Daniela. There was no question. This was Jana's granddaughter.

Jeremy held Daniela for a moment, letting the two, his daughter and her grandmother, survey each other. Then he said, "Daniela, this is your grandmother. That means she is your mommy's mother. So she is allowed to take care of you."

The little girl looked from her father back to Jana. Jana leaned toward her.

"Hello, Daniela. Is it all right with you if you stay with me in the park for a while?"

After a moment of hesitation, Daniela nodded.

"You can only have her for an hour." Jeremy tried to soften his tone. "Then we will come back to pick Daniela up."

"Perhaps a little longer?" Jana asked, surprised to hear the plaintive quality in her voice. "We need to get to know each other."

"Look, Jana, at the last minute Katka changed her mind. She begged me not to leave Daniela with you. She has been screaming at me during the entire ride over here. It has not been easy, for her or for me, or for Daniela. Please, agree to a one-hour limit on this visit."

There was no choice. Jana nodded. One hour: brief, but just the start of a long series of meetings in which they would see each other over the course of their lives.

"You ready to stay with Grandma for a little while, Daniela?" Jeremy quietly asked his daughter.

Daniela nodded at her father, then turned to Jana, holding out her arm to hand her Raggedy Ann doll over to her grandmother. Then Jana swept Daniela into her arms and held her close.

"I want to stand," said Daniela.

After a quick kiss, Jana set her down.

"Be good," said Jeremy.

"Okay," Daniela replied.

"I'll be good also," Jana put in.

Daniela looked at Jana to make sure she had heard correctly, than solemnly nodded. "We'll be good together."

"That's great." Jeremy managed a smile, stooped to kiss Daniela, then hesitated before giving Jana a quick kiss on the cheek. "Take care of her."

"With my life," Jana promised.

Jeremy trotted back to his car, the argument with Katka recommencing as soon as he got in. It was even louder than before. Through the windshield, Jana saw Jeremy angrily throw up his hands and start the car, then, tires screeching, drive to the exit. The car took the road leading down to the bottom of the hill.

Katka had never looked at her mother.

Jana walked with Daniela over to the bench. Daniela clambered up. Jana sat next to her, as Daniela reached for her doll.

"What's your dolly's name?" Jana asked.

"Missy," Daniela confided.

"Hello, Missy." Jana took the doll's hand and shook it in greeting. "My name is Jana. I'm Daniela's grandmother."

"Hi," said Daniela, in a high voice.

The sound of a crash broke into their conversation. Metal

against metal, car against car. A shock wave of fear went through Jana.

Jana fought the urge to run toward the sound. She forced herself to move slowly as she picked up Daniela, then walked to the road where it dipped downhill, and went down the incline, hoping she was wrong.

Within 150 meters, Jana saw a Peugeot sitting by the side of the road. Its left front was smashed in. Near the Peugeot, on the cliff side, was a broken fence. The Peugeot's passenger and driver stood by the hole in the fence, looking down.

The driver of the vehicle, a woman, was sobbing, saying something over and over in French. There had been no way to avoid a collision, she was saying. Jana held tight to Daniela and looked down.

Jeremy's car, a crumpled mass, was at the bottom of the hill.

"It went boom!" said Daniela.

Her granddaughter was right.

It had all gone "boom."

Chapter 59

Jana had to identify the bodies, direct the French police to the U.S. consulate, and, most of all, keep the terrible events from her granddaughter. Daniela would have to be told, but not now. A mangled mother and father locked in a crushed automobile were things that little girls should not be forced to confront.

As for Jana herself, she could not afford to grieve openly; she had to keep her emotions in check, except for the love she felt for Daniela.

The U.S. consular people were very efficient. They took care of the arrangements. They selected the mortuary, arranging to ship the bodies back to Jeremy's home state at government expense. After a cursory examination by a vice-consul, Katka's and Jeremy's personal effects were packed and sent to his parents. Daniela would also return to the U.S. Jana might escort her. In the meantime, the consul had retained a French nurse as a caregiver until Daniela was actually on the plane.

Jana's pleas to keep her grandchild were denied. The child had been born in the United States and was an American citizen. She would be sent to live with her other grandparents.

After a brief spell of hope, Jana now had to live with that disappointment, along with her grief for the loss of her daughter.

Jana changed hotel rooms, obtaining one with twin beds,

one for her and the other for Daniela. As for Daniela's emotional state, she appeared not to have realized yet that her mother and father were dead. Perhaps she didn't know what death meant, Jana thought. And, fortunately, she had a new grandmother, and their relationship seemed to occupy Daniela's thoughts. Jana had visited every child's shop she could find, buying any toys and picture books that she thought might occupy Daniela's mind.

Jana and her granddaughter were sitting on the floor of the room, playing with a dollhouse and dolls that Jana had purchased, when Jana's cell phone rang.

He did not give his name, but she knew that the man speaking was Koba. As Mikhail had said, there was no question: When the man called, you *knew* who he was. Perhaps it was the timbre of the voice, which left a cold, metallic echo inside you. So you listened, you knew. Or, perhaps, it was the absolute, unquestioning belief in himself that the man projected, which forced you to obey.

Koba spoke softly, distinctly, without stress.

"I was sorry to hear about your loss, Commander Matinova."

Jana hesitated. Then, she asked, "Koba?" There was no reply. Her question was answered solely by the continuation of the conversation.

"I called to thank you for carrying out my request."

"I don't remember you asking me to do anything. If you had, I would not have done it."

"Perhaps." There was a pause. "I would like to see you."

"Why?"

"To return a favor." He gave her an address in the hills on the outskirts of the city. "I will be there for half an hour."

He hung up.

Jana's first impulse was a policewoman's response. She started to dial Vachon's number. Then she stopped herself. A half hour was very little time to set up a police operation that would keep Koba pinned down in his house. If they sent just a few duty police officers, Koba being Koba, the man would escape. In any case, Koba would know if the police were called! That sense was built into the man's genes.

Jana realized she had to go alone.

She kissed her grandchild, told her she would be back in a very short time, and paid the nurse to borrow her car. Jana drove herself to the outskirts of Nice and up into the hills.

It was a large house surrounded by a wall made up of tall steel pickets spaced a few inches apart. Cameras were discreetly positioned well inside the fence to take in everything happening on the grounds and in the street beyond.

"No unwanted visitors, no salespeople, no human beings allowed inside," Jana thought to herself. She walked to the front gate. There was a call button at the gate to push in order to catch the attention of whoever was inside. Instead, Jana pushed at the gate. It swung open. She hesitated, then stepped inside, closing the gate behind her. It had been left open for her.

She walked up to the front steps, then to the front door. Again, the door was slightly ajar. She scanned the front of the building. She had come this far; there was no reason to remain outside. She went in.

The rooms seemed to be surgically clean. There was furniture, sparse, all neutral. Aside from the furniture, there was not the slightest personal touch, or even the smallest sign of human presence to indicate real occupancy: no newspapers or magazines, no pictures on the walls, no matchbooks, not even a scrap of superfluous detritus. Not even a speck of dust. The rooms were so clean, it seemed to suggest that they could never get dirty. The owner had made a statement: I am not here, but I am here. Be warned.

The whole house was like that: furnished, but not for living. Except for the master bedroom, there was no one in the house.

There was someone in the bedroom.

Moira Simmons lay on the bed. Her makeup was perfect, her hair coiffed; she looked like she was posing for a woman's magazine.

Of course she was dead.

To be sure, Jana felt for her pulse. Her skin was cold to the touch. Jana studied the body for a moment, then rolled the head slightly to one side. There was a small bloodstain on the pillow. She rolled the head back to its original position. Jana wondered if Koba had used an ice pick again.

Knowing that Vachon would be upset if she disturbed the scene, Jana wiped her hand on a corner of the bedspread, then retraced her steps to the living room. A man was seated in the room now, relaxed. He was still tanned.

Koba.

Jana seated herself in a chair, facing the man. There was a small ball of fear in her stomach. Being in the presence of this man would do that to anyone.

"Thank you for coming alone." His voice had the same qualities as on the phone. "This was her house, not mine."

"You killed her?"

"She really killed herself. If you don't kill the king, if you only wound him, he will kill you. She thought I was the king. She tried to kill me; she didn't succeed."

"You retaliated."

"The king has to rule his realm."

"The killings in Slovakia?"

"My people were in the van. The old woman found in the river, mine. They were *her* work."

Jana smelled the faint but familiar scent of cologne. The

jacket in the closet of the van driver's apartment had smelled of the cologne.

"The jacket we found in the van driver's apartment was yours."

"You arrived at the apartment very quickly. Almost too quickly for me."

"That apartment, all neat, all new. As if never used, except for a few pieces. It was a setup, meant to catch someone."

He smiled, grimly. "The driver she killed had to have an apartment for her to find. Otherwise, how could she obtain the ledger?"

"You knew she would go after him?"

"I knew her. She unquestionably would go after the king's subjects."

"We found the ledger. But *she* was supposed to find it," Jana ventured.

He nodded.

It encouraged Jana to ask the next question. "Do you like sausage?"

He watched her for a moment, a bemused expression on his face. "Yes, I like sausage."

"You left some in the refrigerator in the apartment."

"The apartment had to look lived-in." He reached down. At his feet were two books: the ledger, and the book of *Montaigne's Essays* she had given Moira Simmons. "I thought you might like these back, as mementos."

"I have a copy of the ledger at the hotel."

He nodded and put the ledger back on the floor. He kept the book of essays. "As you wish."

She thought of the other killings. "Who killed Foch in the house in Alsace?"

"He was on her side; a terrible mistake on his part."

"The body had a finger cut off. Why was the body transported to the UN building?"

"He had worn his wedding ring on that finger. The building was where she worked. All warnings."

"Tutungian in Strasbourg?"

"He was a Simmons lapdog. A killer she liked to use. He was going to kill you. When Foch died, she panicked. She thought you might figure things out. So she pointed Tutungian in your direction."

"You killed him?"

"The business with the ledger was not finished." He thought about it. "Tutungian following you saved your life. It showed me that the loss of the ledger was creating havoc. It kept them off balance. While they were looking for it, they were paying no attention to anything else. To keep them distracted, your life had to be preserved so they would keep hunting for the ledger, and for you."

He got up. "It's time."

Jana tensed, getting to her feet warily. "You haven't told me why you killed Uncle Viktor."

"It should be apparent. He mistreated a particular woman. He deserved his death."

He took a step toward Jana.

She stepped back.

"Are you going to try to kill me now?"

"On the contrary: You are being given your life back."

"It's not like you to be so generous."

"It is in appreciation for what you did for a friend. Indirectly, it was for me. You need not be afraid every time you hear footsteps behind you any longer. Be assured, it is over."

He laid the Montaigne essays on a cocktail table in front

of her, stepped back to let her pick it up, then indicated the door.

"You will have to go now."

Jana took the book and went to the door. For the last time, Jana looked at Koba.

"I am still a police officer. I will continue to do my job. If I can, I will come for you."

"Naturally. Those are the rules of the game.

"One more thing," the man said. "Sasha sends her love to you and to her brother."

Jana nodded, then left, walking quickly to the gate. When she reached the corner, she made a call to Inspector Vachon. By the time the police arrived, the house was totally engulfed in flames.

Of course, Koba was gone.

Chapter 60

Levitin drove Jana and her granddaughter to the airport. He had arranged with the Russian government representative to have the body of his uncle, the minister, shipped back, then decided to stay a few more days in the hopes of picking up a lead to his sister. So he had time to help Jana.

He maneuvered the vehicle cautiously through the French traffic jam. Jeremy and Katka's deaths had put the fear of God in Levitin, softening the traditional Russian driver's lead foot. He was now operating the car like a careful old man.

Before they started, Daniela had insisted on having a pillow to sit on so she could look out the window. Her mouth and nose, and the Raggedy Ann dolly's mouth and nose, were pressed against the window as she pointed out objects on the street to it. Otherwise, it was quiet until Jana, at last, broke the silence.

"You won't find your sister," she told Levitin.

"Thank you for your vote of confidence." He swerved slightly to avoid a scooter traveling on the wrong side of the road. He was pleased he had avoided a crash. "I am getting better."

"At what?"

"Avoiding being killed."

"That is important."

"I am sure I will find her, given enough time."

"I hate to say this, but 'No.'"

"Why 'No'?"

"She has found him, he has found her, and the two of them don't want to be found by anyone else. She has been very good at staying hidden before. With him helping, they will completely vanish."

"Nobody just vanishes."

"Yes, they do, all the time."

"What do I tell my mother?"

Jana glanced at the back seat to make sure Daniela was all right, then shifted her attention back to Levitin.

"Tell your mother that your sister has found a new man who will take care of her, at least for a while."

Levitin fell in behind an airport bus that was going slowly enough to satisfy him.

"Will he take care of her? Or will he kill her?"

"A short time ago, you told me that you have this little trick of remembering numbers."

"Any and all combinations," he acknowledged, a note of pride creeping into his voice. "They stick like good adhesive tape."

"Is it a family trait? Your sister, does she also have this adhesive tape?"

"A family trait. Together, we used to do magic memory tricks for guests when we were younger. She's even better at it than I am. Much better."

They turned off the main boulevard, circling back to the road that led to the airport parking lot, then onto the road leading to the international terminal. The bus they had been following took a different path. No longer protected by his moving shield, Levitin drove even more cautiously, eyeing the passing cars with suspicion.

"She was Pavel's bookkeeper," Jana continued. "Only

there was no book; there was no 'ledger.' Her mind was the book. That's why everyone wanted her."

"We have Koba's ledger, the one you found in Slovakia."

"No, that was a diversion. To keep them from looking for your sister. He wanted it found to keep everyone misdirected until he could locate her. She was the ledger."

"And the ledger we have?"

"A fake. There is no code. There's just organized garbage in the book to make anyone who looks at it think it's real. Like you and me; like your uncle; like Moira Simmons; it fooled us all."

Levitin took the news calmly, as if he had already had a surfeit of shocks and could no longer react.

He finally managed to park the car and let out a sigh.

"I thought Russians learned early on how to drive."

"I just took you over a very dangerous route." He put the gearshift into Park and put on the emergency brake. "Beautifully done." He sat for a moment, relaxing. "The car wreck in Bratislava. Who killed the man and the prostitutes?"

"He was Koba's manager. Hence, competition."

He thought about this. "How do we know the man didn't work for Moira? How do we know Koba didn't kill him?"

"Moira Simmons asked that I be put on the UN committee because I was the primary officer investigating the killings in Slovakia. She wanted me close so she could follow the investigation. I also had the ledger. If she played it right, she thought, she could get it from me. She and Uncle Viktor finally got their ledgers. But not the real one: not your sister."

They got out of the car. Jana unstrapped Daniela and picked her up, giving her a big kiss. The little girl clutched her dolly, sucking the thumb of her other hand. Levitin took the bags from the trunk, and they walked toward the terminal.

"Why didn't *they* find the ledger?"

"I moved too quickly. Koba had placed it in the freezer. When it wasn't found, he moved it to the couch." Jana smiled ruefully. "It was too easy to find. After all, Seges, my generally incompetent aide, discovered it under the couch. That told the whole story. It was meant to be found.

"He knew they would discover that we had it. Grisko, the Ukrainian cop whose club was blown up, would pass on that information. He created a false trail, away from your sister, who is the real ledger."

They walked into the terminal and saw Inspector Vachon waiting. The inspector walked up to Jana, giving her a kiss on each cheek.

"Good to see you." He fell in with them as they went to the ticket check-in counter.

"You know, I thought of France as relatively crime-free before you arrived," the inspector joked. "Your imports from Eastern Europe are very bad for a French police officer's stomach."

"Eat more Russian food," suggested Levitin. "It will get you used to dealing with us."

The inspector grimaced. "I will stick to my country's cuisine."

Jana set Daniela down, handing the ticket clerk her tickets and passports for the two of them. "Tell me about the burned house."

The inspector gave her a very Nicean shrug. "One body. In the place you told us to look. Not much left."

"Moira Simmons."

"We found enough teeth to make an identification if and when we get her dental records. You say it was her, so I believe it was her. But we have to make it official."

Jana waited impatiently. "And what else?"

"No other bodies, nothing. It was a hot fire. There are signs that incendiary materials were used to make it so. But there should have been other remains, some remnants, if there were more bodies. We're still sifting the ashes, but I don't think we will find Koba."

"I was hoping."

Levitin shook his head. "He is alive."

"Yes," Jana said.

"Somewhere," added the inspector.

Depression and sorrow suddenly swept over Jana. Police training in dealing with tragedy went only so far.

"You have conducted a good investigation," Vachon told her. "I am truly sorry about the other things that happened."

Levitin touched Jana on her shoulder, trying to convey his own condolences.

She thought of her daughter. There would be no closure for them.

Jana picked up her granddaughter, hugging her tightly. The little girl's warmth gave her comfort. She was an innocent, without the flaws of an adult. She was still without sin. A thought began to germinate in Jana's mind: Maybe the other set of grandparents would let Jana see her more frequently; perhaps they'd let her come to Slovakia. A few months out of the year was not too bad, and Jana, after all, *was* her other grandparent.

Jana became aware of the check-in clerk asking her a question. The clerk had their passports open in front of her. She was asking Jana her relationship to the little one in her arms.

Without thinking, Jana answered, "My daughter."

Chapter 61

On the Dalmatian coast, about seventy-five kilometers north of the last island he had called home, the tanned man walked through a newly constructed house, admiring the craftsmanship. Everything had been done according to his requirements by the best workmen in the area. The rooms were spacious, the walls painted an egg-white. The sun splashed freely through the open space. The furniture was covered in soft pastels; the oriental rugs, from Qum and Khafkaz, spread their richness over the white tile floors.

He looked through the thick windows overlooking the sea. All were triple-glazed. It kept the cold out in the winter, a cold that swept in with frigid fingers that made it almost unlivable unless you were well insulated. The winds were due soon.

The man stepped closer to one of the windows, gazing down. Sasha lay on the rocks at the edge of the sea. She was already tanning. Comfortable in the sun, she was already at ease inside the house with him. Pavel had been right: She had been a treasure for Pavel, and she would be for him.

Sasha stood, looked up at him, and waved. He waved back. She rose and dove into the water, a perfect arc. She surfaced, and he saw the glistening drops of water on her arms as she stroked.

Yes, he thought. Thank you, Pavel. Thank you, Commander Matinova. Thank you, everyone, even the dead. They had brought the Siren of the Waters to him. All was right again in his world.